Jayne Ann Krentz is the critically-acclaimed creator of the Arcane Society world, Dark Legacy, Ladies of Lantern Street and Rainshadow Island series. She also writes as **Amanda Quick** and **Jayne Castle**. Jayne has written more than fifty *New York Times* bestsellers under various pseudonyms and more than thirty-five million copies of her books are currently in print. She lives in the Pacific Northwest.

Visit Jayne Ann Krentz online:

www.jayneannkrentz.com
www.facebook.com/JayneAnnKrentz
www.twitter.com/JayneAnnKrentz

JAYNE ANN KRENTZ

SECRET SISTERS

piatkus

PIATKUS

First published in the United States in 2015 by Berkley,
A division of Penguin Random House LLC, New York
First published in Great Britain in 2015 by Piatkus
This paperback edition published in 2016 by Piatkus

1 3 5 7 9 10 8 6 4 2

A CIP catalogue record for this book
is available from the British Library.

ISBN 978-0-349-40937-5

Printed and bound by CPI Group (UK) Ltd, Croydon, CR0 4YY

Papers used by Piatkus are from well-managed forests
and other responsible sources.

MIX
Paper from
responsible sources
FSC
www.fsc.org   FSC® C104740

Piatkus
An imprint of
Little, Brown Book Group
Carmelite House
50 Victoria Embankment
London EC4Y 0DZ

An Hachette UK Company
www.hachette.co.uk

www.piatkus.co.uk

This one is for my fabulous editor,
Leslie Gelbman,
who knows the secret.

SECRET SISTERS

CHAPTER ONE

Cooper Island, eighteen years earlier . . .

He stood in the shadows of the kitchen and tried to decide which girl he wanted. An hour ago they had both fallen asleep in front of the television. Now they slept the way only the young could sleep—deeply, soundly.

Both were the right age—twelve, maybe thirteen—right on the cusp of womanhood. That was the way he liked them. Pure. Innocent. Virginal. They were small-town girls who lacked urban street smarts—the kind of girls who usually could be terrified into keeping the secret. *If you tell anyone, I will come back and kill your parents and then I will kill you.*

The cottage was some distance from the main hotel building where the wedding reception was taking place. The smaller girl's grandmother owned the Aurora Point. Her friend's mother worked there. Both adults were fully occupied with the crowd in the hotel tonight. There were no men in the picture—no fathers, no brothers; just the grandmother and the mother. No need to worry about them.

He had watched the girls closely ever since he had checked into the hotel. They had helped with the preparations for the wedding reception, setting up folding chairs and placing the flower arrangements on the tables.

Once the festivities had begun, the girls had taken off to entertain themselves. They had played Ping-Pong for some time and then disappeared into the cottage to watch television.

The taller girl was the prettier of the two, but with her slim, long-legged body, she might be more of a problem to control simply because of her size and reach. If she struggled—and some did struggle in spite of his threats—she might knock over an object or make some noise that would attract attention. Still, there was a sweet, dreamy air about her that was very appealing. Earlier in the evening she had taken obvious delight in arranging the silly decorations and then she had fussed with the flowers on the buffet table. The adults had smiled and let her tweak things.

The smaller girl wasn't as pretty, but there was something intriguing about her attitude and self-confidence. She had been working behind the front desk when he had checked in. She had given him his key and instructions concerning his room with all the poise and assurance of an adult. She would grow up to become one of those bitchy women who were always giving orders, he thought. A real ball-buster. She needed to learn her place.

Now, standing in the shadows, he decided that she would be easier to handle. He could crush her with one arm and squeeze the air out of her lungs so that she couldn't scream. But she was also the one who might be the hardest to subdue with threats. He might have to kill her afterward to be sure she didn't talk.

In the end, fate made the decision for him. It was the smaller girl who awakened and padded, barefoot and yawning, into the kitchen to get a drink of water.

She never knew he was there until he put a hand over her mouth and carried her outside into the night.

CHAPTER TWO

Sanctuary Creek, present day

"You're still grieving, Madeline." Dr. William Fleming folded his hands on top of his desk. The professional concern in his eyes was infused with a gentle, more intimate vibe. "It's been less than three months since you lost your grandmother. You were very close to her. She was your only surviving family member. Naturally you've been traumatized. It is very unwise to make serious, life-altering decisions when you are in a psychologically fragile state."

On the other side of the window the Arizona sunshine blazed in a cloudless spring sky. But inside William's office the air-conditioning was cranked up very high. Madeline Chase was chilled to the bone. She decided that it probably wasn't fair to blame the AC system. It was William who made her so aware of the intense cold. The all-too-familiar sensation of feeling trapped seethed deep inside. She needed to escape and soon.

She crossed her legs and sat back in the padded leather chair. She had been raised in the executive suite of her grandmother's small but very successful boutique hotel chain. She knew how to look like a woman in charge. And now that Edith Chase was gone, she *was* the woman in charge. She was the sole heir of her grandmother's innkeeping business.

"If you knew me as well as you think you do, you'd know that I'm well aware of what I'm doing," she said. "My decision is final. We will not be seeing each other again."

He removed his stylish, titanium-framed glasses, set them on the desk, and exhaled deeply, making it clear with his body language that although he was very disappointed in her, he was willing to be patient and understanding.

Her attention was briefly caught by his hands. They were among his best features, she reflected—one of the many assets that she had placed in the plus column of the spreadsheet she had prepared a month ago at the start of their relationship. William's hands were smooth, well manicured, and, like the rest of him, not intimidatingly large or powerful. They often moved in graceful little arcs when he talked. They were the hands of a man who read books that came from the literary end of the bestseller lists; the hands of a man who enjoyed dining in trendy restaurants and touring museums that featured modern art. They were soft, nonthreatening hands.

The rest of William went well with his hands. He was on the short side for a man. When she was wearing high heels, as was the case today, they were the same height. She also liked the fact that while he was certainly physically fit, he was slightly built, not heavy or thickened up with muscle.

She had begun to conclude that they might be compatible in bed, at least for a short time. Her relationships never lasted long once things moved into the bedroom. William had certainly been pushing for full sexual intimacy. But she never allowed herself to rush into that aspect of a relationship because sex was always the beginning of the end for her. The only part she ever truly enjoyed was the getting-to-know-you stage. That was the stage when she could still dream, still imagine that she had found the right man, the one with whom she could have a family of her own.

"You don't want to end our relationship, Madeline." William assumed his lecturing tone, the one he employed in the classroom. He was a part-time instructor at a local college. "As I've explained, we are ideally suited to each other."

She laughed. She couldn't help herself. It was either laugh or pick up the nearest heavy object and hurl it in the general direction of William's head. She was an executive who knew it never paid to lose her cool, so she went with the laugh. But there was no real humor in it. The sheer irony of his words was breathtaking. William was, after all, a therapist who specialized in couples counseling.

"That's certainly what you've been telling me for the past month," she said. "But you're wrong. In fact, I would go so far as to say you've been lying to me."

"That's ridiculous. Not to mention offensive."

"I suppose it was all about getting funding for your couples ther-apy research, wasn't it? I realize it's a tough world out there for those who need grant money. But did you actually think you could seduce me into paying for your study? Really?"

"Madeline, it's obvious that something has upset you. Why don't you calm down and tell me what's going on here? Between the two of us we can sort things out."

Too late for that, she thought. She was filled with the same unshak-able determination that she felt when she concluded that an employee's skill set was no longer a good fit with the business culture of Sanctuary Creek Inns. Firing members of the well-trained staff was, thankfully, a rare event at Sanctuary. Nevertheless, there were occasions when it had to be done. Her goal at termination interviews was to *counsel out* the employee and suggest that he or she resign to pursue other career opportunities. The cardinal rule for conducting a termination interview was to *never explain*. Once you started listing reasons for terminating someone's employment, you opened the door to arguments and counter-arguments. Things got messy fast. That was only one of the many lessons she had learned from her grandmother.

The difference between getting rid of an ineffective employee and dumping Dr. William Fleming was that, in the case of the employee, she would have sent the person away with a handsome severance package and the conviction that leaving Sanctuary was his own brainstorm.

She had no intention of offering William a damn thing.

"I'm afraid there is nothing to sort out," she said. She uncrossed her legs and got to her feet. "I appreciate your concern for my *psychologically fragile state*, but my decision is final. We will not be seeing each other again. Do not attempt to contact me in any way."

She started across the room, heading for the door. She had stayed too long, she reflected. She was on the verge of losing her temper.

William shot to his feet behind his desk.

"This is nonsense," he snapped. "Sit down and tell me what is wrong. You owe me that much. I know you have some serious intimacy issues, but we've made excellent progress in that area."

A tide of soul-searing anger swept through her without warning. Her palms tingled with an icy-hot sensation. It was similar to the unpleasant adrenaline rush that accompanied a missed step on a flight of stairs. The realization that a bad fall had barely been averted was always a shock to the system.

She wasn't furious with William—okay, she was definitely pissed at him. She had a right to be pissed, she thought. But she knew her rage was mostly directed at herself. She shuddered to think that she had been considering an affair with the little creep.

She stopped at the door and turned around to face him. Probably a mistake, she thought. The smart thing to do was to leave immediately and close the door on the near disaster that she had just avoided.

And maybe she could have kept going if he hadn't made the crack about her intimacy issues. A woman could only take so much.

"Let me clear up an apparent misunderstanding, William," she said. "I wasn't seeing you as a client. As far as I was concerned, our relationship was personal."

"Of course it was."

He'd switched his tone of voice with the agility of a trained actor. He sounded soothing and reassuring now. He came out from behind his desk and moved toward her. Instinctively she tightened her grip on the doorknob.

"I told myself your deep concern about my intimacy issues was a sign that you cared about me," she said. "It was irritating, but I believed that you meant well. In fact, you might even have been correct with the diagnosis."

He came to a halt in front of her and smiled a modest smile.

"Well, intimacy issues are my specialty, darling," he said. "But if you're not ready to discuss them, we can wait."

"Here's the thing, William. I wasn't looking for therapy when we met. I was hoping for a serious, meaningful relationship. But now I know for a fact that you aren't any good at relationships."

"What are you talking about?"

"I'll try to keep this simple. You are a lying, deceitful asshole."

William looked as if he had been poleaxed. "What has happened to you?"

"Data happened," she said.

"What?"

"I'm a businesswoman, remember? I thrive on data. I asked an investigator to look into your background."

"What?"

The look of horror on his face would have been entertaining in other circumstances.

"Don't take it personally, it's routine for me." She smiled. "I always commission a background check on my dates if things look like they might get serious. I was a bit late getting around to ordering the research on you because I've been so busy dealing with my grandmother's estate. But the report came in this morning, and let's just say that it doesn't make you look like the kind of man I want to date."

"Are you crazy?"

"Maybe. But that is no longer your problem."

She started to open the door, but he moved much faster than she had expected and planted one hand against the wooden panel. When she tugged on the door she discovered that he was stronger than he looked. So much for judging a man by his size.

The trapped sensation threatened to explode through her. She fought it with logic. She was in no immediate danger. William's receptionist was a few feet away in the reception area. Even more reassuring was the knowledge that her own personal hired gun, Jack Rayner, was in the hall outside the office, waiting for her. As far as she had been able to determine, Jack didn't actually carry a gun, but he was definitely on her payroll.

She was not alone. She was not trapped.

"We both know it's in your best interests to let me leave quietly," she said. "You don't want a scene. You will only make yourself look like a fool and worse if you actually try to keep me here by force. Think of your professional image."

"You can't hurl accusations around the way you just did and then walk out," he snarled. "You owe me an explanation for this wild talk."

"All right, here's what I know about you, William. You took advantage of your position as a trusted therapist to seduce at least two of your clients in the past year."

He flushed a dull, angry red. "That's a lie. Who told you that?"

"Both women were married at the time you seduced them. Their husbands were also coming to you for counseling. Do you know what that makes you, William? It makes you a real bastard. If the women ever came forward, your career would go down in flames."

"I don't know who you hired to dig up dirt on me, but I can assure you the accusations are false."

"How many female clients have you seduced? I know of at least two. But that's definitely enough to suggest a pattern. Shall I ask my investigator to keep digging?"

"A client's files are confidential. Your investigator had no right to hack into them."

"Relax. He didn't hack into any files. He just started asking questions. Here's the thing about affairs, William. They never stay secret. Sooner or later someone always talks."

He seized her arm, his fingers biting through the fabric of her dark blue blazer.

"Listen to me," he said, his voice low and harsh. "I was providing therapy to those two clients. They needed to know they were still sexually attractive so that they would have the courage to realize that divorce was the correct decision. There was nothing personal about the relationships, certainly not on my end."

She reached into her shoulder bag with her free hand and took out her cell phone.

"Let me out of this room now or I will call the police. That won't be good for business, will it?"

For a second or two William just stared at her as if she had spoken in another language, one that was utterly incomprehensible to him. Then he glanced at the phone in her hand.

He released her and moved back a step.

"Get out," he said.

She opened the door and walked into the outer room. The receptionist flushed and quickly became very busy on her computer. Madeline nodded at her politely. The woman did not look up.

Madeline went out into the hall and closed the door very calmly, very deliberately.

CHAPTER THREE

The name on his new business cards was John Santiago Rayner, but everyone called him Jack.

He was waiting for her, right where she had left him a short time earlier: one broad shoulder propped against the wall, his arms folded across his chest. He was dressed in dark trousers, a denim shirt that was open at the collar, a rumpled sport coat, and low boots. He was descended from an Arizona ranching family with a history in the state that stretched back several generations to the days when Arizona had been a territory.

Years ago the Rayners had traded the cattle business for commercial real estate development, but Jack was a throwback. He had the hard, unreadable eyes of an Old West lawman. In the mythic past that infused the modern Southwest, you gave a man like Jack a badge and sent him out into the dusty street at high noon to stop the bad guy.

Okay, so Jack had chosen a career in hotel security and he didn't carry a gun on his hip. But those concessions to the modern age did not make him any less formidable. Even wearing the sport coat, he would not have looked out of place in Tombstone.

He glanced briefly at the door of William's office.

"Any problem?" he asked in a voice that carried the deceptively laid-back cadence of an Arizona accent.

Some of the tension inside her dissipated at the sight of him. He was all the things William was not—too tall, too powerful in too many subtle ways, and his hazel eyes were too difficult to read. But at that particular moment, he looked good. Very good.

She reminded herself that he was a man of many layers. She'd had a glimpse of the hidden side of Jack Rayner the day she had attempted to fire him. It had not gone well. Jack was not the kind of employee you could *counsel out*. As it happened, he was not at all interested in pursuing other career opportunities. He wanted the Sanctuary Creek Inns account and he had been willing to fight for it.

The upshot was that Rayner Risk Management was still under contract with Sanctuary Creek Inns.

In the business world, a contract was a contract, and shortly before her death in a hotel fire, Edith Chase had signed one with Jack's security firm. Madeline had argued against the move because Rayner Risk Management was a very new and very small player in the competitive world of corporate security.

Madeline had tried to talk her grandmother out of signing the contract, but Edith had dismissed her qualms with a few casual reassurances. *I think we can assume he's qualified, even if he lacks experience in the hotel business. He did some consulting work for the FBI.* Madeline had responded with, *That's great, but we're in the hospitality industry. We're not dealing with serial killers or the mob.* Edith had come back with, *Rayner Risk Management is headquartered here in Sanctuary Creek. It's always good to do business with a local firm whenever possible.* Whereupon Madeline had pointed out that Jack probably wasn't a very good businessman because his previous firm, a security agency located in Silicon Valley, had recently gone bankrupt in a rather spectacular fashion.

In the end, she had lost the battle and now she was stuck with Jack Rayner. It did not help that his social graces were minimal. The day they had met in her grandmother's office, Madeline had offered her hand to him in an attempt to be professional, even in defeat. He'd stared at her for a couple of seconds and then looked down at her hand as though baffled about what to do with it. When his fingers had finally closed around hers, she had been intensely conscious of the heat and strength in the man. It had taken some effort to extricate her hand. She got the impression he had forgotten he was holding it.

Ever since that moment she had been telling herself that Jack was not her type. But he did have a few very important things going for him—he was on retainer, he was convenient, and he had signed a confidentiality agreement.

When her intuition warned her that there was something off about William, she had called Jack and commissioned the background check. He, in turn, had made it clear that the small, routine assignment irritated him. Why, she had no idea, because part of his job was to run background checks on prospective new hires. A background check was a background check, regardless of whether the subject was applying for a job in one of the hotels or dating the president and CEO of the chain.

"No, there was no problem," she said. "It wasn't pretty, but it's done." She hitched up the strap of her shoulder bag and walked briskly toward the elevators. "There was no need for you to escort me here today. William is a lot of things, but he's not the violent type."

Jack fell into step beside her, shortening his stride to match hers. He seemed to loom over her, even though she was wearing her highest heels.

"Anyone can become the violent type under the right circumstances," he said.

She shivered. "Yes, I know. I'm not naïve. But I honestly don't believe that William will be a problem."

"You're probably right." Jack looked back toward the office door. "He's not accustomed to having his target turn on him. He'll move on."

"Uh, *target?*"

"That's what you were to him at the start."

She winced. "I suppose so."

"His type prefers easier prey."

"You sound like you know his type," Madeline said.

"Met a few in my other life."

"That would have been when you were some kind of consultant for the FBI?"

"Right."

"I accept your analysis of William Fleming. Nevertheless, I would appreciate it if you would stop using words like *target* and *prey* to describe me."

Jack ignored that. "Make sure you don't accidentally take one of his calls. Don't respond to any texts. Don't agree to talk to him or meet him for coffee so that you can talk things out."

She stopped in front of the elevators and punched the button. "I know the drill. As it happens, I'm leaving town tomorrow morning, anyway. I'll be gone for a couple of days."

"Where are you going?"

"Cooper Island." Not that it was any of his business, she thought. "It's one of the San Juan islands in Washington State. My grandmother had a property there. It's mine now."

"The Aurora Point Hotel."

She glanced at him, genuinely startled. "You know it?"

"Came across some property-tax records associated with it when I did my initial research on your company."

She took a deep breath. "Your research was very . . . thorough."

"I asked Edith about it. She told me that she wasn't concerned with security for the hotel. She said it was personal property—not part of Sanctuary Creek's portfolio."

"That's right."

The elevator doors opened. She moved inside. Jack followed her in and pushed the lobby button.

"Are you going to Cooper Island to take some time off?" he asked. "Not a bad idea. You've been going a hundred miles an hour ever since your grandmother's death. You look like you could use some R-and-R."

She groaned. "First I'm a target and now you tell me I look like hell warmed over. Got to hand it to you, Jack, you really know how to flatter a girl."

He frowned. "I just meant that you need to give yourself some downtime. You've been through a lot in the past three months. Edith left you with a solid management team. They're more than capable of handling things for a couple of weeks or even longer now that the initial shock has worn off the company."

"Forget trying to explain what you meant. I don't think that's your forte. But to be clear, I'm not going to Cooper Island for a vacation. Something has come up regarding the Aurora Point property, that's all."

"Something that needs your on-site attention?"

"Evidently. I got a message from Tom Lomax, the caretaker my grandmother paid to look after the hotel. He said he wanted to speak to me in person."

"He wouldn't tell you on the phone?"

"Tom doesn't trust phones, or email either, for that matter. He's a little old-fashioned."

"He sounds paranoid."

"Okay, Tom is rather eccentric, I'll give you that."

"So you're going to fly all the way to Washington to talk to this

Tom Lomax about a problem related to an abandoned property your grandmother didn't even care enough about to insure," Jack said.

She glanced at him. "Yes, I am. As you pointed out, my management team is perfectly capable of handling company business while I'm out of town. If you have any questions relating to security issues, feel free to contact Chuck Johnson directly."

"Johnson is a good man."

"I know."

Jack looked at her. "You're not going to tell me why you're dropping everything to fly to Cooper Island, are you?"

The doors opened. Madeline walked out of the elevator.

"No," she said. "Partly because, as I just explained, I don't know what the problem is. But mostly because it's none of your business. This is personal, Jack."

But she was learning that once Jack Rayner sank his teeth into a problem, it was very hard to shake him loose. He followed her out of the elevator.

"Your grandmother told me that the two of you left Cooper Island nearly two decades ago," he said. "Ever been back?"

"No."

She kept going across the building lobby, heading for the glass doors on the far side.

"You didn't need me to do the research on William Fleming," Jack said.

She glanced at him, wary of the sudden change of topic. "What do you mean?"

"You were never even close to marrying him."

"I was thinking about it." But that sounded weak, even to her own ears.

"No," Jack said. "You would have ended the relationship sooner or later."

Now she was getting mad. "How do you know that?"

"You wouldn't have asked me to vet him unless you were looking for a way out. I made it easy for you to escape because I found a good excuse you could use. But if I hadn't been around, you would have ended things on your own."

"What makes you so sure?"

"There's a look people get when they feel cornered or trapped. You had that look."

"What kind of look is that?"

"Hard to explain. Let's just say I know it when I see it. Like I said, you were looking for a way out, so you asked me to hand it to you on a silver platter."

She thought about that. She wanted to argue, but he had a point. "You're right. William was a little too perfect. It bothered me. I was going to end the relationship, but I wanted a good reason."

"A good reason to give to yourself, not to him."

She reached into her shoulder bag, took out her dark glasses, and very deliberately put them on so that he could not see her eyes.

"I think we're finished here," she said.

He didn't say anything. Instead he took his own sunglasses out of a pocket, slipped them on, and opened the heavy glass doors.

They walked outside into the brilliant warmth of the spring day. The sun sparked and flashed on the cars parked in the lot in front of the office building. It was only March, but the heat coming off the pavement was already palpable.

Beyond the parking lot was the main street of Sanctuary Creek. The town had been founded well over a century earlier, but it had remained little more than a dot on the Arizona map for most of its history. Eighteen years ago Edith and Madeline had moved to the small community. Edith had opened a B&B to make ends meet. The property had been the first in what had become a chain of boutique inns.

In recent years the town had been discovered by tourists, retirees, and those seeking winter homes in the Sunbelt. The developers had soon followed. Sanctuary Creek was now a picturesque Southwestern destination that rivaled Scottsdale and Sedona.

Jack walked her to her car. His continuing silence worried her. There was another boot waiting to drop.

She got in behind the wheel and looked up at him.

"What?" she asked when she couldn't take the suspense any longer.

Jack looked out at the view of the desert and mountains for what seemed like a very long time.

"I know about commitment issues," he said. "Got a few myself."

She clamped her hands around the steering wheel. *Just breathe.*

"Excuse me," she said in her iciest executive accent. "I don't recall discussing commitment issues with you."

He looked down at her, sunlight glinting on his dark glasses.

"Next time, use someone else to dig up the dirt on one of your dates," he said, his voice cold, flat; emotionless. "I'm good with the business side of things, but I don't want to get involved in your personal relationships."

She felt as if the wind had been knocked out of her.

"Use someone else?" she repeated. "But doing background checks is part of your job."

"My firm provides business-related background-check services. Not the personal kind."

"No offense, but from what I can tell, your company could use whatever work it can get. Why don't you want this kind of business?"

"We all know what happens to messengers. Sooner or later they bring news that the client doesn't want to hear. The outcome is never good for the messenger."

He closed the car door, turned, and walked toward a silver-gray SUV parked a couple of slots away. He did not look back.

She fired up the ignition and drove out of the parking lot, heading for the corporate headquarters of Sanctuary Creek Inns. She had things to attend to at the office before she went home to pack for the trip to Cooper Island.

She glanced once in the rearview mirror. There was no sign of the silver-gray SUV.

So much for thinking of Jack Rayner as her personal hired gun.

CHAPTER FOUR

Jack splashed some whiskey into a glass and went to stand at the window of his condo. From where he stood he had a sweeping view of the valley and the town of Sanctuary Creek. The lights of houses and condominiums and resorts scattered on the hillsides overlooking the community glittered like fool's gold beneath the desert moon.

On the far side of the valley he could see the glow of the gated community in which Madeline's condo was located. She would be packing for the trip north tonight. Tomorrow she would be on her way to an island that she and her grandmother had left eighteen years ago. As far as he had been able to determine, neither of them had ever returned, nor had they shown any desire to go back to Cooper Island.

Yet Edith Chase had never sold the Aurora Point Hotel.

Edith had been a savvy businesswoman. Why had she hung on to a property that was evidently rotting into the ground?

He wished he'd had more time to get to know his first major client. He'd certainly been impressed with Edith. He had also been very grateful to her. She had taken a chance on him and he had been determined to prove that his firm, tiny though it was, could handle security for her hotel chain. But now Edith was gone and he was left to deal with Madeline Chase.

He told himself that he had done his job today. He had given his client the data she needed to make an informed decision. He recalled Madeline's fierce expression when she had emerged from the encounter with Fleming. She had been every inch the warrior queen. Her coffee-brown hair had been knotted in a severe twist at the back of her head. The style emphasized her amber eyes and her striking, sharply etched features. In that moment she had been radiating so much energy he was surprised that there were no lightning bolts in the atmosphere around her.

She had been coldly furious—not with Fleming; with herself. He understood. He'd been there.

He swallowed some of the whiskey. It wasn't her fault that she had been deceived for a time by the bastard. She was a very smart woman, but guys like Fleming were very, very good with camouflage. It was their greatest talent and they honed it because it was pretty much the only thing that kept them alive. If the true nature of a narcissistic manipulator ever surfaced, the logical response from decent people would be to slay the beast.

There was nothing in Fleming's background to suggest that he fell into the category of violent sociopath, but that didn't mean he hadn't done a lot of damage in his time. He had taken advantage of Madeline's grief to move in on her while her natural defenses were down. But in the end her personal firewall had held. She had summoned the messenger and asked for a background check. The messenger had delivered the bad news.

The warrior queen had been singed but not badly burned.

She was right about one thing—background checks on her dates were routine for her. He'd found records of investigations going all the way back to her high school prom.

He drank a little more whiskey and turned his attention to the Cooper Island property. It was reasonable that in the wake of Edith Chase's death, the eccentric caretaker would want to discuss the future of the old hotel and his own job. It was even possible that he might have insisted that the conversation take place in person.

But there seemed to be a lot of fog around the Aurora Point property. Edith Chase had never wanted to answer any questions about it. Now her granddaughter was proving to be just as secretive.

There was very little information about the old hotel online. It had been a struggling property when Edith had purchased it, and it had continued to struggle even as Edith tried to transform it into a Northwest vacation retreat. At some point Madeline's parents had been killed in a car accident, and Edith had taken her five-year-old granddaughter into her home.

According to the records, the Aurora Point Hotel had eventually begun to turn a profit. But eighteen years ago, for no obvious reason, Edith had closed the hotel and left a caretaker to look after the grounds. Then she and Madeline had moved to Sanctuary Creek and apparently never looked back.

But now, after all these years, Madeline felt compelled to make the long trip to the San Juan Islands to discuss the future of the property— not with a real estate agent or a developer but with the caretaker.

He let the questions simmer while he finished the whiskey. When the glass was empty he went into the kitchen and turned on the oven.

He opened the refrigerator and considered his options. He liked cooking. It relaxed him. But cooking for one was not particularly inspiring. Sharing a meal with another human being on a nightly basis was one of the things he missed most whenever he was between relationships. Okay, he missed the sex, too.

Unfortunately, ever since the disaster in California, he tended to spend a lot of time between relationships—and the few he did manage to fire up never lasted long.

He took out the block of feta cheese, a few green onions, and some green olives and closed the refrigerator door. There was a can of diced tomatoes in the cupboard. He sautéed the onions in a pot and added the tomatoes and some white wine. A little salt and cumin finished it off.

While the tomato mixture was heating, he arranged several chunks of the feta cheese in the bottom of a baking dish and sprinkled the olives across the cheese. He poured the tomato sauce over the cheese and olives and stuck the dish into the oven.

He spent the next twenty minutes at his computer, reviewing reports from his small—two-person—staff. Then he went back into the kitchen and took a couple of eggs out of the refrigerator. He cracked them, one by one, into the bubbling casserole. He covered the dish with aluminum foil and stuck it back in the oven for another eight minutes.

When the eggs were set, he removed the dish from the oven and put it on the counter to cool. He poured himself a glass of red wine and thought about what he had said to Madeline that afternoon.

He had meant it when he told her that he didn't want the job of messenger again—not when it came to running background checks on her dates. She could get someone else to do that work.

The problem with doing those checks was that it presented him with a serious conflict of interest—because he was seriously interested in Madeline Chase.

He drank some wine and carried the tomato and feta cheese dish to the kitchen table. He turned on the television news for company and thought about Madeline while he ate his solitary dinner.

He needed to give her time to recover not only from her

grandmother's death but also from the Fleming situation. Madeline had a long history of being very cautious about relationships, but she would be even more careful now. It would not be a good strategy to rush her.

He wondered who Madeline would hire to look into his past if he did manage to convince her to take a chance on him. He wasn't concerned about what an investigator would find. One of the useful things about being in the security business was that you knew how to bury your own secrets.

CHAPTER FIVE

Tom Lomax was dying. Blood and other matter draining from the terrible head wound soaked the threadbare carpet. His thin, wiry body was crumpled at the foot of the grand staircase that once upon a time had graced the lobby of Aurora Point Hotel.

He looked up at Madeline with faded blue eyes glazed with shock and blood loss.

"Maddie? Is that you?"

"It's me, Tom. You've had a bad fall. Lie still."

"I failed, Maddie. I'm sorry. Edith trusted me to protect you. I failed."

"It's all right, Tom." Madeline held her wadded-up scarf against the horrible gash on Tom's head. "I'm calling nine-one-one. Help will be here soon."

"Too late." Tom struggled to reach out to her with a clawlike hand that had been weathered and scarred from decades of hard physical labor. "Too late."

The 911 operator was asking for information.

". . . *the nature of your emergency?*"

"I'm at the Aurora Point Hotel," Madeline said, automatically sliding into her executive take-charge tone. "It's Tom Lomax, the caretaker. He's had a bad fall. He needs an ambulance immediately."

"I've got a vehicle on the way," the operator said. "Is he bleeding?"

"Yes."

"Try to stop the bleeding by applying pressure."

Madeline looked at the blood-soaked scarf she was using to try to stanch the flood pouring from the wound.

"What do you think I'm doing?" she said. "Get someone here. Now."

She tossed the phone down on the floor so that she could apply more pressure to Tom's injury. But she could feel his life force seeping away. His eyes were almost blank.

"The briefcase," he whispered.

Another shock wave crashed through her.

"Tom, what about the briefcase?"

"I failed." Tom closed his eyes. "Sunrise. You always liked my sunrises."

"Tom, please, tell me about the briefcase."

But Tom was beyond speech now. He took one more raspy breath and then everything about him stopped. The utter stillness of death settled on him.

Madeline realized that the blood was no longer pouring from the wound. She touched bloody fingertips to Tom's throat. There was no pulse.

A terrible silence flooded the lost-in-time lobby of the abandoned hotel. She knew that Tom was gone, but she had read that the first responder was supposed to apply chest compressions until the medics arrived. She positioned her hands over his heart.

Somewhere in the echoing gloom a floorboard creaked. She froze, her gaze fixed on the broken length of balcony railing that lay on the threadbare carpet beside the body. For the first time she noticed the blood and bits of hair clinging to it.

There were probably several scenarios that could explain the blood and hair on the broken railing, but the one that made the most sense was that it had been used to murder Tom.

The floorboards moaned again. As with the blood and hair on the strip of balcony railing, there were a lot of possible explanations for the creaking sounds overhead. But one of them was that Tom had, indeed, been murdered and the killer was still on the scene.

She listened intently, hoping to hear sirens, but the wind was picking up now, cloaking sounds in the distance.

The floorboards overhead groaned again. This time she was almost certain she heard a footstep. Her intuition was screaming at her now.

Instinctively she turned off the phone so that it would not give away her location if the operator called back. She scrambled to her feet.

Somewhere on the floor above, rusty door hinges squeaked. One of the doors that allowed access to the upstairs veranda had just opened.

She looked down at Tom one last time and knew in her heart that there was nothing more she could do for him.

"I'm sorry, Tom," she whispered.

Her car was parked in the wide, circular driveway in front. She slung the strap of her heavy tote over one shoulder and sprinted toward the lobby doors.

The vast, ornate room was drenched in age and gloom. The dusty chandeliers were suspended from the high ceiling like so many dark, frozen waterfalls. The electricity had been cut off eighteen years earlier. When her grandmother had closed the old hotel she had left all the furnishings behind.

Edith had claimed that the heavy, oversized chairs and end tables, the graceful, claw-footed sofas, and the velvet draperies had been custom designed to suit the Victorian-style architecture and would look out of place anywhere else. But Madeline knew that was not the real reason why they hadn't taken any of the furniture with them. The real reason was that neither of them wanted any reminders of the Aurora Point Hotel.

In its heyday at the dawn of the twentieth century, the hotel had been a glamorous destination, attracting the wealthy travelers and vacationers of the era. Her grandmother had tried to revive the ambience and atmosphere of that earlier time, but in the end it had proven too expensive. In the wake of the violent night eighteen years ago, there had been no way to get rid of the property. Selling the Aurora Point Hotel was never an option after that night. There were too many secrets buried on the grounds.

Madeline was halfway across the cavernous space when she saw the shadows shift beneath the rotting velvet curtains that covered one of the bay windows. It could have been a trick of the light caused by the oncoming storm, but she was not about to take a chance. The shadow had looked too much like a partial silhouette of a figure moving very rapidly toward the front doors. It was possible that she had seen the shadow of the killer. The bastard had used the veranda stairs at the back of the building to get down to the ground and was now moving toward the front lobby entrance to intercept her.

In another moment whoever was out there would come through the lobby doors. She had to assume the worst-case scenario—Tom's killer was hunting her.

Madeline retrieved her keys from her shoulder bag and dropped the tote on the floor. She could hear the muffled thud of running footsteps on the lower veranda now.

She bolted behind the broad staircase and went down a narrow service hall. She had grown up in the Aurora Point. She knew every inch of the place. In the many decades of its existence it had been remodeled and repaired countless times. The gracious, oversized proportions of the public rooms concealed a warren of smaller spaces that made up the back-of-the-house. There was a large kitchen, a commercial-sized pantry, storage rooms, and the laundry.

There were also the back stairs that the staff had used to service the guest rooms.

She summoned up a mental diagram of the layout of the sprawling hotel grounds. It was clear that there was no way to get to her car without being seen by whoever was on the veranda.

She heard the lobby door open just as she emerged from the small, dark hallway into the pantry. The silence that followed iced her nerves. Most people who happened to walk in on a dead body would have made some noise. At the very least they would be calling 911.

So much for the fleeting hope that the intruder might be an inno-cent transient or a high school kid who had stumbled onto the murder scene and was as scared as she was.

She heard more footsteps—long, deliberate strides. Someone was searching the first floor, looking for her. It would be only a matter of time before she was discovered. If the person stalking her was armed, she would not stand a chance of making it to her car.

She tried to think through a workable strategy. On the positive side, help was on the way. She needed the equivalent of a safe room until the authorities arrived.

She went to the doorway of the pantry and looked out into the big kitchen. The old appliances loomed like dinosaurs in the shadows. Beyond lay the service stairs that led to the guest rooms on the upper floors.

She rushed across the kitchen, not even trying to conceal her move-ments. Her shoes rang on the old tile floor. She knew her pursuer must have heard her.

Muffled footsteps suddenly pounded across the lobby, heading for the kitchen.

Madeline opened the door of the service staircase and raced up to the next floor, praying that none of the steps gave way beneath her weight.

She reached the first landing, turned, and went down the hall. Most of the room doors were closed. She chose one at the far end of the corridor, opened it, and rushed inside.

Whirling, she slammed the door shut and slid the ancient bolt home. A determined man could kick the door down, but it would take some work.

She could hear the intruder coming up the service stairs. But her pursuer would have to check the rooms one by one to find her.

Heart pounding, her breath tight in her chest, she looked down and was vaguely surprised to see that she was still clutching her phone. She stared at it, oddly numb. Very carefully she switched it on and tapped in the emergency number again. She set the phone on the top of a dusty dresser.

"Don't hang up again," the operator said earnestly. "The ambulance and police should be there any minute. Are you all right?"

"No," Madeline said.

She went to the nearest piece of stout furniture, a heavy armchair, and started to drag it across the room.

"Are you in danger?" the operator demanded.

"Yes," Madeline said. "I'm upstairs in one of the bedrooms. Someone is coming down the hall. He'll be here any second. I've locked the door but I don't know how long that will stop him."

"Push something in front of the door."

"Great idea," Madeline gasped. She shoved harder on the heavy chair. "Why didn't I think of it?"

The big chair seemed to weigh a ton, but it was moving now. She managed to maneuver it in front of the door.

She heard the footsteps stop outside her room. She grabbed her phone and headed toward the French doors that opened onto the veranda.

The storm struck just as she stepped outside. Wind-driven rain lashed at her. But she could hear the sirens in the distance.

She knew the intruder had heard them too because the footsteps were retreating down the hall, heading toward the rear stairs at a run. She knew the killer was headed for the safety of the woods that bordered the rear of the property. She remembered the old service road that wound through the trees.

A short time later she heard a car engine roar to life. The intruder was gone.

She reminded herself that there were not a lot of ways off Cooper Island. A private ferry provided service twice a day. There were also floatplanes and charter boats. The local police might have a shot at catching the killer.

Or not. Most of Cooper Island was undeveloped. A great deal of it was covered in forest. There were plenty of places where a determined murderer could hide until he found a way off the island.

She rushed to meet the emergency vehicles pulling into the drive. Mentally she made a list of what she could—and could not—tell the cops.

She had spent eighteen years keeping secrets. She was good at it.

CHAPTER SIX

The following afternoon she was standing at the window of the Cove View B&B, watching rain fall on the small community of Cooper Cove, when Jack knocked on the door. Just two short, imperative raps. It had to be Jack, she thought. His tough, brusque, no-nonsense style came through in even the smallest actions. There were few wasted motions. It was as if at some point in his life a fierce desert wind had scoured away any veneer of polite polish that he might have once possessed, leaving only the hard rock behind.

She hurried across the room and opened the door. She was startled by the wave of intense relief that cascaded through her when she saw Jack standing in the hall. His dark hair was damp with rain. Water dripped off his scarred leather jacket. He gripped a battered black duffel bag in one big hand.

"What's the problem?" he asked.

That was Jack for you, Madeline thought. Mr. Cordial-and-Charming he was not. The man didn't believe in wasting time with the customary social greetings. That was probably a good thing because it was doubtful that he would be any good at the cheery platitudes and courtesies that smoothed conversations and connections between people. She doubted that he had ever uttered the words *Have a good day* in his entire life. Even if he got the right words out, the chill in his hazel eyes would completely nullify the warmth of the sentiment. In his opinion, your failure to have a good day was your problem, not his.

On the positive side, Jack was not a whiner. She had phoned him late last night after a great deal of thinking. She knew that he had flown out of Phoenix at the crack of dawn and had been traveling ever since—planes, cars, and a couple of ferry rides. It wasn't easy getting to Cooper Island. But she had called and he was here. That was Jack.

She reminded herself that he wasn't exactly doing her a favor by coming to Cooper Island. She was a client, after all. He was here because there was money in it for him and for his fledgling security business.

Even though she had been expecting him—pacing the floor, if the truth be told—she was not only reassured but oddly rattled by the sight of him looming in the doorway. It was always like this when she was near him. He had a weird effect on her senses, she thought.

Yet on some deep level she felt like she understood Jack in some ways. There were shadows around him and the *No Trespassing* signs were glaringly bright, but she understood shadows and warning signs. She possessed a few herself.

People like William Fleming interpreted the signs as an indication of commitment and intimacy issues. In past generations there had been more respect for personal secrets, she thought; even an expectation that everyone had a few and had a right to keep them private. But in the modern era, when people impulsively posted every thought and emotion on social media sites, keeping a secret was generally regarded as a mental health issue.

But if you had kept secrets yourself, you understood why others might choose to do the same.

"Come in," she said.

He moved through the doorway, quartering the suite with a quick, sweeping glance as though assessing potential security risks. She was suddenly very conscious of the king-sized bed.

"I booked the room next door to this one for you," she said. "If you'd like to settle in first—"

"Later." He dropped the duffel bag on the floor near the door. "Right now I could use a cup of coffee."

"Let me take your coat," she said. She nodded toward the in-room coffeemaker. "Help yourself to the coffee."

"Thanks."

He stripped off his jacket, handed it to her, and then headed straight for the coffeemaker.

That was another thing about Jack, she thought as she hurried into the bathroom with his jacket. If he said *thanks*, you could be pretty sure he meant it.

The inside lining of the jacket was still warm with his body heat. She caught a trace of his scent when she hung the garment on a hook.

She stood there for a beat, watching the rainwater drip onto the white tiles, and composed her thoughts. Jack would demand answers. Supplying them would mean giving up secrets that she had kept for eighteen years, but she no longer had a choice.

She took a deep breath and went out into the other room. "Thank you for making the trip here today on such short notice. I couldn't think of anyone else to call."

"No need to thank me." He hit the switch on the coffee machine and looked at her. "This is what I do. It's why you keep my company on retainer."

She cleared her throat. "Right."

"Here's what I know based on what little you told me on the phone. You came here to meet with the man who had been looking after the Aurora Point property."

"Tom Lomax, yes."

"You found him badly injured."

"He was dying." She folded her arms very tightly beneath her breasts. "I called nine-one-one and I tried to stop the bleeding, but there was no hope."

"Head injury, you said?"

"Someone struck him from behind with a length of broken staircase railing. I found him at the foot of the lobby stairs. There was . . . a lot of blood. The police believe that Tom surprised an intruder who had broken into the hotel to search for anything that might be worth stealing."

"I'm assuming there is more to the story or you wouldn't have called me."

This was quintessential Jack, she thought. He pretended that he worked for you, but somehow he always seemed to be in charge. Jack might not be the warm and fuzzy type, but he had the vibe of a man who could handle just about any crisis. And she had a crisis on her hands.

She sank down onto one of the two reading chairs near the window and looked out at the obsidian-dark waters of the cove. For the past few hours she had pondered various ways to explain her situation. But now that Jack was there she was not sure where to begin. It wasn't easy to start talking about a secret that had been kept for eighteen years.

"Here's what I didn't tell you on the phone," she said. "Tom spoke to me before he died. He said he was sorry, that he had failed. He mentioned a briefcase and reminded me that I had always liked his sunrises. I assume he was talking about his photographs. He is— was—a very avid photographer. I think he was hallucinating there at the very end. That was when I heard the footsteps overhead."

Jack went as still as a sniper waiting to take the shot. "What?"

Okay, this was not going well. She took a breath and prepared to race through the rest of the explanation.

"I heard the intruder go down the outside staircase at the back of the lobby. At first I thought the person was running away. Instead—" She paused to take a breath. "Instead I heard footsteps on the lower veranda. I was afraid that whoever it was intended to intercept me if I tried to get to my car. So I ran upstairs and locked myself in one of the rooms until the cops arrived. The intruder tried to follow me but gave up and ran off. I think the emergency vehicle sirens scared him away."

Jack watched her with an unblinking gaze. "Him?"

"Or her. I honestly couldn't tell. Whoever it was went out the rear of the hotel and drove off in a car. The cops conducted a search but they couldn't find anyone. I've been assured that an officer will monitor outgoing ferry traffic for a while, but there are a lot of ways you can bring a boat ashore on the island without being spotted."

There was a short, ominous silence. Jack did not take his eyes off her.

"When you called last night you never mentioned that there was anyone else in the hotel when you arrived on the scene," he said in a voice that was much too neutral.

"I was afraid that it would only alarm you, and it wasn't like there was anything you could do from Arizona. And besides, I was safe here at the B-and-B."

She hated being put on the defensive. She reminded herself that Jack worked for her, not vice versa.

"Shit," Jack finally said very softly. "I knew it was a mistake to let you come here alone."

That stopped her cold for a beat. She had never heard him use rough language. It was probably not a good omen.

"Look," she said, "maybe this was not such a great idea. I've got a problem on my hands and I need your professional assistance. If you don't feel that you're in a position to provide it, I'll find someone else."

"No," he said. "You won't find anyone else. We've got a contract. You told the police about the intruder?"

"Yes, of course. But I wasn't able to give them a description. Like I said, they think poor Tom surprised a burglar. And that might be true. But I've got my doubts."

"Because of what Tom told you before he died?"

"It's possible that he hallucinated everything there at the end—got the past and present mixed up. But he knew who I was. What concerns me were his comments about the briefcase and his belief that he had failed."

She got the feeling that Jack was fortifying himself for what he anticipated would be a difficult conversation.

"All right," he said finally. "Let's start with the briefcase."

She took a breath and let it out slowly. "Give me a minute. I haven't talked about the briefcase in eighteen years. Family secret."

"I'm listening."

She forced herself to focus. "The briefcase Tom mentioned belonged to a man who checked into Aurora Point Hotel eighteen years ago. He used the name Porter but that was probably not his real name."

"What happened to this Porter?"

She gripped the arms of the chair.

"My grandmother and Tom killed him with a couple of heavy-duty gardening tools. They buried the body in the woods behind the hotel. Tom poured a concrete slab over the grave and built a nice little gazebo on top."

CHAPTER SEVEN

She watched Jack very closely but as far as she could tell, he took the news of Porter's death the same way he took everything else—as just another fact. He did not appear shocked or even mildly surprised; merely thoughtful.

It occurred to her that after what he must have seen in the course of his FBI profiling work, death by garden tools was probably a fairly tame scenario. Still, they were talking about her grandmother, a very nice woman who had never killed anyone else in her entire life.

After a moment Jack poured two cups of coffee and handed one to her without a word. She got a little spark when their fingers brushed against each other. The jolt caused her to flinch. The coffee threatened to splash over the edge of the rim. But she managed to regain her control.

Jack moved to stand in front of the window. He contemplated the view, evidently unfazed by their brief physical contact. She wondered what it would take to shake him.

"And the briefcase belonged to Porter?" he said.

"Yes."

"Walk me through everything that happened at the hotel the day Porter died."

"Aurora Point was my grandmother's first hotel. She and my grandfather picked it up for a song. They were determined to renovate it. But my grandfather died in the same car accident that killed my parents. I came here to live with Grandma. She worked hard to reopen Aurora Point. She was just starting to turn a profit when Porter checked in. There was a big wedding event going on in the main building. Grandmother and the rest of the staff were all very busy. My friend Daphne and I spent the evening together playing games and watching TV in the cottage where Daphne and her mother lived."

"Daphne?"

"Daphne Knight. She was my best friend at the time. Her mother was a single mom who worked on the hotel's housekeeping staff. She was busy in the main building that night, along with everyone else."

"Go on."

"It grew late. Daphne and I fell asleep in front of the television. I woke up and went into the kitchen to get a glass of water. There was a man waiting there. He grabbed me. Slapped a hand across my mouth and said he'd kill me if I struggled. But I struggled anyway. It didn't do any good. He was big. And so much stronger. I couldn't breathe. I think I passed out for a moment. Not long, though, because the next thing I remember he was carrying me into the maintenance building. By then I was literally frozen with terror. I thought I was in a nightmare. None of it seemed real."

The cup trembled ever so slightly in her hand. She set it down with great care. She had spent eighteen years trying not to think about the events of that terrible night. It was unnerving to talk about them now after the years of keeping the secret; years of nightmares in which she was trapped under the weight of a man's big, sweating body. Years of coming awake gasping for air. Years of intimacy issues that inevitably spelled doom for all of her relationships.

She fell silent for a moment and tried to order her thoughts. Jack did not urge her to continue. He stood at the window, drinking coffee and watching the storm clouds roll over Cooper Island as if he had all the time in the world.

The fact that he wasn't pushing told her in some mysterious way that he understood something of what she had experienced. That made it easier to go on with the story.

"As it turned out, Daphne awakened just as Porter carried me out the kitchen door. She didn't know what to do. She was terrified but she was incredibly brave. She followed us and saw Porter take me into the maintenance building. She ran to Tom's cottage and pounded on his door. He headed for the maintenance building but he told her to find Grandma, who happened to be in the kitchen checking on something involving the buffet. Daphne dragged her outside and tried to explain that something terrible was happening in the maintenance building."

Madeline stopped again. Again Jack waited.

"The next thing I knew, first Tom and then Grandma came through the door like a couple of avenging angels. They each grabbed a garden tool and went after Porter. He had me pinned down on a sack of garden loam, trying to get me out of my jeans. In the end I think Grandma and Tom went a little mad. There was . . . a lot of blood."

"They killed Porter."

"Yes."

"Good." Jack nodded, satisfied. "Were you . . . hurt?"

"He didn't succeed in raping me, if that's what you mean."

"But you were traumatized."

She shuddered. "I think all four of us were traumatized. Daphne witnessed the whole thing."

Jack turned his head to look at her. "And Porter's briefcase? Was it buried with Porter?"

"No. The Aurora Point was undergoing renovations at the time. Tom and Grandma walled it up in room two-oh-nine."

"Why didn't Edith and Tom call the police?"

"Because of what was in the briefcase," Madeline said. "And before you ask, no, I don't know what was inside. I just know that after Grandma and Tom opened the briefcase, they decided not to call the police. They told Daphne's mother what had happened but they didn't tell her what was in the briefcase—just that it was very dangerous. Maybe they thought she would feel safer if she didn't know exactly what was inside. Who knows? But that was when the three of them—Grandma, Tom, and Daphne's mother—decided to bury the body and make every bit of evidence disappear."

"They wanted to make it all vanish, but they didn't bury the briefcase or burn the contents?"

She hesitated. "For what it's worth, I overheard Grandma tell Tom and Daphne's mother that the contents of the briefcase were an insurance policy. With luck they would never have to use it."

Jack's eyes tightened at the corners. "Edith used that phrase? *Insurance policy*?"

"Yes. Grandma told us that the stuff inside the briefcase was very dangerous because it could get some powerful people in trouble. She said if that happened, we would all be in mortal danger. We all promised each other that we would never tell anyone about Porter and his briefcase."

"How many people, in all, knew about Porter's death and the briefcase?"

"Just the five of us—Grandma and me. Tom Lomax. Daphne and her mother, Clara Knight."

Jack shook his head. "That's four people too many to keep a danger-ous secret."

Anger splashed through her. "Well, we did manage to keep it for all these years."

"As far as you know."

"We each had a very good reason to keep it."

"Let's do a head count. How many people who knew the secret are still alive?"

The question chilled her. "Grandma and Tom are both gone. I haven't been in touch with Daphne or her mother for eighteen years." Tears burned in her eyes. "I don't know what happened to them. Daphne was my best friend. She saved me that night. But I don't even know if she's alive. How is that possible?"

The tears got hotter and started to trickle down her cheeks. She lurched to her feet, intending to go into the bathroom to find a tissue, but Jack handed her a small napkin from the coffee service tray. She sank back down into the chair and blotted her eyes.

Jack watched her pull herself together. He was giving her some space, but she knew that whatever he was about to say, he was not going to try to soften the blow. Jack probably didn't know how to soften bad news.

She sniffed one last time and tossed the crumpled napkin into the trash.

"Sorry, it's been a long day," she said. "What now?"

"Here's what we've got," he said. "Your grandmother and Tom are dead within three months of each other and some unknown person—presumably Tom's killer—may have tried to kill you. Meanwhile, we don't know the whereabouts of the two other people who featured in the events eighteen years ago—Daphne and her mother."

Madeline stared at him, reeling from his words. "Grandma's death was an accident, according to the authorities. Even the insurance com-pany didn't question it, and you know how they hate to pay out."

"A fire in the penthouse of an old hotel caused by faulty wiring.

Only one victim, your grandmother. That kind of accident is not difficult to arrange if you know what you're doing. And if you don't have the skill set, you can hire someone else to set it up."

"It wasn't even one of her hotels," Madeline whispered. "Grandma was the guest of an old friend in the business, someone she had known for decades."

"I know. I've had someone on my staff looking into your grandmother's death ever since I got a copy of the insurance company's final report last month."

"What?" She bolted up out of the chair. "You thought my grandmother might have been murdered but you didn't say anything?"

"At the time, I didn't have any reason to suspect that she had been murdered." Jack's mouth twisted. "As you said, the insurance company signed off on an accident. There was another problem, too. The only one who might have had a possible motive was you."

"Good grief." She dropped back into her seat, stunned all over again. "Because I inherited the Sanctuary Creek chain."

"I didn't see you as the type to murder your own grandmother for a business she had been slowly handing off to you anyway."

"Gosh, thanks for that rousing vote of confidence."

"There were other reasons I didn't tell you that I had looked into the circumstances of Edith's death. You were swamped. Not only were you dealing with the loss of someone you loved, you didn't even have a real opportunity to mourn because you had to become the face of Sanctuary Creek Inns. Your employees and your execs were looking to you for direction and stability. You had to reassure suppliers and accounts. On top of that, you were starting to get uneasy about William Fleming."

"Fine. I was busy and grieving and I had issues with the guy I was dating. That is absolutely no excuse for not coming to me with your concerns about my grandmother's death."

"I used my best judgment."

"Bullshit. You weren't using good judgment. You were trying to protect me from bad news. That's not in your job description."

"I didn't have anything solid indicating that Edith's death was anything other than an accident. For that matter, I still don't."

"Bullshit, the sequel. I have recently been made aware of the fact that you have issues with being the messenger who brings me the bad news. But you need to understand that I am paying you for the news— good or bad. I do not pay you to protect me from bad news. If you screw up one more time I will find a new security firm—even if I can't find a way out of our contract. I'll pay for two consultants if that's what it takes to make sure I'm getting what I want. Are we clear?"

He studied her for a long moment. She got the impression he was seriously considering whether he should resign. That was the last thing she wanted. But some things were nonnegotiable.

Jack finally came to a decision. "All right. I'll make sure you know whatever I know regarding your grandmother's death. But understand up front that a lot of the information that comes in at the start of an investigation leads nowhere. It can be confusing."

She allowed herself to breathe again. "Understood."

He gave her a reluctant smile. "You are definitely Edith's grand-daughter, all right. Sanctuary Creek Inns is in good hands."

"Thank you. Now stop trying to placate me. Just so you know, you're not very good at soothing ruffled feathers."

"You're not the first person to say that."

"Tell me what you've got relating to my grandmother's death."

"I had nothing until now," he said patiently. "That's why I didn't talk to you about the investigation."

She gave him a warning look.

"But now I've got something," he said.

"Tom Lomax's death?"

"Yeah." Jack finished his coffee and put the cup down. "Now we are starting to see the first ripples of what could be a very disturbing pattern."

"Because you have a problem with coincidence."

"Sure." He raised his brows. "Don't you?"

"Yes, of course."

"One accident involving a person who is keeping a secret that four other people know is a coincidence. The death of someone else who knew the secret is a pattern."

She absorbed that thought. "But why is the past surfacing now?"

"I warned you that at the start of an investigation all the data points come wrapped in fog."

She folded her arms. "What do we do?"

"We move on a couple of different fronts," Jack said. "First, we find Daphne and her mother."

"We need to warn them, don't we?"

"I think so, yes." He paused, looking a little wary. "But there is another possibility."

"That one of them had something to do with the deaths?" Madeline shook her head. "No. I admit I haven't seen or spoken to Daphne or her mother for the past eighteen years, but I can't believe either of them would kill Grandma or Tom. Setting emotions aside, there's no logic to that theory."

"You were the one who told me that Edith referred to the contents of the briefcase as an insurance policy. Maybe someone has decided to collect."

"That is a very unnerving thought."

"Either way, we need to find Daphne and her mother. I'll get someone on it immediately."

"Okay." Madeline paused. "You mentioned a second front."

"It looks like we'll be spending a fair amount of time on Cooper

Island. We need to put together a cover story to explain my presence here."

"The investigation starts here?"

"Yes," Jack said. "And it will probably end here."

"What makes you so sure?"

"If I'm right, this thing has its roots in the past. And this is where the past is buried."

"Under a gazebo."

"Some of it is under the gazebo. Evidently the rest is walled up in room two-oh-nine of the Aurora Point Hotel."

CHAPTER EIGHT

Daphne Knight stood in the doorway of the spare bedroom of her new condo and contemplated the chaos the intruder had left behind. The bastard had invaded her new home—her private space. It dawned on her that she ought to be feeling some strong emotion—rage, violation, fear—something.

Instead, she was strangely numb, just as she had been for most of the past year. The Mediterranean cruise had done little to boost her spirits. Walking into her home a short time ago and discovering that it had been vandalized while she was away had not caused the appropriate degree of shock and outrage. She was just exhausted.

Her phone rang. She turned away from the sight of her ruined home office and looked at the screen. For a couple of seconds she stared at the unfamiliar number, trying to make sense of it.

She took the call and pressed the phone very tightly to her ear. "Yes?"

"Daphne? This is Madeline Chase."

"Maddie? Is that really you?"

"Yes, it's me," Madeline said. "Daphne, it's so good to hear your voice. It's been too long. Eighteen years."

Eighteen years, Daphne thought. But the bloody scene in the maintenance building was as sharp and clear as ever. She knew that memory played tricks over time and over distance. It was entirely possible that she had invented and reinvented some of the details of that terrible night in an effort to deal with the trauma.

But some things had been seared into her so deeply that she could never forget them. Even after all this time they came back to haunt her dreams. The sight of Maddie crushed beneath the man named Porter. The image of Edith Chase plunging the huge pruning shears into Porter's back again and again. The vision of Tom Lomax smashing Porter's head with a gardening hoe. The blood had spurted in fountains.

So much blood she was afraid that she was too late, that Maddie was dead.

"Daphne, are you still there?" Madeline's voice, already strained, tightened still further. "I've been so worried. Please tell me that you're okay."

"Yes, yes, I'm okay. I'm fine. Hearing your voice is a shock, that's all. I'm afraid you caught me at a bad time."

"I'm so sorry. I would offer to call later but this is really important. I have to talk to you."

"It's all right. I'm just a little shaken up at the moment. My condo was burglarized while I was away on a cruise. The police just left."

"Oh, damn. Are you sure you're safe?"

Daphne took the phone away from her ear and looked at it, bewildered by the alarm in Madeline's voice. It seemed a little over the top. House burglaries were hardly uncommon. And it wasn't as if she and Madeline had remained close. Eighteen years was a long time.

She put the phone back to her ear.

"Yes, of course," she said. "The police took a report and asked me to draw up an inventory of any stolen items. They were very nice and very professional, but they didn't hold out much hope of catching the creep."

"What was taken?"

"As far as I can tell, just my computer. Standard procedure for home burglars, the cops said. But all my important files are stored in the cloud. The place is a mess, though."

She looked at the papers and files that littered her office. The sketches she had done for the proprietor of a clothing boutique in Boulder had been dumped from a file drawer. Her collection of books written and illustrated by nineteenth-century architects and interior designers had been yanked out of the glass-fronted bookcase and dropped on the floor. Framed photographs of the finished interiors she had created for clients in and around the Denver area had been yanked off the wall and smashed. Here and there shards of broken glass sparked in the late-afternoon light.

"Daphne, I'm calling about something really important."

"I assumed as much. I heard that your grandmother was killed in a hotel fire. I'm so sorry."

"You knew she was gone?"

"My mother found the obituary online and sent it to me. To be honest, I hadn't realized that Mom was still watching for that sort of thing. For a few years after we left Cooper Island she was obsessive about any hint of news relating to the island and your grandmother, but I thought that she had put it all behind her by the time she remarried."

"Your mother is married?"

"She was. She's widowed now. Her second husband suffered a stroke a few years ago. Mom is alone again but this time she is a very wealthy widow. Turns out rich widows are never alone, at least not for long. She's having a good time."

"Where is she?"

"I'm not sure. I'd have to check the itinerary. She's on a round-the-world cruise with some friends. I joined her for a couple of weeks while her ship was touring the Med, but she's still on board. She's got another month before she returns to Florida."

"But she's alive."

"Very much so. Maddie, don't get me wrong, it's great to hear from you after all this time, but what's going on here? Why are you so nervous?"

"I have some very disturbing news. We need to talk."

Daphne caught her breath. "This is about the past, isn't it?"

"I'm sorry, but yes, it's about the past. It may be nothing. Or it may be something terrible. We need to figure out what is happening. I'm going to have to ask you to come to Cooper Island."

Daphne went cold. "You're serious."

"This is secret-sisters serious, Daph. Please believe me."

Secret sisters. The words were a beacon of light in a world that had gone uniformly gray. Secret sisters did not lie to each other.

"You've got my full attention," Daphne said.

"The company that handles security for Sanctuary Creek Inns has someone standing by to escort you here to the island," Madeline said. "He's in Phoenix now. He can be in Denver by early this evening."

Daphne tightened her grip on the phone. "Just to clarify, you're talking about a bodyguard, aren't you?"

"I'm afraid so. Here's what we know—there's a possibility that Grandma was murdered because of what happened that night. And now Tom Lomax is dead, too."

"Tom? The nice old man who helped your grandmother—?" She could not finish the sentence. Eighteen years of silence was like quicksand. You couldn't just step out of it all at once. You had to pull free inch by inch.

"Tom was killed in the lobby of the hotel late yesterday," Madeline said. "I was the one who found him."

"*Maddie.*"

"I think the killer was still there when I arrived."

"My God."

"It's okay, he heard the sirens and ran off. But now you tell me you've had a break-in and your computer is gone. This could be nothing, but we can't take any chances. We need to get to the bottom of this thing. Hang on; Jack Rayner, the head of my security firm, wants to talk to you."

In spite of everything, Daphne almost smiled. At the age of twelve, Madeline Chase had talked like a future executive, and it sounded like she had fulfilled her destiny. Even as a girl, she'd had a knack for going straight to the bottom line. *Stop dreaming, Daph. You don't want to be an actress when you grow up. The odds of actually becoming a star are horrible. Besides, you're my best friend. I can't stand the thought of you having a lot of bad cosmetic surgery.*

Another voice came on the line—a man this time. His voice was infused with the calm, professional authority of someone who knew something about dealing with dangerous people.

"This is Jack Rayner. Where are you?"

"My condo. Why?"

"I want you to leave now," he said. "Do not take time to pack. Don't try to grab any valuables—just your car keys, ID, and whatever you've got in your purse."

"Go where?"

"The airport. Plenty of built-in security. I just gave my agent the go-ahead to fly to Denver. His name is Abe Rayner. He'll have ID. He'll escort you to Cooper Island."

Daphne groped to keep ahead of the flow of instructions. "Rayner?"

"My brother. Now focus on getting to the airport. You'll be safe there."

For the first time in a long while, Daphne experienced a surge of strong emotion—fear. Tom Lomax and Edith Chase were dead and someone had just vandalized her condo. Her survival instincts were kicking in.

"Okay," she said. "I'm leaving now."

"I'll stay on the phone until you're in your car," Jack said.

Daphne turned away from the ruined office. She went back downstairs. The luggage she had taken on the cruise was still sitting, unpacked, in the front hall. She grabbed the roll-aboard suitcase—it wasn't as if she had disobeyed instructions and taken time to pack it, she thought. It was already packed.

No matter what happens, we will be secret sisters forever.

It was an oath sworn by two terrified girls of twelve who were forever bound by the terrible events of a night filled with blood and panic.

Daphne ran for the door.

Some things you had to believe in. An oath taken in girlhood between best friends who had seen more violence than anyone should have to witness in a lifetime was one of those things.

Besides, it was not like there was anything left for her in Denver.

CHAPTER NINE

Louisa Webster paused in the doorway of the great room and looked at her husband. Egan stood at the wall of windows, meditating on the sweeping view. In the distance other islands in the San Juans could be seen; some, like Cooper, were large enough to support small communities. But many were so small that they were only visible at low tide.

The fading light of the rain-stricken day transformed the dark, cold water into hammered steel. The cloud cover hung low over the island. She knew there were plenty of sunny days on Cooper Island, but it seemed to her that it was always like this when she and Egan were in residence—an unrelenting shade of gray.

A fire burned in the big stone fireplace, but no one had turned on the lights in the room.

She remembered her first impression of Egan all those years ago. He had been so arrestingly attractive in so many ways—a tall, broad-shouldered, athletically built man with a mane of blond hair, brilliant blue eyes, and classically chiseled features. Very little had changed over the years. Like a charismatic televangelist, he managed to project the image of a man endowed with the wisdom that came with maturity coupled with the energy of a man in his prime.

And like a successful televangelist, he'd always been able to seduce his audience—investors, politicians, friends, women. He had a gift for convincing others that he could make dreams come true. He had employed that talent to make a fortune.

Unlike the average televangelist, Egan had delivered on at least some of his promises—specifically those relating to wealth. He'd made a good living as a stockbroker in the early years, but after establishing his own hedge fund, Egan had been golden. It was as if he could not miss. His ability to predict markets had made him a legend and opened doors in the political, social, and financial worlds.

But the glossy trappings of his successful fund concealed a secret, one that was growing more dangerous by the day. From the outside, Egan still appeared to be the master of his universe, but she knew the truth. The great moneymaking engine that he had constructed twenty years ago had begun to wind down. Egan had privately blamed the problems on the volatile nature of the global economy—the unpredictability of oil, the financial troubles in the Eurozone, the surging influence of China.

She listened to his excuses, but she knew the truth. She wondered when his investors would start to get nervous. There had been some turnover among the top clients recently, but most were still satisfied with their monthly statements. After all, those statements still glowed with the luster of gold. But she wondered how long Egan could continue to dazzle his audience. Successful hedge funds often followed a predictable trajectory—fast out of the gate, astonishing results for a time, and then a crash-and-burn.

But if there was one thing she knew for certain about Egan, it was that he was a survivor.

She walked partway into the gloom-filled room.

"Travis and Patricia have agreed to join us for dinner this evening."

Egan turned away from the gray vista. "And Xavier?"

With the ease of long habit she suppressed the little whisper of despair that always fluttered, wraithlike, at the edge of her awareness. Xavier was better now. Stable.

"His assistant phoned with regrets a short time ago. The campaign team is due in from Seattle this afternoon. He wants to take them out for drinks and a meal at a local restaurant. Something about giving them a taste of life here on the island so that they can convey a sense of Travis's small-town upbringing to the media."

Egan grunted. "For the most part Travis and Xavier were raised in Seattle."

"Yes."

The silence stretched taut between them. She had stopped loving Egan years ago when she realized that the womanizing would never cease. She had finally accepted the reality of their relationship. He had never truly loved her. He had coveted her beauty and her family's money. She had brought him both, but she had made the mistake of giving him her heart, as well.

Whatever they'd had back at the start of their marriage had long since evaporated. But they were forever bound by their two sons. Xavier and Travis had inherited so many of their father's gifts—his striking looks, his blue eyes, and his talent for mesmerizing an audience.

But beneath the surface they were very different men. It was Travis who held the promise of a brilliant future in politics. He was preparing for his first run for office, and Louisa knew that meant Egan now had to deal with the one thing he was not good at—accepting the fact that he was not going to get something he wanted very badly.

He had long been obsessed with the vision of one of his sons becoming a U.S. senator and eventually taking the White House. Egan's problem was that he had always believed it was Xavier who was destined to wield great political power, not Travis. For years he had convinced himself that Xavier was his true heir——the strong one; the son who was capable of the ruthlessness it took to survive in the tough worlds of finance and politics. But it had become clear that Xavier's flaws ran too deep. It was Travis who was headed for the Oval Office.

Egan turned back to the window. "I talked to Travis about the wisdom of making Xavier his campaign manager."

"What did he say?"

"The same thing he told you."

Louisa's stomach tightened in a knot of anguish. "'Keep your friends close but keep your enemies closer.'"

"In this case, keep a certain member of your family where you can watch him." Egan snorted softly. "He may be right. Travis is weak in some ways, but he is not naïve——at least not when it comes to Xavier."

"Xavier has been stable for some time now," Louisa said. But she knew it was the mother in her speaking, not the realist. "The medication they started him on at the Institute last year has been working well, and managing Travis's campaign seems to have given him direction and focus. Travis says Xavier is doing an excellent job. He knows how to charm the media."

Egan clasped his hands behind his back. "We both know it's just a matter of time before there's another . . . incident. We've managed to keep things under control in the past, but we had the advantage of privacy. That's gone now. If Xavier has another break he could destroy Travis's election chances. That can't be allowed to happen. There is too much at stake."

"What can we do?"

"I've been considering our options. There aren't many. But Xavier has been demanding access to his inheritance. He wants to prove that he has a talent for the hedge fund business. I'm thinking of granting his request. Let him set up his own fund with his name on the wall.

That may satisfy him and occupy his attention, at least long enough to ensure that Travis gets elected."

Hope flickered somewhere deep inside Louisa. It had been so long since she had experienced the sensation, she almost failed to recognize it.

"That is . . . a brilliant idea," she said slowly, thinking it through. "It just might work."

Egan's jaw jerked once. "For a while."

"Yes. For a while."

Nothing could cure the darkness in Xavier. They both knew it, just as they both knew that it was only a matter of time before the fire inside their golden boy exploded into flames again—possibly quite literally.

Louisa turned to leave. "I have an appointment with the event planner."

"I heard that Edith Chase's granddaughter is in town," Egan said over his shoulder. "What was the girl's name? Margaret? Mary?"

"Madeline," Louisa said. "Madeline Chase."

"I understand that she was the one who found the body of the old man who was taking care of the Aurora Point property."

Louisa paused in the doorway. "That's true. There's a rumor going around that now that Edith Chase is gone, Madeline will sell the hotel. Evidently she's brought in a consultant to help her evaluate her options."

"If she has any sense, she'll sell," Egan said. "Never could understand why Edith hung on to that old hotel."

CHAPTER TEN

"This settles one question," Jack said. He studied the gaping hole in the wall of room 209. Chunks of broken wallboard and insulation littered the floor. "Looks like whoever murdered Tom Lomax has the briefcase."

"I was afraid that was what Tom meant when he said he had failed." Madeline shook her head. "And we have no clue what was inside. We don't even know if it's still dangerous. After all, a lot can happen in eighteen years. Maybe whatever was in the briefcase is harmless now."

Jack looked at her. She stood in the center of the dusty room, bundled up against the damp chill of the rainy day. The collar of her black parka was pulled up around her neck, framing her expressive face and arresting eyes. There was an edgy tension about her. He knew that in spite of everything that had happened, she had been clinging to the possibility that the killer had not found the briefcase. He wanted to reassure her, but offering false hope was not part of his job description. Besides, he was no good at faking unfounded optimism.

"Someone murdered Lomax for the briefcase," he said. "Trust me, whatever is inside is still dangerous."

She flinched a little at the unvarnished statement of fact, but she dipped her chin in a single crisp nod.

"You're right," she said.

He glanced at his watch. "We've got some daylight left. Time to take a look around Lomax's place. You say he lived in one of the cottages on the grounds?"

"Yes, I'll show you." She turned away from the ripped wall and went toward the door. "We don't have to worry about the daylight. The electricity was turned off in the main hotel buildings but not at Tom's cottage."

He followed her, circling a sagging bed draped in several hundred generations of spiderwebs. With the exception of the damaged wall, the hotel room looked as if it had been caught in a time warp. A shroud of dust lay over everything. The layers of grime on the window were so thick that very little daylight made it through the glass.

But the floor had been swept. Recently.

Nevertheless, he took out his penlight, switched it on, and aimed the beam at the floor. There was one faint set of prints.

"Huh."

Madeline halted. "What is it?"

"Whoever wore those boots was here within the past few days," he said. "After the floor was swept."

"Tom was murdered yesterday."

"If those are his footprints then he came up here recently, presumably to retrieve the briefcase."

"That doesn't make any sense. Why would he do that after all this time?"

"Let's go take a look at Lomax's cottage."

They left room 209 and went down the hallway toward the main staircase. With most of the room doors closed and no electricity, it was a trek made in deep shadows. The only natural illumination was the weak daylight coming through the windows at opposite ends of the corridor. Jack aimed the beam of the flashlight at one of the rusted metal numbers on a nearby door.

"Did the person who pursued you yesterday seem to know his or her way around in here?" he asked.

Madeline considered briefly. "Somewhat. The intruder knew enough to follow me into the hallway beneath the lobby stairs. But whoever it was didn't know about the service stairs in the kitchen. I could hear him stumbling around, opening and closing doors before he found the service stairs. That's what bought me enough time to get into one of the rooms and lock the door."

"Just wondering how long the killer had been hanging around the hotel."

"Long enough to know about the service road in the woods behind the place," Madeline said grimly. "That's where the car was left."

"Why was your grandmother so afraid of the local cops eighteen years ago?"

"She wasn't, at least not that I know of, not before she opened the suitcase. But whatever she found in the briefcase convinced her that she couldn't call the police." Madeline paused a beat. "There is one thing I do know, though."

"What's that?"

"Egan Webster pretty much owned this island eighteen years ago, including the local cops. Money was rolling in off his hedge fund and he used it to buy anything and everyone who was for sale."

"So it's possible that Edith was afraid that the contents of the briefcase were connected to the Webster family and she assumed the Websters would not have wanted the material made public."

"That's been one of my working theories over the years. But there are other possibilities. What if it was a shipment of drugs or cash connected to a violent cartel or the mob or terrorists? But every time I tried to talk to Grandma about it, she just said, *Let sleeping dogs lie*."

They left the main building through a back door and walked through what had once been a gracious garden. The area looked like a scene from a dark fairy tale now, Jack thought. The foliage was wildly over-grown and choked with forbidding weeds. It was as if nature were trying to reclaim what had once been a civilized part of the island.

Madeline led the way through a narrow opening in a sagging trellis clogged with half-dead vines.

On the other side of the trellis Jack saw a dilapidated wooden structure with a low roof. The small windows were murky with the evidence of decades of weathering. No one had bothered to clean them in a very long time. A garage door was set into one wall. At the far end of the building there was another, regular door secured with a padlock.

The maintenance building, Jack thought. He glanced at Madeline. She did not look at the building.

The maintenance building, he decided. No doubt about it.

He had to work to suppress the icy fury that threatened to sweep through him. He reminded himself that Edith Chase and Tom Lomax had killed Madeline's attacker.

"That's Tom's place," she said, indicating the first cottage in a row of small, rustic structures. "It's the only one that isn't boarded up."

Years ago the quaint little houses perched on the bluff above the rocky beach would have appeared cozy and welcoming to guests, Jack decided. But now they were just more elements in the bleak fairy tale of Aurora Point.

Behind the cottages was a thick stand of trees. He caught a glimpse of a gazebo.

"Is that——?" he asked. He did not finish the question.

"Yes."

Madeline did not look at the gazebo, just as she had not looked at the maintenance building.

She went around to the front of the cottage and climbed the steps. When she tried the doorknob, it turned easily. She paused on the threshold. ·

"Brace yourself," she said. "Eighteen years ago Tom was something of a hoarder. Also, he had a passion for photography. He never threw any of his photos away."

"I've been warned," Jack said.

Madeline opened the door and moved into the shadows of the tiny front room. She flipped a switch. Somewhere in the shadows a dim light came on. A dank, musty miasma swirled amid the accumulated clutter of decades.

"Ugh." Madeline wrinkled her nose.

Jack glanced at her. "Don't worry, it's not the kind of smell you get when there's a dead body around."

She flicked him a quick, startled glance. "Good to know. Thanks for that cheery observation. Should I ask where you learned about the difference between the smell of a hoarder's house and a dead body?"

"I used to do some consulting work for the FBI, remember?"

"Grandma mentioned it. I got the impression you didn't profile folks engaged in art fraud or Internet gambling."

"Sometimes. But not often enough. The company I was with specialized in behavioral analysis of other kinds of bad guys."

Madeline whistled soundlessly. "Serial killers."

"I changed career paths a while back."

"I can certainly understand why."

He looked mildly surprised. "Thanks. Not everyone does understand."

"They watch too much TV." She swept a hand out to indicate the interior of the cottage. "What does all your experience tell you about this place?"

Jack surveyed the interior. "I'd say Lomax's hoarding tendencies did not improve in the past eighteen years. And I see what you mean about the photography thing."

The cottage had clearly been furnished with leftovers from the hotel—a shabby armchair covered in worn leather, a floor lamp with a torn and badly yellowed shade, odd chunks of carpeting from assorted eras, and curtains decorated with faded floral prints.

The room was crammed with the flotsam and jetsam of a life lived on the fringe of paranoia. Crumbling, yellowed newspapers were piled high in various corners. Books and magazines were stacked everywhere. There were plastic containers filled with assorted lightbulbs and small batteries that were probably no longer viable. Boxes held frayed extension cords and small tools. What looked like a century's worth of mail—bills, catalogs, and requests for charitable donations—overflowed old packing boxes.

And everywhere there were photographs of all descriptions and every conceivable size—black-and-white, sepia toned, and full color. The subjects, as far as Jack could tell, were mostly Cooper Island scenes. There were dramatic shots of the northern lights over the island—brilliant images that captured the spectacle of waves of green and purple fire rippling across the night sky. Striking photos of fierce storms. Atmospheric scenes of the Aurora Point Hotel caught in various stages of renovation and decay.

More than a dozen large prints had been framed and hung on the walls.

"Those were his favorites," Madeline explained, "the only ones he signed. He considered himself an artist. This was his own private gallery."

Only a few of the images featured human subjects, usually the same two people—young girls on the brink of womanhood. In some of the scenes they raced carelessly, wildly, across a rocky beach. Other images featured the pair in a more pensive mood, dreaming at the edge of the cliffs. In a few photographs they were silhouetted against sunsets and sunrises. But in every picture there were storm clouds gathering in the distance.

The inescapable takeaway from every photo was the same. You knew that the innocence of girlhood would not last. Real life was bearing down on them in the form of a storm.

Jack looked at Madeline. "You and Daphne?"

"Yes." A wistful smile curved her mouth. "Tom was a brilliant photographer, but he didn't like to take pictures of people. Mostly he preferred landscapes. Grandma asked him to take some shots of Daphne and me so that we would have them to give to our children. He agreed. But in the end we left the island without them. I don't think any of us wanted any reminders of Cooper Island or the hotel."

"Understandable."

Jack turned away from the pictures.

"Doesn't look like Tom ever threw anything away," Madeline said.

"He was paranoid. Seriously paranoid people are afraid to toss things into the trash. There's always a chance that someone will find something that could be used against you—a bank account number or a compromising photo. You never know."

Madeline smiled faintly. "Sounds like you've dealt with the type on more than one occasion."

"Oh, yeah. My favorite kind of suspects. There's always plenty of stuff to find."

"Because they never throw stuff away. Got it."

"Tomorrow we can take a closer look, but right now I just want to get a feel for the place."

He walked through the living room and into the miniature kitchen. There were not a lot of pots and pans and only a handful of plates, cups, and silverware, but what there was looked as if it had come from the hotel's kitchen.

The refrigerator was mostly empty, but the old freezer was full of frozen meals. The cupboards were crammed with canned goods. There was an old-fashioned calendar pinned to the wall. Jack took it down and flipped through it quickly. At first glance he saw no helpful notes in any of the squares. But he rolled it up and stuck it in the inside pocket of his jacket.

He was about to leave when he noticed the newspaper clipping thumbtacked to the wall. The picture showed a handsome couple smiling over a picnic basket.

PATRICIA WEBSTER SHARES FAMILY
CORN BREAD RECIPE AT COMMUNITY PICNIC

Madeline came to stand in the doorway. "Find something interesting?"

"Just a recipe for corn bread." Jack gave the kitchen another cursory glance. "Doesn't look like Lomax was into cooking."

"Not that I remember." Madeline moved into the kitchen and glanced at the photo. "So that's how Travis Webster turned out. A younger version of his father."

"Wonder why Lomax cut out the recipe."

"I have no idea."

Jack glanced through the article.

. . . Patricia Webster, the new bride of island resident Travis Webster, arrived at the annual Cooper Days picnic with a basket of corn bread that brought raves from attendees. In response to requests, Mrs. Webster explained that it was an old family recipe with a secret ingredient . . .

Jack read the list of ingredients. "Huh."

"What?"

"The secret ingredient in Patricia Webster's corn bread is sour cream."

Madeline raised her brows. "You have a problem with that?"

"Yes, I have a problem with that. There are rules when it comes to corn bread."

"No sour cream?"

"Not in my corn bread."

"Oh, wow." Madeline smiled. "You cook."

"Got a problem with that?"

"Nope. I like to eat."

He was not sure how to take the teasing lilt in her voice. He wondered if she was flirting, just a little, but he was afraid to ask.

He left the kitchen and went down the hall to the bathroom.

He did not spend much time on the small, spare space. It, too, was crammed with stuff, including enough plastic-wrapped rolls of toilet paper to get a survivor through the tough times following Armageddon.

The last stop was the bedroom. He studied the bed for a moment.

"Only one pillow," he said.

Madeline hovered in the doorway. "Meaning?"

"Meaning you were right when you said there probably wasn't a girlfriend, at least not one who was in the habit of spending the night on a regular basis."

He made his way around the bed and opened the closet door. The clothes inside were exactly what he'd expected to find—several identical plaid flannel shirts and half a dozen pairs of identical, well-worn twill pants.

And work boots.

Two pairs of scuffed, battered work boots. Same brand. Same style. Same vintage.

Jack took out one boot and examined the tread on the sole. He measured the length of the boot with his pen. When he looked up he saw that Madeline was watching him with a resigned expression.

"It was Tom, wasn't it?"

"I think it's a good bet that Lomax was the last person to go into room two-oh-nine before we arrived."

"The question is, why would he do that, and why now?" Madeline paused. "And who swept the floor in that room?"

"That last part is easy," Jack said. "Whoever has the briefcase swept the floor—to erase his footprints."

CHAPTER ELEVEN

Daphne clamped her phone to one ear and watched the passengers stream off the plane from Phoenix. She had no idea what to expect in a security escort, but she assumed Abe Rayner would bear a strong resemblance to a nightclub bouncer or a football player.

Her attention fell briefly on the short, compact man with the nerdy, black-framed glasses, a backpack, and a computer case. Automatically she tried to assess his personality on the basis of his style. It was an old game she had played since she was young. He was dressed in cargo pants festooned with pockets that bulged with tech gear, a short-sleeved sport shirt, and sneakers. His dark hair was secured in a ponytail with a leather thong at his nape. The finishing touches were a well-worn suede jacket and a leather bolo tie trimmed with a discreet chunk of turquoise.

Something about the way he moved suggested that he did not spend all of his time sitting in front of a glowing screen. Computer-Geek-Meets-Man-of-the-West, she concluded. If she hadn't been so tense she would have smiled at the fashion mashup.

She went back to studying the other men coming off the plane. The one thing she knew for certain about Abe Rayner was that he was male and that he would show her some ID when he arrived. Not much to go on, considering the circumstances. Maybe this was all a mistake. Maybe she had allowed herself to be panicked for no good reason. Maybe she was losing her mind.

A masculine voice infused with an Arizona drawl spoke behind her. "Daphne Knight?"

She jumped a good inch or two. Her system kicked into fight-or-flight mode. Heart racing, she looked around, searching for a face that fit the voice.

She saw Computer-Geek-Meets-Man-of-the-West. He gave her an apologetic smile and pushed his glasses a little higher on his nose.

"Sorry, didn't mean to startle you," he said. "Abe Rayner. I had the benefit of a photo of you that Jack sent to me. I've got some ID to show you."

"Mr. Rayner." She collected herself and got to her feet.

Now that she was upright she realized that Abe Rayner was an inch or two shorter than she was and definitely not built like a nightclub bouncer or a football player. He was lean and wiry and there was a lot of energy about him, as if he couldn't wait for the next computer problem to solve. So much for the mental image she had conjured. Maybe Abe Rayner carried a very big gun. He worked for a high-end security firm, so presumably he was reasonably good at his job.

If he was aware that she was trying to assess his capabilities, he showed no indication. He simply held out his identification without comment. She looked at the Arizona license and then she examined the business card.

ABRAHAM RAPHAEL RAYNER

INFORMATION ANALYST, RAYNER RISK MANAGEMENT

She looked up from the card and met his dark eyes. She got the feeling he was slightly amused by her reaction.

"What exactly is an information analyst, Mr. Rayner?" she asked.

"I analyze information. Call me Abe."

"All right," she said. She handed him his ID. "Please call me Daphne."

"A pleasure to meet you, Daphne. Sorry about the circumstances. Your friend Madeline said to tell you hello. She also said she's really looking forward to seeing you again. We've got another hour and a half until our flight to Seattle. What do you say we grab a cup of coffee and a bite to eat? Don't know about you, but I'm hungry."

"Coffee will be enough for me," she said. "I'm not hungry."

The words came automatically. She had not been very hungry for a long time.

Abe's eyes narrowed a little. He did not appear to believe her lack of interest in food, but he didn't argue.

"Let's go find someplace where we can sit down and talk," he said. "You've probably got a lot of questions. I don't have all the answers, but I do have something that I think will interest you."

"What's that?"

"Our cover story."

"We've got a cover story?"

"Sure." He grasped the handle of her roll-aboard and started walking down the concourse. "We at Rayner Risk Management believe in being proactive when it comes to security. How do you feel about operating undercover as a hotel consultant?"

Unable to think of anything else to do, she hurriedly fell into step beside him.

"Undercover?" she repeated, still trying to orient herself to her rapidly changing world.

"Jack wants a reason to explain why all four of us have suddenly descended on Cooper Island. So for now, at least, we're all going in as your friend Madeline's hotel consultants."

"What exactly are we consulting on?"

"The idea is that she called us in to help her decide what to do with the old Aurora Point Hotel property—rehab it or sell it."

"That's easy." Daphne tightened her grip on the strap of her purse. "My advice is sell it."

"Yeah? Why?"

"Why do you think? It's an abandoned hotel. It's haunted."

He nodded. "Good reason for selling."

He guided her into one of the airport restaurants and sat her down at a small table. He sank into the chair across from her and opened the computer case. She watched him remove a small computer, vaguely aware of a growing sense of curiosity. It had been a year since she had felt even the smallest stirring of the once-familiar sensation.

"Tell me about this undercover job," she said.

"I will do that." He picked up the menu. "Right after we order some food."

A waiter appeared. Without consulting Daphne, Abe ordered two cups of coffee and two grilled cheese sandwiches.

"I told you, I'm not hungry," Daphne said.

"Don't worry, if you don't eat your sandwich, I will. Now, about our cover story."

She glanced around. There was no one seated close enough to over-hear her, but she lowered her voice anyway and leaned across the table.

"Are you carrying a gun?" she whispered.

"Of course not." He did not look up from the computer screen. "I just arrived on a commercial airplane with no checked baggage, remember?"

"Okay, but how about when you're not flying?"

"This is the modern age. The boss says that private investigators no longer carry firearms. We depend on computers and intelligent analysis of data."

"The boss being your brother?"

"Right."

"That's all well and good, but I got the impression we might be dealing with someone who is very dangerous."

"You're safe with me, Daphne." He flashed her a brilliant grin. "I am a professional."

"But I shouldn't try this at home, right?"

"Exactly."

She concluded that Abe Rayner was going to be irritating. However, there was something reassuring about him.

When the sandwiches arrived she picked up one and bit into it without thinking. The cheese was warm and gooey and the bread was fried to a crispy golden brown.

She finished the first half and picked up the second half.

Abe watched her with a calculating expression.

She swallowed.

"What?" she said.

"How is the sandwich?" he asked a little too innocently.

She examined the partially demolished sandwich in her hand, vaguely astonished. It was just an airport restaurant sandwich but it was the tastiest thing she had eaten in a very long time—a year, in fact.

"Good," she said. "It's good."

"Maybe you were hungry after all."

"Maybe I was. Probably the adrenaline. It's been a very long day."

"I know. Jack told me about the burglary at your place," Abe said. "When was the last time you ate a real meal?"

"I had some yogurt this morning. Why the keen interest in my food intake?"

"You look a little thin, that's all."

She felt the heat rise in her cheeks. "Hasn't anyone told you that you're not supposed to make personal remarks about your clients?"

"No. Is there a rule?"

"There's definitely a rule. I think we'd better change the subject. Tell me what is happening on Cooper Island."

"We're not sure yet, but according to your friend Madeline, it's linked to an incident that occurred eighteen years ago."

"Mom always said that night would come back to haunt us."

CHAPTER TWELVE

"Your brother makes me nervous," Patricia said.

Travis watched her slip an earring into one earlobe. The small, deft movement was infused with graceful femininity. Everything about his beautiful wife was graceful and feminine, he thought. The media would love her once the campaign was launched.

"Xavier makes me nervous, too," Travis said. He met Patricia's eyes in the mirror. "Hell, he makes everyone in the family nervous."

Patricia smiled in sympathy. "I know."

She reached for the second earring.

Ethereally blond and elegantly slender, she wore designer clothes with the refined aplomb of a supermodel. She had a long, delicate jaw, a fine, aristocratic nose, and wide blue eyes that were slightly tipped upward at the outer corners. Her most important attribute, however, was that she had the inner drive and ambition it would take to survive the campaigns that lay ahead of them.

A year ago when they had been introduced by a mutual friend at a Seattle charity event, he had known immediately that Patricia would make the perfect candidate's wife. She had proven to be a shrewd partner.

He also appreciated the fact that she was not complaining about the weeklong stay on Cooper Island. It wasn't as if it was the most exciting place on the face of the earth, he thought. But everyone on the staff had agreed that it was critical that the media got the right image of the candidate. This week was all about demonstrating that he was bonded with a solid family and grounded in small-town values. Patricia had been gallantly pretending to enjoy the scenery and the locals ever since they had arrived two days ago.

That was the easy part, of course. It was dealing with his family—especially his brother—that required real acting talent.

"We can't go on indefinitely with Xavier in his current position." Patricia slipped the other earring into her ear. "I know he's been on his best behavior for months, but we both know that sooner or later he'll have another break. If that happens at the wrong time—if he does too much damage—he'll destroy everything we're working so hard to build."

Travis moved to stand behind her. He put his hands on her elegantly curved waist.

"Believe me, I know," he said. "But until we figure out how to deal with him, it's best to keep an eye on him. There's no better way to do that than to involve him in the campaign."

Patricia raised her brows. "The interesting thing is that he's actually quite good at producing useful media hits."

"My brother has always had a gift for charming people. And let's face it, the media are an easy target for someone with his talent. The twenty-four-seven news beast must be fed on a daily basis. The best zookeepers are people like Xavier—people who can frame even the smallest event in a way that makes the candidate look brilliant, farsighted, and dedicated."

Patricia laughed. "You *are* brilliant, farsighted, and dedicated."

"Thanks." He bent his head to kiss the curve of her throat. "I do like hearing that from my wife."

Patricia grew serious. "My concern is that when—not *if*—Xavier turns on you, he'll be so clever about it we won't know what's happening until it's too late. All he has to do is create a few twisted stories for the media. He can make them up out of thin air, but it won't matter. Once the rumors start, they'll be hard if not impossible to stop."

"Believe me, I'm well aware of just how dangerous Xavier can be. But I know him, Patricia. You could say I've studied him since the day he was born. I had to figure him out fast in order to protect myself. I know his triggers and flash points. I recognize the warning signs. Trust me, it's better to have him in sight where I can keep an eye on him. It would be far more dangerous to have him out there somewhere, lurking in the shadows."

"He's jealous of you."

"Always has been. He was supposed to be the golden boy, the true heir to the throne. He was the son Dad hoped to put into the Senate and, ultimately, the White House. Not me."

"Do your parents understand how dangerous he is?"

"On some level, yes, I think they do. But both of them are reluctant to admit that there's no fixing Xavier. Deep down they still think of him as their golden boy. They've spent a fortune on counseling and medications and rehab over the years. Eventually they packed him off to a private psychiatric hospital. They told everyone it was a very exclusive boarding school, but that wasn't true."

"What happened?"

"A year later the Institute pronounced him cured and sent him home." Travis shrugged. "It wasn't long before Mom and Dad sent him back. He spent most of his teenage years there, and he's been back a few times since then."

"It must have been devastating for your parents," Patricia said.

"The problem is that Xavier is a hell of an actor. Each time he comes back from the Institute he looks normal. Balanced. Back in control.

But he can't maintain the charade indefinitely, and I think Mom and Dad understand that. They've seen the cycle often enough to know that sooner or later he'll always explode again."

"It's probably pure good luck that he hasn't killed someone when he flies into one of his rages."

Travis took his hands off her waist. "You want the truth? I'm not so sure that he hasn't killed someone."

She whirled around, eyes widening. "Are you serious?"

"I never joke when it comes to my brother. But Xavier is very smart and his survival instincts are well honed. If he has committed murder, you can bet he didn't leave any evidence. I guess that's the good news for us. It's highly unlikely that Xavier will ever be arrested."

Patricia's shoulders straightened. "Something has to be done about him."

"I know." He turned toward the closet and selected a shirt.

"Soon."

"Soon," he promised. "I'll talk to Mom and Dad. They've always been able to handle him in the past."

"We can't let him destroy your future."

"Trust me, Mom and Dad won't let that happen."

His wife was damn near perfect, Travis thought, buttoning the shirt. There was just one small thing that worried him. He was pretty sure that if she decided he had too much baggage in the form of a dangerous brother, she would bail.

Women like Patricia did not hang around with losers.

CHAPTER THIRTEEN

"Of course I remember you, Madeline." Heather Lambrick emerged from the steamy restaurant kitchen, wiping her hands on her chef's apron. "Welcome to the Crab Shack." She pulled Madeline into a warm hug. "I was so sorry to hear about your grandmother. I always liked her. She gave me a job when I really needed one, you know."

"I miss her," Madeline said.

"We always miss the good people. That's how it's supposed to be." Heather stepped back and gave Madeline a head-to-toe assessment. "My goodness, how you've changed. You were just a kid when you left Cooper Island."

Heather was in her midfifties. Madeline remembered her as a hard-working single mother who had always looked exhausted and more than a little frazzled. To support her son she had held down two jobs. Days, she had been behind the counter at the Crab Shack. In the evenings, she had worked the dinner shift at the Aurora Point.

"It's good to see you again, Heather." Madeline smiled. "You look great."

Heather did look great. She was flushed from the heat of the kitchen, but it was obvious she was no longer the desperate, anxious woman she had been eighteen years ago. Now she looked like a person in command of her own life.

Madeline was suddenly very conscious of the curious glances that Heather was giving Jack.

"This is Jack Rayner," Madeline said quickly. "He's a consultant in the hotel industry. I've asked him to help me decide what to do with Aurora Point."

Heather beamed. "A pleasure, Jack."

He nodded. "Heather." He glanced toward the kitchen. "Whatever you've got going on in there sure smells good."

Heather glowed. "It's my own special seafood chowder. Comes with sourdough bread."

"That's what I'll have," Jack said. "At least to start."

Heather chuckled. "Don't you want to look at the menu first?"

"Sure, but I already know I want the chowder."

"Sounds good to me, too," Madeline said.

"You got it." Heather waved Madeline and Jack toward a booth. "Have a seat. I'll send Trisha over to take the rest of your order. We're not very busy tonight, but the town will be filling up for the weekend starting tomorrow. Cooper Cove has changed since you left. We pull in a lot of tourists on the weekends."

"I saw the new shops and taverns," Madeline said.

Heather disappeared into the kitchen and reappeared on the other side of the service window.

"I suppose you heard the news that Travis Webster is getting ready to run for Congress?" she said.

Madeline sank into the red vinyl booth. "I heard."

"There's going to be a big event at Webster's place out on Cooper Point later this week. The whole island is invited. You know, hometown-boy-goes-to-the-other-Washington thing."

"Will you be doing the catering?"

"Are you kidding? No way." Heather rolled her eyes. "They're bringing in outsiders from Seattle. The local talent isn't good enough to impress a lot of rich potential donors and the media. But we'll get plenty of spillover. People gotta eat."

The young waitress cruised over. "Get you anything from the bar?"

Jack ordered a beer.

"Whatever red you're serving by the glass will be fine for me," Madeline said.

"On it."

The waitress hustled off and disappeared into the adjoining tavern.

Madeline watched Heather moving around on the other side of the service window.

"You know, Grandma always said you'd be running your own restaurant someday, Heather. She told me that you were forever asking questions and watching to see how things were done in the kitchen."

Heather raised her graying brows. "Did she tell you that she gave me the no-interest loan I needed to buy this place after the owner died?"

"No, she never mentioned it." Madeline's vision suddenly got a little blurry with unshed tears. "Grandma always did have an eye for talent."

"Thanks, but like I said, she was a good person." Heather shook her head. "Can't believe you got here yesterday and found Tom Lomax dead."

"News travels fast."

Heather snorted. "Small towns." She paused to peer through the opening. "They say poor Tom surprised an intruder."

"Apparently."

"What a shame." Heather shook her head again. "Tom was always a little weird, but harmless."

"One of the police officers mentioned that Tom might have become more eccentric than ever."

"Yeah?" Heather looked surprised. "If you ask me, he seemed fine the last couple of times I saw him. Better than normal, in fact."

"How's that?" Jack asked.

Madeline glanced at him. It was the first time he had become active in the conversation.

Heather paused, as though trying to come up with a good reason for her statement. Finally she shrugged.

"Hard to explain," she said. "Little things. I saw him coming out of Tally's barbershop a few months ago. First decent haircut he'd had in years. Looked like he was shaving regularly again, too. I teased him a bit. Asked him if he'd found a girlfriend."

"How did he react?" Jack asked.

"He turned red, said I should mind my own business, and then he took off in that old rattletrap pickup of his. I felt bad. I shouldn't have teased him about the girlfriend."

The front door opened just as the waitress delivered the beer and red wine to the table. A draft of damp night air blew into the restaurant. A handful of people garbed mostly in stylish black and carrying a lot of flashy tech gadgetry trooped into the room. Several were checking their phones for messages. The others were talking to each other in fast, urgent tones that ensured that those who overheard understood that these were Very Important People having Very Important Conversations.

". . . *Back-to-back interviews, no more than five minutes each. We make it clear that Webster is here for a family event . . .*"

". . . *Working up a new set of talking points. This is all about quality time with his family . . .*"

". . . *Going for the close-knit-family-and-small-town vibe . . .*"

One of the men stood out from the crowd, not because of his sleek black clothes or his blond hair but because of the energy in the atmosphere around him. Madeline hadn't seen Xavier Webster in the past eighteen years, but there was no mistaking Egan and Louisa's younger son. In his youth, Xavier Webster had been an astonishingly beautiful boy. He was now an incredibly beautiful man with a larger-than-life rock-star vibe. She was pretty sure he had put a few highlights in his hair.

"Bar's this way, people," Xavier called out.

He led the crowd into the tavern. His crew followed obediently. The original Pied Piper, Madeline thought.

"Call it a wild hunch, but I think we're looking at the Travis Webster campaign team," Jack said.

"I'd say that's a very good guess." Madeline swallowed some of her wine. "We were lucky to get rooms at the B-and-B." She looked at Heather, who had just emerged from the kitchen with two large bowls of chowder. "Looks like you're going to be busy tonight, after all."

Heather winced and set the bowls on the table. "Heard he got into town a couple of days ago. I was sort of hoping he wouldn't feel the need to eat local."

"I haven't seen him since Grandma and I left Cooper Island," Madeline said.

"Count yourself fortunate." Heather's jaw hardened and she lowered her voice. "The only good thing anyone in this town can say about that pretty bastard is that he hasn't been around much in recent years. Excuse me, I'd better go give Sarah a hand with that crowd. I don't want her behind the bar on her own, not as long as Xavier is in there."

"I understand," Madeline said quietly.

"Let me know if you need any backup," Jack said.

Heather glanced at him, startled. Then she gave him an approving look.

"Thanks," she said. "With luck he'll behave himself. After all, the Webster family has a lot riding on Travis's campaign."

"Which only gives a guy like Xavier all the more reason to screw things up for his brother," Madeline said.

Heather exhaled heavily. "Yeah, there is that." She lowered her voice all the way to a whisper. "Someday, someone is going to do something permanent about Xavier Webster. And that day can't come too soon if you ask me."

She hurried away.

Jack folded his arms on the table and gave the tavern doorway a thoughtful look.

"What's the bad news about Xavier Webster?" he asked.

Madeline folded her napkin into precise origami shapes. "Who knows? When I lived on the island I remember the adults speculating about him. Some thought he was flat-out crazy. Others said he needed help. When he was good, he was very, very good."

"And when he was bad?"

"He was damned scary. Luckily the family spent most of their time at their home in Seattle in those days, so we only saw them on occasional weekends and summer vacations. But that was more than enough, believe me. Eventually we heard that Xavier had been shipped off to some fancy boarding school. Everyone on the island breathed a sigh of relief. Unfortunately, he still showed up here from time to time."

"He was trouble?"

"Oh, yeah. He was in his early teens when I knew him. He was very smart and very clever. There were some bad incidents, but somehow they were never his fault."

"What kind of incidents?"

"Xavier liked to play with fire—literally. And he liked to hurt things. One day Daphne and I found the remains of some poor cat on the beach. It was obvious that . . . Never mind. I can't even talk about it. We were pretty sure it was Xavier who had tortured the cat, but no one could prove it. Still, everyone knew to keep an eye on him.

Then one day he got careless. Tom Lomax caught him trying to set fire to one of the Aurora Point cottages. There were guests inside at the time. It was late at night. They were all sound asleep. If Tom hadn't spotted Xavier—"

"What happened?"

"Tom went to Grandma, who went straight out to Cliff House."

"Cliff House?"

"The Webster family compound. I don't know what she said to Egan and Louisa Webster, but whatever it was, the family packed up and returned to Seattle the next day. It was shortly after that we learned Xavier had been sent off to some exclusive school."

"Take a deep breath. He's coming this way."

"And here I thought this day couldn't get any worse."

"Madeline Chase, I didn't recognize you when we came in a few minutes ago." Xavier swooped across the restaurant like some brilliantly plumaged bird of prey. His smile dazzled. "You sure turned out great. Good to see you again." Without warning, the too-vivid pleasure on his face metamorphosed into an expression of sincere sympathy. "Heard about your grandmother. So sorry. A real tragedy."

Xavier had grown up to be a shockingly good actor, Madeline thought. When he was a kid the mask had slipped from time to time. But it was clear that in the intervening years he had perfected his talent.

"Xavier," she said.

She kept her own tone as cool as possible in an effort to end the conversation before it could get off the ground. Jack watched Xavier the way any sensible man would watch a poisonous snake.

"Hey, is that any way to greet an old friend?" Xavier reached down, grabbed Madeline around the shoulders, and hauled her up out of her seat. "Don't I at least get a kiss?"

For a beat she was too stunned to react. Xavier's hands were gripping her very tightly. She was caught, trapped, overwhelmed by his superior strength. Panic and rage flashed through her.

"Let me go," she hissed through clenched teeth. "Let. Me. Go."

He ignored the command and hauled her against his chest. She caught a glimpse of vicious triumph in his eyes. Instinctively she brought up her hands to try to push him away.

There was a blur of movement at the corner of her eye. Jack was coming up out of his seat.

In the next instant she was free, staggering backward, clutching the back of the booth to catch her balance.

She was dimly aware of a heavy thud. She looked down and saw that Xavier was sprawled on the floor. Jack had kicked his legs out from under him.

It was all over in a couple of heartbeats, but she knew from the icy fury in Xavier's glacial blue eyes that there would be repercussions.

Other people were just starting to notice the commotion. The scattered diners turned their heads, trying to figure out what had happened. Heather appeared in the tavern doorway. She took in the scene in a single glance. She looked stricken.

"My fault," Jack said easily. "I'm sorry about that. These booths are a tight fit, aren't they? Lost my balance." He reached down as though offering to help Xavier to his feet. "Didn't mean to stumble into you like that. Name's Jack Rayner, by the way. Tell you what, let me buy you a drink by way of apology."

Madeline held her breath. She knew everyone else in the vicinity was doing the same. For one tense moment it looked as if Xavier might not take the face-saving way out that was being offered. Something dark and menacing flared in his eyes.

But he did not lose control.

Ignoring Jack's extended hand, he rolled to his feet and dusted himself off. For a split second his features twisted into a mask of raw fury. But in the next instant he was suddenly smiling his neon-bright smile.

"Clumsy bastard, aren't you?" he said in a chatty tone. "You might want to be careful in the future. There are a lot of dangerous places on Cooper Island. We usually lose a couple of tourists every year." He turned back to Madeline. "I'll catch up with you later, Maddie. It will be fun, hmm? I hear you recently inherited your grandmother's hotel chain. Nice."

He walked away without a backward glance and vanished through the tavern doorway.

Madeline realized that she was shivering with reaction. She dropped onto the vinyl seat and reached for her wine. Jack sat down, watching her intently. Everyone else in the room suddenly went back to whatever they had been doing, but the conversations were a little louder than they had been prior to the small, tense scene.

"Are you all right?" Jack asked quietly.

"Yes." She took a deep breath. "Thank you. But I'm afraid it isn't over."

"No," Jack said. "Guys like that can't let anything go."

Madeline gulped a little wine and put the glass down very carefully. "This is not good, Jack. I appreciate what you did, believe me, but now you've made yourself a target."

"That was pretty much the point of the exercise," Jack said.

CHAPTER FOURTEEN

Madeline sat on the edge of the bed and watched Jack prowl through her room, checking the locks on the windows and the door. Satisfied, he went to the connecting door that separated his room from hers and opened it.

"You've had a long day," he said. "Try to get some sleep."

"Sure," she said. She knew she wasn't going to get much sleep, but there was no good reason to whine about it.

"I'll leave this door ajar," he said. "If I hear anything that doesn't sound right in your room, I'll come in and check, okay?"

"Okay." She made a face. "No, it's not okay. I'm worried, Jack."

"About Xavier Webster?"

"About you. Xavier looked like he had some control tonight, but the thing is, he was always sneaky as a kid. I told you, he rarely got caught. Now that he's an adult I've got a hunch that he's probably even better at hiding in the shadows."

Jack contemplated her for a long moment.

"This isn't the first time I've dealt with a bastard like Xavier Webster," he said finally. "Let me do my job."

She winced. "Sorry. Didn't mean to imply you don't know what you're doing. It's just that guys like Xavier are scary."

"And you don't like feeling that you need someone else to protect you. It makes you feel vulnerable."

"Is it that obvious?"

"Everyone is vulnerable to something. The trick is to recognize your own weaknesses and blind spots so that you can come up with a way to protect them. In this case you did the smart thing and brought in a professional. That's what smart people do when they're facing situations outside their sphere of competence."

She smiled. "Do you have to give that lecture to every client?"

"Only the stubborn ones."

"Good night," she said.

"Good night."

He went into the other room and pulled the door almost but not quite shut behind him.

She held it together all the while she was getting ready for bed. She brushed her teeth, washed her face, and changed into her nightgown without losing it. She wrapped the B&B's complimentary robe around herself, tied the sash, and turned out the lights.

By the time she was ready, the other room had gone silent and dark. Evidently Jack's nightly routine was more efficient than hers. The stillness that seeped through the narrow opening between their rooms made her wonder if he was already fast asleep.

She went to the window and pulled the drapes aside. From where she stood she could see the lights of the Webster family compound crowning the cliffs on one side of the cove. The windows of the sprawling main house and both guest cottages were illuminated.

The Aurora Point Hotel loomed on the opposite cliffs, dark ruins of a haunted past.

She thought about the shock of finding Tom dying; her panicky flight up the service stairs, fleeing an unseen killer; and the decision to summon Jack to Cooper Island. She pondered the fact that her best friend from childhood might be in mortal danger. And then she thought about how Jack had made himself the target of a man who was probably a dangerous sociopath. Last of all she made herself consider the possibility that someone had murdered Edith Chase.

And she knew that it was all her fault. The past was coming back to haunt all of them because of her. Tears burned in her eyes.

She turned away from the dark view and headed toward the bathroom. At the very least she could do the decent thing and spare Jack the sound of a weeping woman. He was dealing with enough problems as it was.

Inside the bathroom she closed the door, turned on the light, and sank down on the cold side of the white porcelain tub. She grabbed a fluffy towel off the rack and buried her face in the thick cotton.

She gave herself up to the tears. It was not the first time she had cried alone since Edith Chase's death.

CHAPTER FIFTEEN

Jack waited for the bathroom door to open again. When it didn't, he systematically ran through the various explanations for the unnatural silence in the next room. He could think of only two or three logical possibilities—illness, an anxiety attack, or tears. He figured he could eliminate illness because there had been no flushing of the toilet and no water running in the sink. That left the anxiety attack theory or tears. Madeline had a right to either or both.

She wasn't pacing the floor. He concluded that ruled out the anxiety attack. Tears, then.

Damn.

He waited a moment longer. When the bathroom door still failed to reopen, he pushed aside the covers and sat up on the edge of the bed. There was a hotel robe in the bathroom, but he never actually felt dressed in a robe. When you were dealing with a client, it was generally a good idea to keep your clothes on.

He got to his feet and reached for his trousers. He took his time stepping into them, hoping that the bathroom door would open. It didn't. He collected the shoulder holster and the gun. Accessories made the outfit, he reminded himself. Also, he had a policy when it came to weapons—if he was convinced that the job required one, he made sure it was always close at hand.

Satisfied that he met the minimum sartorial requirements, he pushed the connecting door open and went into the other room. The bed had been turned down but was otherwise undisturbed. There was enough moonlight to reveal the little chocolate on the pillow.

He paused halfway across the room and listened closely. Still no sound from the bathroom. If Madeline was crying, she was doing it very quietly.

He braced himself and reluctantly knocked on the door.

"Everything okay in there?" he asked.

There was a short silence from the other side.

"Yes. Fine."

Madeline's voice was tight and hoarse. He tried to figure out where to go next. There was nothing in the Detecting for Dummies manual that covered these situations. It wasn't the first time he'd dealt with a client who broke down in tears, but such events usually occurred in an office setting. There was a reason he had made the executive decision not to take divorce and missing-person cases; a reason why he had skewed his career toward corporate security since leaving the FBI consulting work.

"Do you want to talk about it?" he asked, for lack of anything more inventive.

"No." There were some sniffs. "Please go away. I'm okay. Just tired."

He heard water splash in the sink.

"Are you wearing a robe?" he asked.

There was a pause from the other side of the door.

"Why?" Deep suspicion underlined the single word.

"Because I think we should talk, and it's never a good idea to have conversations with an undressed client."

"Oh, for pity's sake." She yanked open the door. Her face was flushed and a little blotchy from the crying jag. Her hair was down around her shoulders and somewhat damp from the hasty cold-water splash. But she was in full command of herself. Irritation sharpened her glare. "I told you, there's nothing wrong." She stopped, taking in the sight of him standing in the shadows. "You're dressed."

"Well, sure. Like I said, there's a rule about being dressed while engaging in conversations with clients."

She surprised him with a misty but real smile. "We in the hotel industry have similar rules. Sorry. Didn't mean to make you think there was a major crisis going on over here. You can go back to bed now."

She started to take a step forward but stopped abruptly when she noticed the holster and gun in his hand.

"I didn't know you brought a gun," she said.

She looked a little nonplussed, as if she wasn't quite sure where to go with the observation.

"You said you thought someone had been murdered," he reminded her.

"Right. Okay."

He could almost see her making the decision not to question the weapon.

"I'd better let you get to bed," he said. "As you pointed out earlier, it has been a very long day."

"Yes."

He couldn't think of anything else to say. There was no excuse to hang around in her room for another minute. But he did not want to leave.

He turned away, checked the lock on the door again, and walked resolutely toward the entrance to his room.

"Jack? Thanks for everything you've done today."

"It's my job."

She gave him a wan smile. "I know."

He couldn't take it any longer. He did not want her gratitude any more than he wanted to be the guy who vetted her potential dates. He went into his own room, leaving the connecting door just slightly ajar.

He stood there for a while, listening. She did not go to bed. He heard her move back to the window. He knew that she was just standing there, looking out into the darkness.

And he was suddenly very sure what she was thinking. He had been there more than once.

He opened the door again. She was at the window, as he had known, her arms folded, her hands tucked into the long sleeves of her robe.

"Don't," he said.

She turned her head. "What?"

"Don't blame yourself. It's not your fault, not any of it. Not Lomax's murder. Not the fact that your friend may be in danger. Not that scene with Xavier Webster tonight. Not the decisions your grandmother made eighteen years ago. None of it is your fault."

She watched him very steadily. "I feel like I'm standing at the center of a slow-burning fire that was ignited by what happened all those years ago."

"We're going to put out the flames."

"Jack—"

He set the holstered gun on the table and moved toward her. Carefully, remembering her reaction to the way Xavier had grabbed her up out of her seat, he rested his hands on her shoulders. She did not flinch or pull away.

"You and I are going to figure out what is going on, and then we're going to make it stop," he said.

"Okay," she said.

He smiled. "And in return, you will never again ask me to vet one of your dates."

She shook her head, reluctantly amused. "That really irritated you, didn't it?"

"A hell of a lot more than I anticipated."

"Why?"

"Probably because there's a conflict of interest involved. When this is over I want to be your next date. If you say yes, you're going to have to ask someone else to do the background check."

He waited for some indication of anger or simple surprise.

She stilled. In the shadows her eyes were unreadable.

"You were right," she said.

"About what?"

"I was relieved to get that negative report on William Fleming. If you hadn't come up with the dirt I would have had to find a polite way to break off the relationship. You got me off the hook. Which means I used you. I apologize."

"No apology needed."

"Yes, there is. Because for the past three months I've been wondering what you would say if I asked you out on a date."

The shock slammed through him. He slid his hands upward to cup her face. She made no move to resist.

"I would have said yes," he said.

"That's good to know. I'm sorry that things have gotten so complicated."

"You really do need to stop apologizing. A good executive never apologizes."

"That is one theory of management," she agreed. "I'm not sure I subscribe to it."

"Either way, the complications don't matter."

"Why not?"

"Because I'm in the business of fixing complications, remember?"

She slipped her hands out from the sleeves of the robe and touched his jaw with one finger.

"How could I forget?" she whispered.

He kissed her carefully, a first-date kiss intended to invite and seduce. It was a kiss designed to reassure, a kiss meant to send the message that she was safe with him. She had been through so much. The last thing she needed was a sexual encounter that she might regret in the morning. The last thing he wanted was to be the source of that regret.

Her response was cautious at first. He expected that.

What he didn't expect was the way the simmering heat between them erupted with the fierce energy of summer lightning. The kiss plunged into the red zone with little warning. Madeline's hands became small claws on his shoulders. Her mouth was hot and wet. She shivered in his arms, gasped for air, and pressed herself against him.

With a near-violent effort, he tore his mouth free.

"This is not a good idea," he managed.

She didn't seem to hear him at first. Then she froze. He could literally feel the chill that swept through her. He gently set her away from him.

"A bad couple of days at Black Rock, remember?" He raised his hand and pushed a lock of hair behind her ear. "You need sleep."

She took a step back, folded her arms very tightly once again, and hid her hands inside the long terry-cloth sleeves. He could not read her there in the shadows—couldn't tell if she was hurt or embarrassed—but either way he was pretty sure he had screwed up.

"You're right," she said. She was clearly back in control. Her brittle smile held a steely edge. "This was a huge mistake. And it was my fault."

"Don't start," he warned.

"I apologize for putting you into such an awkward situation. You were trying to comfort me and I attempted to take advantage of your good intentions."

"That is not what was happening here."

"I hope you won't feel it necessary to terminate our contract; however, I will understand if you do. If you elect to depart, I would appreciate a referral to another security firm, one you feel can handle a job like this one."

Outrage sparked through him. "Are you trying to fire me again?"

"No. You seem to have gotten a handle on this case very quickly. Besides, I don't look forward to going through another learning curve with a different security expert."

"I don't know what you think you're doing here," he said, "but let's cut out the heavy drama."

"You started it with all that crap about not taking advantage of me," she said.

That stung.

"It's the damned truth," he said. "I was trying to do what was best for you under the circumstances."

"As I recall, you don't want to be the messenger when it comes to my personal life, remember?"

"That decision has got nothing to do with this situation."

"I disagree," she said, very crisp and sure now. "The deal is that you will no longer be advising me on the suitability of the men I'm interested in dating. That means you will not make decisions for me regarding your own suitability."

"This is crazy."

"You may, of course, make your own decisions about the wisdom of getting involved in a personal relationship with me," she said.

"No shit."

"It was a kiss, Jack. I was in the mood and evidently you were, too.

It was your decision to end it and I can respect that. But do not try to tell me you did it for my own good. Is that clear?"

"This is what I get for trying to play the gentleman?"

"No, this is what you get for pissing me off," she said.

"Fine. Next time this happens I won't worry about whether going to bed with you is a good idea."

"Excellent. That would seem to settle things, then. Apparently you're not going to terminate our contract and I'm not going to fire you, so I'll see you in the morning."

"Right." He collected the holstered gun and went to the doorway of his room. There he stopped and turned his head to look at her. "Out of sheer morbid curiosity, do you get involved in arguments like this a lot with your dates?"

"Nope, this was a first." She gave him a bright, victorious smile. "And I must say, it did wonders for my mood. I feel a lot better now than I did twenty minutes ago."

"That is a damned frightening thought."

"Sort of cathartic, I guess."

"Yeah, well, glad it was good for you."

He was astonished by how much professional control he was forced to summon to resist the temptation to slam the door on the way out of her room.

CHAPTER SIXTEEN

Abe drove slowly through the heart of Cooper Cove. Daphne sat, stiff and tense, in the passenger seat. She studied the shops and galleries that lined the main street.

"Look familiar?" he asked.

She knew he was trying to make casual conversation, trying to ease her growing tension.

"Yes and no," she said. "A lot of the art and souvenir shops are new. The whole town is a little bigger than it was eighteen years ago. But the overall feel of the place is the same."

"Seaside towns that survive largely on weekend and summer tourism usually have a similar vibe," he said. "They go quiet and dark in the winter and brighten up in the summer."

"But they're small towns, and all small towns seem to be really good at hiding secrets."

"Guess small communities are like families and marriages in that respect." Abe's hands tightened a little on the wheel. "Outsiders never really know for sure what's going on under the surface."

She looked at him, no longer surprised by his occasional, disconcertingly astute observations on human nature. They had known each other for less than twenty-four hours, but in that time she had discovered that Abe was a good deal more complicated than he had appeared at first glance.

She'd had a flash of uncertainty last night when they had checked into connecting rooms at the airport hotel after landing at Sea-Tac. She was certain that Madeline had employed a reputable, first-class security firm; nevertheless, Abe was still very much a stranger. But he had gone about the business of checking locks and making sure the windows were secure with a calm, professional competence that had reassured her.

For the first time in a very long time she had fallen asleep almost immediately after climbing into bed. She had not awakened until Abe knocked on the door that morning. It was the first time she had slept through the night without being troubled by restless dreams and sudden awakenings since Brandon's funeral.

"You're married?" she asked before she could stop to consider the wisdom of such a personal question.

"I was for two years," he said.

"Divorced?"

"Yep. She wanted out."

"I'm sorry."

"Don't be. By the time she left, all I felt was a sense of relief. I knew I was never going to be the man she thought she had married."

"What kind of man did she think she had married?"

A wry smile tugged at the corners of Abe's mouth. "A very rich one."

"I see."

"We were both working at a promising start-up when we met. Most start-ups never get off the ground, but when one does take flight, the payoffs can be big. Our company looked like it would be one of the lucky ones. So on impulse, Alice and I got married."

"But you didn't get rich?"

"Sadly, no."

"What went wrong?"

"The two dudes who founded the start-up had gotten a very good lawyer to draw up the employment contracts. When the big tech firm bought our little operation, the only people who cashed out with the big money were the two guys at the top. The rest of us were let go. The stress undermined the marriage. Alice wanted me to come up with an idea for my own start-up. I decided that what I really wanted to do was security work. Alice concluded that I lacked ambition."

"So she left."

"It worked out well for both of us. Last I heard she married a venture capitalist. He's ambitious and rich. Everyone is happy."

"Including you?"

"I like what I do," Abe said.

"You're fortunate. Not everyone is that lucky."

He glanced at her, his eyes unreadable behind the lenses of his dark glasses. "Don't you like your interior design work?"

She thought about it. "I used to like it—I loved it, actually. I got a lot of pleasure out of creating a living space that came together the way I had envisioned."

"But not anymore?"

"I've just been a little . . . distracted lately."

Abe nodded. "How long did you and your mother live here on the island?"

"Nearly three years. We moved here after my father left us. Mom had some notion that small towns were good places to raise kids. Safe."

"Which only goes to show that bad people can turn up anywhere."

"Yes, it does."

"Here we go," Abe said. "The Cove View B-and-B." He turned in to the parking lot. "This must be the place where Jack and Ms. Chase are staying."

The low-grade tension that had been coiling around Daphne ever since she and Abe had left Seattle that morning tightened like a vise. She finally realized what the problem was. For reasons she could not explain she was suddenly, unaccountably anxious about meeting Madeline again. It made no sense, but there it was.

They were forever bonded by the events of a dark night, but their lives had gone in very different directions. She was a modestly successful interior designer. Madeline had just inherited a successful hotel chain. They were not the same two people they had been when they had forged a friendship. So many things had changed for both of them.

Abe pulled into a parking slot and shut down the engine. He looked at her.

"Don't worry," he said. "My boss and I are good at what we do."

"That's not it." She unclipped her seat belt. "Well, maybe that's part of it. I'm just thinking that under normal circumstances Madeline and I would never have met again. And now we're getting together because of something really bad that happened in the past. It's . . . awkward. We might not even recognize each other."

"Yeah?"

"Eighteen years is a long time." She floundered. "My hair is different now." Okay, that sounded weak.

He eyed her hair. "I like your hair."

She was suddenly acutely conscious of her short, honey-brown hair. In the months following Brandon's death she had made a lot of changes in her life in an attempt to sever her ties with the past. In addition to selling the home she and Brandon had lived in and buying a new condo, she had cut her hair. The stylist had assured her that the look was sassy and arty, but she had a few doubts.

"Thanks," she mumbled.

"Want my professional detective advice?"

She smiled faintly. "Sure."

"Try not to overthink this reunion thing."

Abe cracked open his door and got out. He started around to the passenger side, but she jumped out before he could get to her door. He was a security agent, not a chauffeur or a boyfriend, she thought. Opening car doors for her was not in his job description.

The snapping breeze off the water whipped at the hem of her trench coat. There was a storm moving in. It was midmorning but the sky was darkening quickly. In the old days she and Madeline had loved the energy of an approaching storm, but today it felt ominous.

Abe took her rolling suitcase and his backpack out of the trunk of the car. She seized the handle of her suitcase. He shrugged but did not contest the matter.

Together they walked toward the front door of the B&B.

"I never even sent Maddie a note of condolence when her grandmother died," Daphne said.

She'd been so wrapped up in her own emotions this past year that she hadn't even bothered to do the socially correct thing for an old acquaintance.

"You're doing it again," Abe said.

"Overthinking the situation?"

"Yeah."

He opened the door for her.

She told herself that sort of door opening was okay—just good manners.

Stifling a small sigh, she rolled her suitcase through the entrance. Abe was right about one thing—she was definitely doing too much thinking. A disinterested observer might say she was probably obsessing on the small stuff so that she didn't have to contemplate other, much larger things—things like the possibility that two people she had once known well might have been murdered.

She took in the cozy lobby of the Cove View B&B with a designer's eye. The hardwood floors, open-beam ceiling, and cheerfully blazing fireplace were complemented by comfortably weathered furniture and a lot of warm, earthy colors. The fragrance of warm pastries and hot coffee drifted through the French doors that separated the lobby area from the small breakfast room and tearoom.

It was nearly eleven o'clock and the little restaurant was empty except for two people drinking coffee at one of the tables near a window. Even sitting down the man looked big compared to the woman who sat across from him. She was petite and there was a lot of tension in the stiff line of her shoulders. Her companion looked calm and relaxed, but Daphne knew intuitively that the casual air was deceptive because he was watching the doorway the way a cop or a soldier might watch it.

Abe nodded once to the man at the table and then went toward the front desk.

So that was Jack Rayner, Daphne thought. That meant the tense woman sitting with him was Madeline.

My secret sister.

Jack put down his coffee and got to his feet. There was a small clatter of china as his companion set her cup on a delicate saucer, jumped to her feet, and turned toward the door. For the first time Daphne got a look at the woman's face.

And just like that, the years fell away. Time had wrought changes, but there was something about Madeline's eyes. She knew that Madeline recognized her in that same instant.

"Daphne."

Madeline started across the room, walking quickly at first, and then she was running.

Daphne dropped the suitcase and rushed to meet her. "Maddie. Oh, my gosh, Maddie. I can't believe it."

They hugged fiercely, breathless with the wonder of the reunion. Joyous.

Some things never changed, Daphne thought. She would know the sister of her heart anywhere, anytime.

Madeline took a step back and smiled. "Love what you've done with your hair."

CHAPTER SEVENTEEN

He had not handled the scene in the Crab Shack well. He had come close to losing control, just like in the old days. He absolutely had to be more careful. There was too much at stake.

Xavier made his way down the cliff path to the beach. He needed to think. He needed breathing room, a little time to calm the rage that burned inside him. The storm was moving in fast. The waves slashed at the sand and rocks. The gusty winds howled. The energy sparking in the atmosphere resonated with something inside him.

He reached the foot of the steep path, shoved his fists into the pockets of his jacket, and started walking toward the far end of the beach. He was on fire with his fury, as charged as the storm. He wanted to scream his defiance of his fate into the teeth of the oncoming gale, but he did not dare take the risk. The noise of the fierce gusts and crashing waves would probably muffle the sound, but beach winds were tricky. There was a chance they would carry his roar of fury up the cliffs—all the way to the dark house at the top. The last thing he wanted was to have people come searching for him. He needed to be alone.

He walked faster, trying to burn off some of the anger.

It was Rayner's fault that he had come close to losing it last night. The humiliating fall in the restaurant had not been an accident. Rayner had done something swift and subtle with his foot. Martial arts, maybe. The bastard's expression when he'd extended his hand in that phony offer of assistance had said it all. Rayner hadn't mocked him— mockery was something Xavier understood intuitively because he practiced it often. But there had been no humiliating amusement in the bastard's cold, dark eyes—just a chilling promise.

In that shattering moment he had understood that Rayner knew him for what he was. Rayner could not be charmed or bullied or frightened off. That made him the most dangerous piece on the playing board.

Xavier walked faster. He had learned a lot at the Institute, where they had filled him with drugs and subjected him to their stupid therapies. It had taken him a while to realize the truth: The fools actually believed—or maybe simply hoped—that they could fix him. They yearned to make him look normal because it validated everything they wanted to believe about themselves.

Yes, Mrs. Webster, of course we can teach little Xavier impulse control.

The problem, Mrs. Webster, is that Xavier is so much smarter than the people around him. He does not understand or empathize with normal people, so he becomes impatient with them. That, in turn, leads to socially unacceptable outbursts.

I'm sure we can help your son, Mrs. Webster. With our cutting-edge therapies we can provide him with the social skills and medications that will enable him to gain emotional balance and self-control.

It hadn't been easy at first, especially when he was a kid, but once he had finally realized that the only way to regain his freedom was to adopt the mask of normalcy, he had buckled down and studied hard.

He had become a brilliant, polished actor who gave an award-worthy performance every time he went onstage.

Oh, yeah, he had learned a lot at the Institute.

Acting was stressful, of course. There were times when he simply had to relax, let down his guard, and allow his true nature to emerge for a while. He'd discovered a hobby that worked much better than the meds. Once or twice a year he went on vacation to someplace in the world where lovely young women were bought and sold like cheap jewelry. He purchased one and indulged in the pure luxury of a physical and emotional catharsis achieved through sex and violence. There was nothing else like it to make him feel normal again.

The fires always explained the deaths while simultaneously destroying all the evidence. Fire was so wonderfully cleansing.

The therapeutic vacations calmed him and allowed him to return to the main stage.

But lately the vacations had not proven as therapeutic as they once had. He found himself getting restless more frequently. It was increasingly stressful to put on the mask. The truly worrisome thing was that he was pretty sure his family was no longer buying his performance.

It had taken a while but he had finally begun to suspect that Travis didn't really trust him to handle the campaign's media outreach. No, Travis wanted to keep an eye on him.

He sensed that he was making the whole damn family nervous. They were all on high alert and probably plotting against him because this was supposed to be Travis's moment. Travis, after all, was the *normal* one, the one who was now supposed to become the heir to the Egan Webster throne. But Travis was weak. Soft.

Do you really think I'm going to stand by and let you steal my destiny, you little shit? I'm the golden boy, not you.

In some ways it was very amusing to see them all so scared, but it made for a riskier scenario. He had to be very careful.

It was raining now. Xavier broke into a run. And as he ran into the storm he asked himself a question.

Why would a hotel consultant be an expert in martial arts?

CHAPTER EIGHTEEN

"I can't believe that we're finally getting together again because of what happened here all those years ago," Madeline said.

"It's ridiculous," Daphne said. "But the adults involved meant well. They were trying to protect us. Mom was terrified after she talked to your grandmother that night. She couldn't run far enough or fast enough. We actually ended up in Florida for several years, if you can believe it. Mom still lives there."

"I believe it," Madeline said. "I saw her face the day the two of you packed up your car and drove away. She was scared to death and she was determined to get you as far away from Cooper Island as possible."

"And your grandmother was just as determined to keep you safe."

"I know."

They were standing in the middle of Tom's cottage. There were two empty suitcases open on the bed. The plan was simple. Supposedly the four of them were on-site doing initial walk-throughs and evaluations of the property in an attempt to decide if renovations were worthwhile.

The reality was that Jack had assigned them to search for anything of a personal nature that might provide some explanation of Tom's actions in recent days and months.

Jack and Abe were exploring the maintenance building. Madeline knew that Jack would not ask her or Daphne to go inside the structure unless it was absolutely necessary.

Daphne surveyed the drab bedroom. "Judging by the condition of this cottage, I'd guess that Tom didn't change much over the years. Looks like his borderline hoarding tendencies took over."

"Grandma always said that Tom took the concept of recycling to the extreme." Madeline picked up a stack of old vinyl records. "But he was always clean."

Daphne opened the closet and groaned at what she saw. "Jack seems fairly certain that Tom was the one who opened up the wall to get at the briefcase."

"Yes. But I can't think of any reason why he would do that. I mean, why now?"

"Whatever his reasons, they helped bring you and me back together. I'm glad about that, Maddie."

Madeline put down the records. "I never got a chance to thank you for what you did that night. I was so traumatized I think I sort of zoned out for a while. By the time I was able to process things, you and your mom were gone."

Daphne's expression softened. "All I did was run for help. You would have done the same if the situation had been reversed."

Madeline felt the tears start to gather. "You saved me. And this is the first time I've been able to thank you. I can't believe it."

"Consider me thanked." Daphne blinked several times and wiped her eyes with the sleeve of her jacket. "Damn, Maddie, I've missed you. I didn't even know it until now."

"I missed you, too." Madeline managed a shaky smile. "We should probably stop crying and practice being girl detectives."

"Probably."

"You take that side of the room." Madeline opened a drawer. "I'll take this side."

Daphne smiled a little. "Okay."

Madeline shot her a quick, searching look. "What?"

"Nothing, it's just the way you take charge and start issuing orders. You were that way as a kid, too. Bossy. Born to be an executive, I guess."

Madeline riffled through a small mountain of faded photographs. "You may be astonished to know that not everyone considers it an endearing character trait."

"Is that so?" Daphne pulled a box down from the closet shelf. "Who doesn't admire it?"

"I've got a string of ex-boyfriends who will tell you that they found my management style irritating."

"Is that so? How long is that string of exes?"

"Well, it's not short." Madeline closed the drawer and opened another one.

"But you don't take pride in it?"

"Nope." Madeline examined a pile of assorted flashlights. "Sadly, I can't take credit for being a femme fatale. I do have secret powers, though. Turns out being the heir to a profitable chain of hotels is viewed as a very desirable asset in a wife."

"A-ha. I can see the problem."

"The last bastard I dated wanted me to fund a study to test his theories of couples therapy, one of which apparently involved the therapist sleeping with the client's wife, who was also a client. Let's just say that I discovered that Dr. Fleming was a devoted practitioner of his own theories."

Daphne looked up quickly. "You're joking."

"Unfortunately, no."

"How did you find out Fleming was sleeping with his clients?"

"Had a background check run on him. Standard procedure for me. I've been doing it since I started dating. Grandma insisted."

"Huh. Not a bad idea, actually." Daphne's jaw tightened. "These days a woman can't be too careful."

"That's what Grandma always said."

"So who exactly do you hire to run that sort of check?"

Madeline raised her brows. "Well, in my case I've always had access to the services of an in-house security company."

Daphne's eyes widened. "You used Rayner Risk Management?"

"*Used* is the operative word. I got my report, but the investigator who provided it said he wouldn't do any more for me. He said I'd have to go to another agency."

"Jack Rayner said that? Those were his words?"

"More or less. I got the message."

"Why did he refuse . . . Oh, wait." Daphne got a knowing look. "I get it."

"You do?"

"He probably views running background checks on your dates as a conflict of interest."

Madeline dropped the old-fashioned camera she had just picked up. "That is exactly what he went to great lengths to explain to me. How in the world did you figure that out? Are you psychic?"

"No, but I'm also not an idiot, Maddie. There's something about the way he looks at you. It's clear that he wants you. What's more, I think you're interested in him. There's a kind of heat in the atmosphere between the two of you."

Madeline groaned. "Is it that obvious?"

"It is to a sister."

"Who hasn't seen me in eighteen years and therefore hasn't witnessed the string of disasters that I fondly refer to as romantic relationships. Here's the bottom line—even if I didn't have to worry that every guy I meet might be after Sanctuary Creek Inns, I have to admit I've got some serious intimacy issues. Inevitably, they get in the way."

"Given your history, that's perfectly understandable." Daphne crouched to look under the bed. She grimaced at whatever she saw. "But for what it's worth, I don't think Jack Rayner is interested in your hotels."

"No, I'll give him that." Madeline opened a camera box and looked at the ancient device inside. "But there is still the problem of my issues."

"Did you ever get therapy to talk about those issues?"

"No. There didn't seem to be much point in going to a professional counselor. I knew the source of my problems and I also knew that I could never talk about it."

"The old family-secret thing."

Madeline put down the box and surveyed the cluttered room. "And now, for some reason, it looks like Tom Lomax may have decided to reveal that secret."

"Not necessarily." Daphne got to her feet. "What if he took the briefcase out of the wall because he was afraid that someone had discovered where it was? Maybe he intended to hide it somewhere else for safekeeping."

Madeline thought about it. "I suppose that's possible. Tom told me that he had failed. But I think he was hallucinating at the end."

Daphne circled the bed and hugged her tightly. "From what you've told me, you were nearly killed the other day. And all because of that damned briefcase."

"It's not just a damned briefcase. I hate to bring up the subject, but there is also the little matter of a dead body buried under the gazebo."

CHAPTER NINETEEN

Jack surveyed the long, gloom-filled maintenance building. "This looks like the graveyard where old, worn-out tools and equipment come to die."

The interior of the wooden building was dimly illuminated by the weak daylight slanting through grimy windows. The atmosphere was thick with the odor that was unique to old garages—the unmistakable reek of gasoline, lubricants, and solvents.

The far end of the structure was cluttered with gardening supplies and broken appliances. He and Abe were standing on the opposite side, the portion of the building that had once served as a workshop and garage.

There was an old-fashioned lube pit sunk into the concrete floor. In years past it would have been used to perform oil changes on the hotel's vehicles. But now several ancient mattresses and a lot of yellowed lampshades were stacked inside.

"It's not a graveyard, it's a junkyard." Abe hefted a large hammer and examined it with an admiring eye. "A very nice junkyard." He set the hammer down. "What are we looking for?"

"I've got no idea."

Abe nodded. "That's one of the things I've always admired about you, boss. Your sophisticated, high-tech approach to the business of investigation. Yes, sir, I'm learning a lot from you."

"I've got no idea what we're looking for, but I do have a question," Jack said.

"What's that?"

"I've been wondering what Edith and Lomax did with the car."

Abe gave him a sharp, searching look. "You're talking about Porter's ride?"

Jack played a penlight over an array of rusty drill bits. "We know what they did with the body and the briefcase, but Madeline and Daphne don't have any idea of what happened to the car. All they know is that the next morning it was gone, along with all the records of Porter's reservation."

Abe looked around. "Well, we know they didn't hide it here in the maintenance building, at least not indefinitely. No sign of any vehicle here. No room for one, either."

"Eighteen years ago when the hotel was active there probably would have been room." Jack used the penlight to gesture toward the lube pit and the rows of oil cans on a nearby shelf. "Looks like Lomax did regular vehicle maintenance here back in the day."

Abe glanced at the lube pit. "So they could have parked Porter's car here, out of sight for a couple of days, until they figured out how to get rid of it."

"Yeah. But what do you do with a dead man's car on an island?"

"While we're pondering that question, I've got another one."

"What?"

"What's going on between you and Madeline Chase?" Abe asked. "Seems to be something more developing than just a business relationship."

"It's complicated."

"I'll say. A couple of months ago she tried to fire us. You had to go toe-to-toe with her to keep the contract. This morning I find the two of you having coffee together like you've been married for ten years. Inquiring minds want to know, what's wrong with this picture?"

"She's a client, Abe."

"Right. Our biggest, most important client."

"Where are you going with this?"

Abe turned to contemplate a workbench covered with wrenches and screwdrivers. "Got no idea, boss."

Jack glanced at him. He was pretty sure Abe was smiling a little.

"I couldn't help but notice that you and Daphne Knight seem to be on a first-name basis," Jack said.

"Yeah, well, you know how it is. Spend a lot of time in someone's company and you get to first names pretty fast."

"Sure." Jack relaxed a little. "What's your take on her?"

"Daphne? She's too thin."

"You've been with her since yesterday and that's your considered analysis of Daphne Knight? She's too thin?"

"She needs to eat more."

"I don't suppose you noticed anything else that might be of interest in this little murder investigation I'm attempting to run here?"

"Her husband died a year ago."

"I'm aware of that. Natural causes, though."

"Yeah, but I think she's having trouble dealing with it." Abe bent down and pulled a collection of automobile hoses out from under a bench. "Returning to the subject at hand, I'm thinking that if I were tasked with the problem of getting rid of a vehicle that could tie me to a dead man, I might have driven it off a cliff somewhere on the island."

"I don't think that would have been a good idea, not on this island. The tides around here are pretty extreme. There would have been a very good chance that the dead man's vehicle would have been exposed at low tide or during a storm."

"Okay, point taken. Maybe Lomax just waited a week or two, drove the car onto the ferry, and ditched it somewhere on the mainland."

"Possible." Jack rummaged through a metal cabinet. "But again, there would have been the possibility of someone finding it and tracing it to an owner who had gone missing."

"True. There would also have been the very real possibility that Lomax would have been seen driving off the island in a car that was not his own. Questions would have been asked. Small towns and all that." Abe hauled a wheelbarrow out of the corner and started going through the planting supplies stacked behind it. "Got any idea of what might have been in that briefcase?"

"Whatever it was, it scared Edith Chase and Lomax so badly they covered up what most courts would have viewed as a justifiable homicide."

Abe moved a shovel out of the way so that he could get behind a workbench. "You know how it is with small towns—there's always a hierarchy. The people at the top usually have a lot of influence over local law enforcement."

"In this town the people at the top are the Websters."

"So if you killed the guy who was trying to rape your granddaughter and afterward you decided it would be best not to call the police, it might be because you were worried that the Websters wouldn't be pleased."

"Can't go there just yet. There are plenty of scary people in the world. Mob bosses. Drug cartels. Powerful politicians. Terrorists." Jack crouched to aim his flashlight under a rusted-out washing machine. "But yeah, this thing feels local."

"What else do we know?"

"Lomax's murder was intended to look like an accident or, at the very least, the work of a surprised burglar. Someone bashed him on the head and pushed him down a staircase."

"There are hit men who specialize in making a kill look like an accident."

"Yes, but the timing feels local, too," Jack said. "Why else would someone go after the briefcase now, just as Travis Webster is getting ready to run for office?"

"Maybe the more important question is, how did someone find out that there was something dangerous or seriously damaging in the brief-case?"

"That's easy. One of the five people who knew the secret must have talked, and probably recently."

"Like you say, if more than one person knows a secret, it's no longer a secret. But I'm pretty sure Daphne never talked. She swears she didn't, and she says she is certain her mother didn't, either."

"Same goes for Madeline and Edith Chase," Jack said. "That leaves us with Tom Lomax."

"Daphne and Madeline seem to think he was a confirmed recluse."

"Who recently got a haircut and started shaving."

The flashlight played across the corner of a flat metal object lying under the washer. Jack got to his feet.

"Give me a hand with this washer," he said.

Abe crossed the cluttered space and helped him shove the heavy machine out of the way. Jack aimed the flashlight at the metal object.

"I think we just found out what happened to Porter's car," Jack said. "It's still here."

CHAPTER TWENTY

"What about you?" Madeline asked. She watched Daphne shuffle through yet another stack of old photos. "Did you ever get counseling?"

"No." Daphne tossed the pictures aside. "For the same reason you didn't. I knew the source of my problems but I couldn't tell anyone. Mom talked to me about it a few times, though. Mostly she kept telling me that we were safe and that I shouldn't worry. But I kept having nightmares. Oh, God, Madeline. There was so much blood that night and I was so afraid it was yours."

"You aren't the only one who has had a few nightmares. I still wake up from time to time feeling as if I'm being suffocated."

"To this day I can't read thrillers or watch gory films." Daphne made a face. "My husband used to tease me about having a weak stomach."

"If he had only known the truth. You were the bravest kid in town and you saved me."

"I was terrified."

Madeline looked at her. "It wouldn't be an act of courage in the first place if you weren't scared to death. I want you to know that I have not only been enormously grateful to you all these years, I've also admired you. You were a true heroine that night."

"Not really."

"Yes," Madeline said. "Really."

"You and I should have talked about what happened. We never processed it."

Madeline winced. "Not sure that's even possible."

"So we've both got issues."

"Who doesn't have issues? Personally, I'm trying to embrace mine. I tell myself they're firewalls."

"Good plan. I think I'll do the same."

Daphne's voice was a little too flat, a little too even. Madeline looked at her.

"What happened, Daph?"

"I fell in love. Got married."

"I hear that happens."

"Brandon died a year ago. Brain cancer."

"I know. Jack mentioned that you had lost your husband. It came up when he started looking for you online." Madeline dumped a heap of ancient photography magazines on the bed and put her arms around Daphne. "I'm so sorry."

"I should be moving forward. But it feels like I'm trapped in quicksand."

"Everyone processes grief in their own way. There are no rules."

"It isn't the grief that has me trapped. It's the anger."

"I understand. They say there are several stages to grief. One of them is anger."

"I'm pissed, all right." Daphne pushed her fingers through her spiky hair. "But I couldn't tell anyone else exactly why. It would have been just too damn humiliating."

"What happened?"

"A woman came to the funeral. She was a colleague of Brandon's at the bank where he worked. Her name was Jennifer. I had met her once or twice. She even came to see Brandon a couple of times when he was in the hospital. I thanked her for attending the funeral services. But I noticed that she seemed really broken up by his death."

"Uh-oh."

"Yeah. Uh-oh. When I started going through Brandon's things, I found some of their correspondence on his computer. It went back three years. They had been lovers before Brandon and I met. She was married to someone else. According to the emails, they both agreed to stop seeing each other after Brandon asked me to marry him. And for a while, I guess they called it quits. But it didn't last long. They restarted the affair a few months later."

"That lying, cheating, double-crossing *bastard*."

Daphne looked startled by the fierce reaction. Then she smiled a wry, humorless smile. "I wake up thinking those exact words nearly every morning. I keep remembering all the times he told me that he loved me, especially toward the end."

"When he wanted to make sure you stayed by his bedside because he didn't want to die alone," Madeline said.

"After I found out the truth, I definitely felt used. There is no other word for it. A part of me keeps wishing I could go back in time and tell him that I know everything and then walk away and leave him there in that hospital bed, hooked up to all those tubes and needles."

"Think of it this way. He's gone. You're still alive. As revenge scenarios go, it doesn't get much better than outliving the son of a bitch."

Daphne went blank, evidently stunned. Then she started to laugh. It started out as weak, nervous giggling, but within the space of a couple of breaths she was laughing hard, too hard. It was over-the-top laughter. Hysterical laughter. Tears ran down her cheeks.

Madeline put her arms around her and held her until the cathartic laughter subsided. When Daphne was once again under control, Madeline released her.

Daphne found a tissue in her pocket and blotted her eyes.

"Wow," she said after a moment. "That's harsh."

"We executive types are known for being able to get to the bottom line."

"Unlike some of your ex-boyfriends, I admire that in a woman—especially a sister. Thanks, Maddie. As the old saying goes, I needed that."

"Anytime."

Madeline turned away—and saw the framed photo on the bedside table. Tom had framed only his personal favorites, the pictures he considered art. But this was not one of his startling landscapes. It was a casual photo of Tom himself. In the picture he was a young, handsome man in his prime, proudly dressed in a military uniform. There was a pretty, smiling woman standing next to him. Tom's arm was draped around her shoulders in an unmistakably possessive pose. The woman was dressed in a style that Madeline estimated to be several decades out of date.

"Looks like Tom did have at least one relationship at some point in the past," Madeline said.

Daphne came to look over her shoulder. "Maybe there's a name or a date on the back. Although I don't know what good it would do us to know the identity of a long-lost love. Obviously things didn't turn out well for them."

"Maybe she died and Tom spent the rest of his life grieving."

Madeline carefully disassembled the picture frame and removed the photo.

A second photo fell out. It had been concealed behind the first. The shot had been taken from a distance. The subject seemed entirely unaware that she was being photographed. She was standing on the top of the cliffs in front of the Aurora Point Hotel. Her shoulder-length blond hair was blowing around her face but the flying tendrils did not entirely obscure her striking features.

"Whoever she is, she's stunning," Daphne whispered. "Look, she's dressed in a modern style—not like the woman in the other photo."

Madeline flipped the picture over. Written on the back in Tom's handwriting was the name *Ramona* and a date.

"According to the date, this picture was taken about six weeks ago," Madeline said. "Do you suppose Tom and this woman were in a relationship?"

"She's way too young for Tom," Daphne said.

"Since when does being young, sexy, and stunning stop a man from getting excited?"

Daphne winced. "Right."

They studied the photo intently.

"It doesn't look like she knew Tom was taking the picture," Daphne said. "I wonder if there are any more of our mysterious Ramona."

Footsteps sounded on the front steps.

"That will be Jack and Abe," Madeline said. "Maybe they found something."

She led the way down the short hall and opened the door. Jack and Abe trooped across the porch.

"Any sign of Porter's car?" she asked.

"It never left the grounds," Jack said. "It's stashed in the maintenance building."

Daphne frowned. "I thought you said earlier there was no car parked in there."

"Once we found this, we knew what had happened," Jack said.

He held up a badly rusted sheet of metal cut into a familiar rectangular shape.

Madeline stared at it, her pulse kicking up. "It looks like an old license plate."

"That's exactly what it is," Abe said. He grinned. "We're pretty sure Lomax took Porter's car apart in his very own chop shop. He may have buried a few pieces. But a lot of it is still there in the shed—enough for me to be able to trace the ownership and registration."

CHAPTER TWENTY-ONE

Louisa opened the door of her study, a room she considered her private sanctuary, and walked into the space as if it were the lair of a dangerous reptile. The weak light of the rainy afternoon slanted through the windows.

Xavier lounged in the chair behind her desk.

"Come on in, Mom." He gave her one of his brilliant smiles. "Dad is busy talking to New York. I thought this might be a good time for you and me to discuss a few details regarding the private reception for Dad that's going to be held before the big community birthday party."

She closed the door and steeled herself. It was Xavier's unpredictability that frightened her the most.

"The plans are all in place," she said. "I talked to the caterers in Seattle again this morning."

"I'm sure it will all go off like clockwork." Xavier sat forward in the chair. The light from the desk lamp shone down over his long, elegant fingers but left his face in shadow. "My people will see to it that the right impression of the candidate and his perfect family goes out into the world on all the social media platforms. The press releases are almost ready. By the end of the event Travis will have the traction he needs to go all the way to the U.S. Senate. Trust me. I was born to get my big brother elected."

Anxiety twisted Louisa's insides. Xavier was always at his most dangerous when he was most charming.

"What did you want to talk to me about, Xavier?"

Xavier lounged back in the chair. "Did you know that Madeline Chase is in town? I ran into her last night at the Crab Shack. She was there with her so-called consultant. Pretty sure he's screwing her."

"Madeline is here to deal with the old hotel. It belongs to her now that her grandmother is gone."

"Yeah, I heard the old lady had croaked." Xavier shook his head and clicked his teeth. "Never did like the bitch. Wasn't real fond of Tom Lomax, either. They were the ones who got me sent away to that fucking prison you like to call the Institute the first time, weren't they?"

So much for hoping against hope that this time Xavier had changed, that this time he was staying on his meds. She should have known better, Louisa thought. A mother always knew her child.

"We've talked about this many times, Xavier. You know that your father and I felt you needed help."

"You mean you wanted me locked up because you were afraid I might hurt your precious little Travis."

"That's not true. We did what we thought was best for you. You must admit that you always felt better after you spent some time at the Institute. You outgrew your problems. You've been quite stable— normal—since your last stay at the clinic. Why are you bringing up the past now?"

"Because the past never goes away, Mom." Xavier chuckled. "But you're right. I'm fine now. Never better. Absolutely fucking *normal*, thanks to you and Dad making sure I got the very best of care."

Louisa's growing anxiety threatened to erupt into full-fledged panic. She put her hand on her stomach and promised herself that as soon as Xavier was gone she would go into the bathroom and take one of her anti-stress meds.

"Xavier, I'm very busy today," she said. "What is it you wanted to see me about?"

"I thought you and Dad might be interested in a little background data on Madeline's hotel consultant. He's not exactly an expert in the innkeeping business. He runs a security firm—a very low-rent security firm, I might add. Employs a total of three people, including himself."

Louisa stilled. "Are you certain?"

"Oh, yeah. I'm certain. It makes one wonder, doesn't it? I mean, why would Madeline Chase bring in a security guy to help her decide whether to sell the Aurora Point?"

Understanding struck.

"It's Tom Lomax," Louisa whispered. "She's got questions about his death."

"Yeah, that's pretty much what I concluded, too. Interesting, don't you think?"

CHAPTER TWENTY-TWO

The woman behind the front desk at the B&B looked up when Madeline came through the door, followed by Daphne, Jack, and Abe.

She gave Madeline a tight, frozen smile.

"Ms. Chase, may I speak with you please?" she asked in a thin voice.

Madeline went to the desk. "What is it?"

"I have a message for you." She held out an envelope.

Madeline took the envelope and glanced at the elegant writing on the front. The note was addressed to her. The sender's name was embossed on the flap. *Louisa Webster.*

An icy frisson danced across the back of Madeline's neck. She tucked the envelope into her tote.

The clerk cleared her throat. "Ms. Chase, I'm afraid there's a small problem with your reservations."

Madeline gave her a cool smile. "Is that so?"

"This morning you asked to extend your reservations here at the Cove View for you and your friends. At the time I thought that would be possible. However, there's been a mistake with the bookings. I'm afraid I won't be able to let you have the extension, after all."

Madeline raised her brows. "You're kicking us out?"

"We're booked solid for the weekend. Big art show going on here in town."

There was something desperate and pleading about the clerk's very bright smile.

"What do you suggest?" Madeline said.

The clerk blinked. "I beg your pardon?"

"You're asking us to check out after telling us that we could have the rooms," Madeline said patiently. "So what do you suggest the four of us do?"

The clerk swallowed hard. "I could make some calls."

"Great idea," Madeline said. "You do that. My friends and I will wait right here in the lobby."

She turned her back on the front desk and crossed the room to where Jack, Abe, and Daphne stood.

"What's going on?" Abe asked in low tones.

Jack's mouth thinned. He studied the clerk, who was speaking quickly into her phone. "My fault. This is about what happened at the Crab Shack, isn't it?"

"I think so," Madeline said. "I told you, everyone on the island gets freaked whenever Xavier Webster is in town. He's got a certain reputation for revenge."

"And he likes to use fire, as I recall," Daphne added. "That bastard. The hotel management is afraid Xavier might do something very nasty to the B-and-B if we are in residence."

"Yep," Madeline said.

The clerk looked up anxiously. "Ms. Chase?"

Madeline went back to the front desk. "Yes?"

"The inns and B-and-Bs are all filled up, but some of the summer houses are vacant. I checked with a friend at a local property management office. He suggested Harbor House. It's a very large, older home outside of town. Four bedrooms, three baths. Great views. There's a catch, though. Minimum stay is one month."

"Tell your friend I'll take it," Madeline said. "Tell him to get the rental contract ready. I'll stop by the property management office to sign it an hour from now."

"Great." The clerk was visibly weak with relief. "I appreciate your being so understanding."

"No problem." She turned around to look at the others. "Why don't we get some lunch? I'm hungry."

A short time later they settled into a booth at the Crab Shack. Heather Lambrick greeted them and then disappeared into the kitchen. Madeline picked up her menu.

"I've been kicked out of bars," Abe said. "But this is the first time I've ever been tossed out of a hotel."

"Harbor House will work for us," Madeline said.

"I remember it," Daphne said. "It was built as a summer home by some rich guy from Seattle back in the early twentieth century. It's a beautiful old place, or at least it used to be."

"With luck, we won't be hanging around Cooper Island much longer," Madeline said. She looked up at the waitress. "I'll have the Crab Louie."

"Nothing for me, thanks," Daphne said.

Abe looked at the waitress. "She'll have the fish-and-chips. Same for me."

Daphne frowned. "I'm really not hungry."

Jack tossed his menu aside. "Fish-and-chips for me, too."

The waitress took off before Daphne could correct the order.

Madeline peered at Jack. "Are you feeling okay?"

He raised his brows. "Fine. Why?"

"You usually spend a lot more time studying a menu."

"Got this one memorized."

"You're thinking about something else," she accused.

"I'm thinking about the call I'm going to make to my librarian as soon as we finish lunch."

Daphne's brows rose. "You have a personal librarian?"

Abe chuckled. "He's talking about Becky Alvarez. Technically she's our receptionist, but she's got a degree in library science and she insists we call her a librarian."

"Titles are always important," Madeline said. She turned back to Jack. "So why are you calling your in-house librarian?"

"I'm going to have her overnight some outdoor motion sensors to install around our new location," Jack said. "You know, in case a fire-bug decides to visit us."

Madeline caught her breath. "Okay."

"Good plan," Daphne said, sounding as if she, too, had just taken a sharp breath. "This is getting weird, isn't it?"

"And weirder," Madeline said.

She took the envelope out of her tote. Jack, Abe, and Daphne watched her. No one said a word.

She tore open the envelope and removed the crisp notecard inside. It was embossed with Louisa Webster's initials.

Madeline read the message aloud, keeping her voice low.

Dear Ms. Chase:

I am told that you are in town to deal with aspects of your grandmother's estate. A very sad reason to return to Cooper Island after all this time. Nevertheless, welcome home.

I would like to take this opportunity to invite you to join us for a private reception in honor of my husband's birthday

> *on Monday, the fifteenth. This will be an informal event held*
> *in our home immediately before the community event. We will*
> *be sharing some very special news with our guests.*
>
>   *I understand that you are here with a companion. He is*
> *welcome, also.*

"Louisa Webster is inviting you to a reception in honor of Egan's birthday?" Daphne's brows rose. "Well, that strikes me as creepy."

"Oh, yeah," Madeline said. "Definitely creepy. It's the *welcome home* line that gets me, though."

Abe folded his arms on the table. "I take it that when you and your grandmother lived here, your family was not close with the Websters?"

"I'm pretty sure my grandmother was never invited to any of their receptions," Madeline said. "But then, the Websters weren't close with anyone in town. Their family compound here on the island was just a weekend and summer place as far as they were concerned."

"And now, suddenly, you're being invited to a private birthday reception," Daphne observed. "This is too weird."

"Not necessarily," Jack said. "Madeline recently inherited a nice little chain of high-end hotels. She's just the kind of executive who gets invited to receptions in the homes of people who are trying to attract donors to fund a political campaign."

"Oh, right," Daphne said. "Sometimes I forget about the hotels. Of course the Websters view Madeline as a potential campaign donor. That makes sense."

Madeline sat back. "You know, in a strange way, that is oddly reassuring."

"How's that?" Abe asked.

"Let's just say it's not the first time I've had people suck up to me because of my inheritance. I understand folks like that."

Abe nodded wisely. "Sure."

Madeline looked at Jack. "What do you say? Shall I accept? It might be an opportunity to get a closer read on the Websters."

"What it is," Jack said, "is a convenient, legal way to get inside the Webster compound and have a good look around."

Alarm crackled through Madeline. "Are you crazy? I forbid it. Do you hear me? I absolutely forbid you to take that kind of chance. Don't even think about it."

She broke off because the waitress had arrived with the plates of food. When the woman retreated, Abe gave Jack a speculative look.

"This is where your IT guy gets to say, what could possibly go wrong?" Abe said.

Having evidently forgotten that she wasn't hungry, Daphne forked up a bit of crispy fish.

"Do you two do illegal stuff a lot?" she asked. She sounded curious but not particularly concerned.

"No," Abe said.

"Only for very special clients," Jack said.

CHAPTER TWENTY-THREE

The rental agreement was ready for Madeline when Jack escorted her into the property manager's office. No one brought up the subject of arson. The real estate agent seemed delighted to get the check for a month's rent. Jack concluded that the agent was new on the island and therefore didn't know the locals' secrets.

When they returned to the Cove View, Abe was waiting with a report on the license plate that had been discovered in the maintenance building. They gathered in Madeline's little suite. They had an hour before the checkout deadline.

"The car was registered to a woman named Sandra Purvis," Abe announced.

Jack saw Madeline's anticipation fade. Daphne looked dejected, too.

"That doesn't fit," Madeline said. "The license plate must be from a different car."

"Dead end," Daphne said. "So much for finding our first lead."

"Oh, ye of little faith," Abe chided. "Hang on, I'm not finished. Sandra Purvis was a resident of San Diego, California, at the time the license tabs were issued."

"Where is she now?" Jack asked.

"She's dead. Heroin overdose about five months ago. Evidently she was a career addict."

"Another recently deceased individual who happens to be linked to our case," Jack noted.

"Where is this going?" Madeline asked.

"Turns out our Sandra Purvis had a brother named Norman Purvis," Abe said. "Norman disappeared eighteen years ago. Went straight off the grid. Never seen again as far as I can tell."

Jack watched Madeline and Daphne exchange looks.

"It gets even more interesting," Abe said. "At one time Norman Purvis had a California-issued private investigator's license. But it was pulled because he got arrested for soliciting sex with underage girls. Recognize this guy?"

He turned the computer around with the flourish of a magician pulling a rabbit out of a hat.

They all looked at the screen. The old arrest photo showed a heavily built man with a receding hairline and hard eyes.

"Oh, my God," Daphne whispered. "It's him. That's Porter."

Madeline stared at the photo, mute.

Jack tried to throttle back the rage that clawed at his insides. *The bastard is dead,* he reminded himself.

Daphne put out a hand and touched Madeline's arm. The physical connection broke Madeline's trance.

"It's him," Madeline said.

Her voice sounded unnaturally even, utterly flat.

Jack knew that both women had been braced for the name and the link to the dismembered vehicle, but having it confirmed aloud made it, if not actually more real—it was already very real—somehow more visceral. More immediate. It was as if a ghost had walked into their midst, he thought. He understood because he'd had a few visitations from a dead man in his own dreams.

"So Lomax really did chop the car," he said. "Talk about being thorough."

"I told you, everyone was scared," Madeline reminded him.

He looked at Abe. "Anything else?"

"I checked out Purvis's address in San Diego," Abe said. "Eighteen years ago it was an apartment building. But it was torn down a decade ago to make way for a high-rise condo tower."

"Guess that means there's no going back to see if any of Porter's old neighbors remember him," Madeline said.

"Purvis," Abe corrected absently.

"He's always going to be Porter to me," Madeline said.

Nobody argued.

Jack looked at Abe. "All right, we've got a starting point. San Diego. Did you finish those background checks on the various members of the Webster family?"

"Yes." Abe clicked through a few more screens on the computer. "The headquarters of Egan Webster's hedge fund is in Bellevue, Washington. But it turns out that before he moved to Washington to establish his financial empire, he was a broker at a small firm in La Jolla, California."

"Which is a very nice neighborhood in San Diego," Madeline observed. "And Porter-Purvis was from San Diego."

Daphne frowned. "Where does that take us?"

"Still trying to connect dots," Abe said. "After Webster founded his own hedge fund it took off like a rocket. Almost every single investment was a blockbuster success. And the company's annual reports still look terrific. But when I examined some of the underlying investments, I found some serious anomalies."

"Anomalies are always interesting," Jack said.

"Some of the investments break the golden rule of investing—they look a little too good to be true." Abe checked another screen. "And they are, at least according to my analysis. But those anomalies don't seem to have made any impact on Webster's profits. As far as the investors know, Webster still has the magic touch."

Madeline sat back and shoved her fingers into the front pockets of her jeans. "Fraud?"

"It wouldn't be the first time a miraculously successful hedge fund operation turned out to be not so miraculous," Daphne said.

"No," Abe said. "But in this case it's interesting that Webster was so brilliantly successful for so long before he started losing his Midas touch."

Jack thought about that. "Nobody stays on top forever. The fund was established—what?—twenty years ago?"

"Right," Abe said. "A couple of years before Porter-Purvis showed up here on Cooper Island."

"Webster would have been about forty when he set up his fund," Madeline observed. "Not exactly a young hotshot. You said he was working at a brokerage firm before that. What kind of track record did he have there?"

Abe studied his notes again. "A good one, at least in the last year of his employment. Before that he was just average as far as I can tell. Had a nice list of clients, though."

"That I can believe," Madeline said. "He hit the genetic jackpot when it comes to looks and charisma. He was born for politics or sales. Probably didn't have the money for politics back at the start, so he chose sales."

Jack sat forward and folded his arms on the table. "Webster was running with the herd for his first couple of decades in the financial world. Then, some twenty years ago, he moves to Washington, sets up his own fund, and suddenly becomes Mr. Wizard. And shortly thereafter, a low-rent private investigator who had lost his license due to a penchant for sex with little girls shows up under a false ID here on Cooper Island."

They all looked at him.

"I think we need to find out what happened to change Webster's luck twenty years ago," Jack said.

"I'll keep digging," Abe said. "But I think I've done all I can do online. It's time I started talking to some people who knew Webster during his time in La Jolla, isn't it?"

"Yes," Jack said. "Find some of his old colleagues. Maybe an old girlfriend. Someone who knew him well."

Daphne straightened abruptly and drummed her fingers in a quick staccato. "I'll go with you, Abe."

They all looked at her.

Abe found his tongue first. "What?"

"There's nothing I can do here on the island," Daphne explained. "But I might be able to help you interview people. Interior designers learn to deal with all kinds of clients. I'm pretty good at getting a read on people by analyzing their personal style."

"I think," Madeline said, speaking very deliberately, "that is a very good idea."

Daphne looked satisfied. Jack thought Abe looked secretly pleased. So who was he to argue?

"Okay," he said. "Go pack. We don't have time to waste on the ferries. Go down to the marina and charter a floatplane to take you to Seattle."

CHAPTER TWENTY-FOUR

Ramona Owens was waiting for them in the driveway behind Tom Lomax's cottage. She was sitting in the driver's seat of a small gray compact. She had the door open and one foot on the ground.

Jack brought the SUV to a halt. When she spotted the big vehicle in the rearview mirror, Ramona got out. She hovered near the door of her car as if ready to jump back inside at a moment's notice.

Her phone call had come that morning just as Madeline had been enjoying some of the best scrambled eggs she had ever eaten. Jack had made the eggs in an ancient cast-iron skillet that he had discovered in a cupboard at Harbor House. It had clearly been love at first sight for Jack. She had been about to comment on his instant and possibly unnatural attraction to the piece of cookware when her phone interrupted.

The woman on the other end of the connection had sounded breathy, nervous; downright scared. *My name is Ramona Owens. I really need to talk to you. It's about my grandfather, Tom Lomax.*

Madeline studied Ramona through the windshield. "It's the woman in the photo we found in Tom's cottage."

"Get the license number of her car," Jack said.

She took a pen out of her purse and jotted down the number. "She really is gorgeous. No wonder Tom started shaving. He must have been very proud of her. He would have wanted his long-lost granddaughter to be proud of him."

Ramona's long blond hair was caught back in a ponytail today. Her jeans fit like a glove and accentuated her long legs. Her snug-fitting pullover was cashmere. Her leather jacket looked butter-soft. Her sunglasses were high-end designer gear.

Jack studied her as he unclipped his seat belt. "She's trying to be cool, but she's nervous as hell."

Madeline noticed that he did not seem nearly as impressed with Ramona's looks as most men would have been in that situation. She allowed herself a small burst of satisfaction and then immediately suppressed it.

"Scared to death, probably," she said. "She thinks her grandfather may have been murdered because of something that happened here a long time ago and she feels she can't go to the police. This is the break we've been hoping for, Jack."

"Maybe."

"I detect a lack of enthusiasm."

"You know what they say about something that seems a little too good to be true. Got the plates?"

"Yes." She dropped her notebook into her tote.

"Let's go see what this is about," Jack said.

He cracked open his door and climbed out from behind the wheel. Madeline opened her own door and jumped down to the ground.

The morning rain had moved on, but another front was gathering. The winds were picking up again. There would be more rain, and soon.

"Ramona Owens?" Jack asked without inflection.

Ramona flinched a little at the sound of his voice. "Yes." She switched her attention to Madeline. "Madeline Chase?"

"Yes," Madeline said. "This is Jack Rayner. I'm so very sorry about your grandfather."

"You're the one who found him, aren't you?"

"Yes," Madeline said.

Ramona ducked her head, looking down at the ground for a few seconds. Composing herself.

"They're saying he was probably killed because he surprised a burglar or transient," she whispered. There was a faint shiver in her voice.

"That's what the police are saying," Jack agreed. "I assume you've talked to them."

"No." Ramona took a breath. "I want to but I'm . . . afraid. Tom—my grandfather—said that if anything ever happened to him, I should pretend I never knew him. He said that under no circumstances should I contact the Cooper Island police."

"Any idea why?" Jack asked.

"No. He was a very private person. We were still getting to know each other. He didn't want to talk about the past."

"What made you go looking for him?" Madeline asked.

"I never even knew he existed until a few months ago. It wasn't until after my father died last year that I found some photos of his mother—my grandmother—and Tom. Evidently they had an affair. She got pregnant with my father but she married someone else. She never told her husband the truth. It's one of those complicated family secrets. Anyhow, my parents are both gone so I decided to go looking for the grandfather I never knew. It wasn't easy finding him, let me tell you."

"Why do you say that?" Madeline said.

"He'd changed his name. He never told me why. Just said that some bad things had happened in the past. I was so excited to find him, and he seemed just as thrilled. He said he'd never known I existed."

"I can't say that I knew your grandfather well," Madeline said. "I don't think anyone did. He was a bit of a loner and I was just a kid when I left Cooper Island. But I remember Tom as a good man and I know that my grandmother respected him and liked him."

"Thank you. That's good to know."

"What makes you think that his murder wasn't the result of surprising an intruder?" Jack asked.

Ramona made a visible effort to collect herself. Her chin came up and her shoulders straightened. "Shortly after we met he showed me a small lockbox filled with some old newspaper clippings and photos. He said if anything happened to him I should contact Edith Chase, the owner of Sanctuary Creek Inns. When I found out that he had been killed I tried to locate Mrs. Chase. That's when I discovered that she was gone and that her granddaughter was in charge of the business. I didn't know what else to do, so I thought I'd better talk to you, Madeline. I was shocked to find out you were here on the island getting ready to sell the hotel."

"Where is this lockbox you want to show us?" Jack asked.

Ramona eyed him warily and then looked at Madeline for direction.

"It's all right," Madeline said. "Jack is a good friend. My grandmother trusted him and so do I."

Ramona looked uncertain for a few more beats. Then she shrugged. "It's your call. All I know is that Granddad didn't want the box to go to anyone else except your grandmother. I'm winging it here by showing you where it is mostly because I don't want to be the only person who does know the location. Does that make sense? Guess some of Granddad's paranoia rubbed off on me."

"Where is this box?" Madeline asked.

"Granddad kept it in the maintenance building. There's not much to see. It's just an old metal filing box full of papers and photos. He obviously thought they were very important and dangerous, but I can't imagine why and I'm not sure I want to know."

She started walking toward the maintenance building. Madeline and Jack fell into step beside her.

Jack moved a little closer to Madeline. "I can handle this."

"No." She steeled herself. "This involves me. I need to go in there with you."

He seemed to understand.

"Okay," he said.

"I'm trying to decide whether to renovate the hotel or put the property on the market," Madeline said to Ramona. "But either way, I'm going to have to clear out Tom's cottage. I was planning to have most of his belongings hauled away for disposal. I didn't know he had a granddaughter, of course. That changes everything. His possessions belong to you now. You'll want to go through them and make decisions about what to keep and what to discard."

Ramona shook her head, sadly amused. "Thanks. One of the things that I did learn about my grandfather in the short time I knew him was that he was a hoarder. I'm sure most of his stuff can be tossed out. But there may be a few things that have meaning—the framed photos that he signed, for sure. He was proud of those."

"Yes, of course," Madeline said.

Ramona glanced at her. "I forgot to offer my condolences on the loss of your grandmother. Please forgive me. It's just that I've been utterly focused on my own situation."

"Naturally."

They walked the rest of the way in silence. Madeline was aware of an edgy tension in the atmosphere around Jack. She resisted the urge to keep looking at him. There was no point in trying to read his expression. It would be unreadable.

When they reached the maintenance building, Madeline handed him the key to the side door. He inserted it into the heavy padlock.

The door swung open with a rusty groan.

Madeline hesitated at the entrance, fighting the memories. Nothing had changed, she thought. The smell of gasoline and lubricants seemed even stronger now than it had been that night. The odor intensified the memories. Her pulse began to pound in her veins. Her breath got tighter in her chest. The old, all-too-familiar rage, despair, and helplessness threatened to choke her.

Ramona walked into the gloom-drenched interior and swept out a hand. "Can you believe all this junk? There must be fifty or sixty years' worth of stuff stashed in here."

Madeline gazed into the darkness as if it were a real-life version of an abyss. She did not realize that she hadn't taken more than one step into the space until Jack spoke.

"Wait here," he said. He took off his dark glasses. "I'll get the box."

Ramona glanced back at her, frowning a little. "Are you okay?"

The combination of Jack's protectiveness and Ramona's sudden concern acted like a dash of cold water. *I can do this,* she thought. *I'm not a twelve-year-old kid anymore. And the bastard is dead.*

"Yes, I'm fine." She took off her sunglasses and forced herself to walk into the shadows. "Just waiting to let my eyes get adjusted. It's really dark in here, isn't it?"

"I've got a flashlight," Jack said. He took a penlight out from inside his jacket and looked at Ramona. "Where's the lockbox?"

"I'll show you."

Ramona made her way deeper into the garage, weaving a path through mountains of scrap metal, antique commercial-sized washers and dryers, gardening equipment, and discarded furniture.

Jack gave Madeline another close look. She knew he was assessing her state of unease. She glared at him and pulled herself together with a physical effort.

He got the message. Without a word he followed Ramona into the darkness. Madeline trailed after them, trying not to look at the heap of ancient sacks of garden loam piled in one corner. The ones soaked in Porter's blood were long gone, she reminded herself. Tom had buried them with the body.

Ramona came to a halt amid mountains of battered hotel room furniture. Chairs were stacked to the ceiling on one side. Discarded desks and end tables lined the opposite side, forming a narrow pathway through the clutter.

"The box is on that shelf," Ramona said.

Jack aimed the beam of the flashlight toward the far end of the aisle. Madeline saw an old-fashioned metal filing box sitting on top of some wooden shelving.

"I'll get it," Jack said.

Ramona edged backward, giving him room to go past her to the far end of the aisle.

Jack went toward the box. Ramona wrinkled her nose.

"I'll wait outside," she said. "The smell in here is making me a little ill."

Madeline turned sideways in the narrow space to give her room to retrace the path to the door. Ramona retreated quickly.

Madeline ignored her. Everything inside her was focused on the small metal cabinet.

Jack set the flashlight on a nearby box and reached up to grip the box with both hands.

Madeline heard a sharp click followed by a snapping sound. A spark of light flashed in the shadows just behind the filing cabinet. Running footsteps sounded on the concrete floor.

Ramona was heading for the door.

Jack dropped the box, grabbed the flashlight, whirled, and came toward Madeline. He was moving very fast.

"Run," he said, his voice low and fierce with command. "It's a trap."

She didn't argue. But even as she turned and rushed back through the piles of furniture, she knew it was too late.

The door slammed shut. Instantly the space was plunged into even deeper shadows.

Madeline heard the muffled clink of steel on steel and knew that Ramona had locked the door.

CHAPTER TWENTY-FIVE

He had miscalculated badly and now Madeline might pay the price. *Hell of a time to screw up,* Jack thought.

"There are plenty of tools around here," Madeline said. "We can break down the door."

"We don't have time," Jack said. "Into the lube pit. This place is going to blow in a few seconds."

"What?"

"Go."

He pushed her toward the garage side of the maintenance building. It was their best hope—their only hope—of surviving the blast and fire he knew was coming.

The spark that had flashed in the shadows when he moved the filing box had told him just how badly he had screwed up. Even now fire was racing along the gas-soaked cord draped over the top of the stacked boxes. He'd had one glimpse of the large metal pan and the heap of old propane tanks piled inside, but that was enough. He knew a home-made bomb when he saw one.

At least Madeline was no longer asking questions. She reached the edge of the lube pit and hurried down the steps.

He followed her, tossed the flashlight aside, and went to the mattresses stacked end on end at the far side of the pit.

"Give me a hand with these," he said. "We need a couple on top of us. When those tanks blow there will be shrapnel."

Madeline didn't ask questions. She seized one side of the first mattress in line. He took the other side. The mattresses were old and not nearly as heavy as more modern versions.

They hauled one down.

"Get under it," he said.

Madeline crawled awkwardly beneath the first mattress. He managed to get one more partially down and then calculated that he couldn't push his luck any further.

He got under the unwieldy stack of mattresses and wrapped Madeline as close as possible, trying to give her more cover with his body.

"Ramona," Madeline gasped.

"Yeah."

"Bitch."

"Oh, yeah. Ears."

Madeline clamped her hands over her ears. He shielded his own.

The explosion tore through the garage. The force of the energy blew out and up, obeying the laws of physics. The deep cavity of the concrete lube pit was largely protected, but the ground shuddered and the roar was deafening.

Then the thudding started as debris rained down on the mattresses.

The deadly shower seemed to go on forever, but in reality it was all over in a moment or two.

He knew the fire was just getting started.

He shoved aside the mattresses and hauled Madeline to her feet.

"You okay?" he said.

"Yes." She shook her head. "My ears are ringing, though." She stopped short when she saw the result of the blast. "My God."

They were standing in the rain because the blast had blown the roof off the maintenance building and flattened three of the four walls.

The first thing he noticed was that Ramona's car was gone.

Heavy, dark smoke rolled across the scene.

"We have to move," he said. "Lot of combustible material in the vicinity. Cover your nose and mouth. We sure as hell don't want to breathe any more of the fallout than we already have."

Madeline covered the lower portion of her face with her sleeve and staggered up the steps.

"The car," he said.

"What about Ramona?"

"It's an island. Where can she go?" He glanced at his watch. "Next ferry doesn't leave for a couple of hours. We've got a license number and a damn good description. If the local cops can't find her, they'll have to come up with a really good explanation."

By the time they reached the SUV the fire was feeding on the leftovers of the blast. Jack got Madeline into the passenger seat. He could feel the shivers coursing through her.

"Adrenaline," he said. "And shock."

"No kidding."

He went around the SUV, climbed behind the wheel, unclipped his phone, and cranked up 911. When the emergency operator answered, he gave the details of the situation and then ended the call before she could ask more questions.

Together he and Madeline watched the rising flames.

"I don't think it will spread to the main hotel building," he said after a while. "Too much greenery and concrete in the way."

"I can't believe she tried to murder us with a homemade bomb," Madeline whispered.

"Funny. I have no trouble believing it at all."

"What do we tell the police?" Madeline asked.

"The truth."

"But it sounds so far-fetched. A woman claiming to be Tom Lomax's granddaughter asks to meet us because she has something she wants to show us in the maintenance building. We go inside to retrieve the mystery item and trigger an explosion. We survive, barely, thanks to your quick thinking, but when we emerge from the ruins, the woman has vanished."

"Doesn't make me and my so-called quick-thinking skills look good, does it?"

"You saved both of us, Jack." Madeline watched the fire burn. "But who in the world is going to believe our story?"

"The Cooper Island police, I hope."

"There won't be a lot of hard evidence left after that explosion and fire."

"No," Jack said. "No good evidence at all."

"Well, now at least we have a plausible motive to explain why Tom took the briefcase out of the wall in room two-oh-nine. His long-lost granddaughter, Ramona, convinced him that it was necessary."

He surprised himself with a rough crack of laughter.

Madeline frowned. "What?"

"You." He shook his head. "You're amazing. You barely survive an explosion and a fire and the first thing you do is cut to the chase. Yes, you're probably right. The long-lost granddaughter was deeply involved in this thing."

"Think she really is his long-lost granddaughter?"

"What I think," Jack said, "is that someone figured out that a long-lost granddaughter is the one person who might have been able to convince Lomax to talk about what happened the night Porter-Purvis disappeared. Which leaves us with a few more questions."

Madeline glanced at him. "Someone tracked Porter to the island and all the way to the Aurora Point Hotel. Someone concluded that he got this far and no farther eighteen years ago."

Sirens wailed in the distance.

CHAPTER TWENTY-SIX

"I've been doing a survey for the past fifteen minutes and I can now inform you with ninety-seven percent certainty that there are two distinct breeds of dog here in La Jolla." Abe spoke around a mouthful of fish taco. "You've got your basic Rescue Dog and your Very Expensive Show-Quality Dog."

Daphne sipped some of her milk shake and studied the handsome, elegantly clipped wheaten terrier bouncing along at the end of a lead. Although he was not running, the man attached to the other end of the leash was wearing a pricey-looking running outfit and some equally expensive running shoes.

Coming up fast behind the wheaten terrier and its human was a great, shaggy beast of indeterminate ancestry. It might as well have worn a sign around its thick neck: *Shelter dog. Wanna make something of it?* The human clutching the other end of the lead was on roller skates. She had a long blond ponytail and Daphne was pretty sure she smirked when she and the beast surged past the wheaten terrier and the man in running gear. Terrier and companion pretended not to notice the blonde on skates and her tough escort.

Daphne used her straw to stir the milk shake. "You're right. Two distinct breeds here. But both have style. This is Southern California, after all."

In spite of the strange, unnerving situation into which she had suddenly been plunged, it was surprisingly pleasant to sit there on a park bench with Abe. The warmth of the Southern California sun felt good after the chill of Cooper Island.

They were eating lunch and watching the joggers, skaters, and dog walkers pass in front of them on the shoreline path. It had been a long time since she had enjoyed the company of a man as much as she enjoyed Abe's company. Last night at the hotel near the beach she had enjoyed another good night's sleep knowing that Abe was on the other side of the connecting door.

She was sure that he was not her type. She had always been attracted to men who shared her love of design in all its myriad forms. Men who respected her talent for creating a space that reflected the individual taste and style of a client. Men who had an intuitive appreciation of the arts; men who dressed with taste and style.

Brandon had been that sort of man.

As far as she could tell, the only art that Abe responded to with true passion was whatever creativity lay at the heart of computer algorithms. Definitely not her type, but for some reason it was good to sit there with him in the sunshine.

Beyond the path was a sandy beach and the sparkling waters of the Pacific. The day wasn't quite warm enough to draw the bathing suit crowd and the waves weren't high enough to lure the surfers, but in Southern California any day was a good day to do some people watching at the beach.

She was also vaguely amazed to discover that she was enjoying the milk shake that Abe had insisted she drink. The clerk who had sold her the milk shake had assured her that the ice cream was made from milk supplied by happy cows that were never given hormones or antibiotics.

"What are you thinking?" Abe asked.

"I was thinking about contented cows and designer dogs, but now I'm thinking about Maddie and Jack."

"Don't worry about your friend. Jack will take good care of her."

"He seems to have taken a very personal interest in Maddie's security problem."

Abe nodded, thoughtful now. "Understandable. Sanctuary Creek Inns is by far our biggest and most important account. Jack wanted to take a hands-on approach."

Daphne stirred her milk shake. "Have you noticed the way he looks at Maddie whenever she's in the vicinity?"

Abe frowned. "What of it? He's a suspicious man by nature. Goes with the territory. He used to do some work for the FBI, you know."

"Oh, for heaven's sake, Abe. Your brother doesn't look at Maddie as if he's suspicious of her. He looks at her as if he wants to *date* her. There's a difference."

"See, there's where you're wrong," Abe announced with grave authority. "Jack is suspicious of her for exactly that reason."

"Because he's falling for her?"

"That makes him extra cautious. Downright suspicious."

"Why?"

"Because this is Jack we're talking about." Abe munched a bite of taco. "He isn't what you'd call an emotional guy. I mean, it's not like he doesn't have any emotions. He does. But they don't show up very often. And when they do, I think it makes him uneasy."

"So he gets suspicious of whatever is causing him to feel some strong emotion? Okay, in a weird kind of way that makes sense."

"Jack also has a rule. He never sleeps with the clients."

"I doubt if Maddie is in the habit of sleeping with her consultants, either. But I've got a feeling this situation is different for both of them. What would you say if they had an affair?"

"I'd say it's their business. But I'd also say it probably wouldn't last long." Abe paused a beat. "Unfortunately."

"What makes you say that?"

Abe shrugged. "Jack's affairs haven't lasted long since his fiancée ditched him a couple of years ago. Actually, I don't think he's had any relationship that lasted long enough to be called an affair. Mom has been after him to get out of his shell and meet more people. She's afraid he's developed commitment issues. But I think he's just focused on building the business now. See, Jack tends to be really intense when he focuses on something."

"I got that impression."

"He's like a freight train. Once he starts down the track, he just keeps going. Anyone standing in his path has two options—get out of the way or get on board." Abe tossed the taco wrapper into a nearby trash can. "Enough about Jack and Madeline. Let's talk about us."

An odd little tingle of awareness touched the nape of her neck. "What about us?"

"We've got some interviews to conduct, remember? We need to come up with a cover story."

The little frisson of pleasure that she had been enjoying evaporated. But a burst of adrenaline took its place. She slurped up the last of the milk shake.

"Right," she said. "A cover story."

Abe's phone rang just as he started to get to his feet. He frowned at the screen and took the call.

"I don't have any answers yet, Jack. We're just getting started." There was a short pause. "*Holy shit*. Are you both okay?"

Daphne froze. "What's wrong?"

Abe looked at her. "Jack and Madeline were nearly killed in an explosion and fire this morning."

"My God." Daphne stared at the phone. "Maddie? Maddie, are you there?"

"I'm here and I'm fine."

Abe set the phone down on the bench and hit the speaker feature. Jack started talking in a flat, unemotional way that iced Daphne's blood.

"Things are getting interesting here," Jack said.

CHAPTER TWENTY-SEVEN

"You're sure that both of you are okay?" Daphne asked for the third or fourth time.

Madeline looked at the phone sitting on the kitchen table. Jack had hit speaker mode and delivered the report of the explosion as if it were no more eventful than a blip in the stock market. When he had finished he had started to prowl the big, old-fashioned kitchen, listening to the conversation between the two women.

"Depends on your definition of *okay*," Madeline said. "I'm a little shaken up, to say the least, but we executive types pride ourselves on being able to deal with the unexpected."

"A homemade bomb definitely comes under the heading of *unexpected*," Abe said. "Tell me about the tech involved in the bomb, Jack."

Jack stopped in front of the table and looked at the phone. "Low-tech but effective. When I moved the file box I tripped the device that set off a spark. That ignited a cord soaked in gasoline. The cord ran to a pile of empty five-gallon propane tanks—the kind you use with barbecues. They were sitting in a shallow pool of gasoline."

"No such thing as an empty propane tank," Abe mused. "There's always some residue and it's highly explosive under the right conditions."

"Madeline thinks the tanks were left over from the days when each of the cottages had its own barbecue."

"Someone knew what he was doing, that's for sure," Abe said. "What are the local authorities saying?"

"The explosion is still under investigation, but there isn't much left to investigate," Jack said. "Pretty sure it's going to be classified as a suspicious fire, but that will be the end of it. Madeline's grandmother didn't bother to insure the hotel, so there's no insurance company investigator involved."

"What about the Cooper Island police?" Daphne asked, indignant. "There's a would-be murderer running around named Ramona Owens."

"We talked to Chief Dunbar," Madeline said. "He's new, not the guy that was in charge when you and I lived on the island. But we don't know much about him. We gave him the facts. Told him that the woman had claimed to be Tom Lomax's granddaughter and that she wanted to show us some old papers and photos that Tom had kept in a lockbox."

"The cops are looking for Ramona's compact and there will be an officer stationed at the ferry dock for the next few days," Jack said. "But it turns out there are a lot of places where you can ditch a car in the woods and ravines around here. All we know for sure is that Ramona didn't get on the ferry today."

"Anyone at that end got a working theory of the crime?" Abe asked.

"Dunbar seems serious about finding Ramona Owens," Jack said. "But this is a very small town with limited resources, and now he has one unexplained murder and an explosion and fire on his hands. He's a little overwhelmed, to put it mildly."

"Dunbar might have been able to write off the explosion as an accident if you two hadn't survived," Abe said. "No one would have known that there was a woman calling herself Ramona Owens at the scene. But you did survive, and now the cops have to deal with the problem of the mystery woman."

"The chief did trace her license plates," Jack added. "All the way to a rental car agency in Seattle. But the agency had no record of a Ramona Owens. According to them, the vehicle was rented to someone with a different name and a nonexistent address in Las Vegas."

"Get the ID to me and I'll see what I can find out," Abe said. "What's your read on Dunbar?"

"I can't be certain because he's being careful," Jack said. "But he mentioned that he was aware that I was involved in a small, rather public scene in a local restaurant and that the scene involved a certain member of a prominent island family. Got a hunch Dunbar is aware that this individual has a history of playing with fire."

"If he's any kind of halfway decent cop, he knows," Abe said.

"Sure," Jack said. "But at this point he has nothing to connect our individual with the explosion. All he's got is Ramona Owens, who has vanished."

There was a short silence on the La Jolla end of the connection. Madeline got a mental image of Abe and Daphne exchanging glances. She knew that all four of them were now thinking about Xavier Webster.

"Maddie, you and Jack need to get off that island," Daphne said.

"We can't leave," Madeline said. "Not until we figure out what is going on here."

"Maddie, it's not safe there," Daphne said. Her voice was very tight now.

"I know it sounds a little counterintuitive," Jack said. "But I think we may be relatively safer here than we would be in some other place. At least for now. Whoever was responsible for the explosion had a very close call today. He'll be very careful for a while."

"He'll be looking for another opportunity," Abe warned. "I think he's focused on you, Jack. Probably views Madeline as collateral damage."

"But if that's the case, where does this woman who claims to be Lomax's granddaughter fit into this thing?" Daphne asked.

"We don't know yet, but men like the one we're discussing have a reputation for being able to manipulate others," Madeline said. "Especially women."

"We need to find Ramona Owens," Abe said.

"Yes," Jack said. "So much for our excitement. Any leads on your end?"

"Maybe," Abe said. "We've got addresses for a couple of former colleagues of our subject—people who knew him before he became a hotshot in the financial world. We're going to see the first one this afternoon."

"Talk to me when you have something, anything."

"Sure," Abe said.

Jack leaned down and hit *end call*. He clipped the phone to his belt. Madeline drummed her fingers on the table.

He finally noticed that she was glaring at him.

"What?" he asked, genuinely bewildered.

"It's considered good manners to say something polite like *good-bye* or *nice talking to you* when you end a phone call."

He frowned. "There wasn't anything more to say."

Madeline's phone rang before she could continue with her lecture. She picked it up. The number was unfamiliar.

"Yes?" she said.

"Miss Chase? This is Louisa Webster. I got your number from the Cove View B-and-B. I know you've had an absolutely terrible day. The rumors of the accident out at the hotel are all over town. I'm so glad you and your friend Mr. Rayner are all right."

"Word travels fast."

"Well, this is a very small town. But then, you know that. You were once one of us."

Madeline said nothing.

"I realize you must be exhausted," Louisa said quickly. "I hate to impose on you, but I would very much like to talk to you privately. I would suggest some time tomorrow or the next day when you've had a chance to recover from what I'm sure must have been a ghastly shock. Unfortunately, I'm afraid it's quite urgent that I see you as soon as possible. Would you mind coming out to Cliff House this afternoon?"

CHAPTER TWENTY-EIGHT

"It is very gracious of you to make time to see me on such short notice," Louisa said. She took off her reading glasses in a movement that conveyed a sense of great weariness and set them aside. "I do apologize. You've been through a very traumatic experience today. I also want to offer you my condolences on the loss of your grandmother."

"It isn't as though she died of natural causes," Madeline said. "I believe she was murdered."

Louisa stared at her. It was a true deer-in-the-headlights stare. Clearly she had not seen that coming. *Score one for me,* Madeline thought. When you were involved in a negotiation with someone who was accustomed to wielding power, it paid to blindside your opponent.

"I had not heard anything about murder," Louisa gasped, clearly shaken. "I understood that Edith Chase's death was an accident."

"That's what the police said. I have my own opinion."

"I see." Louisa composed herself. "Do you have anything to base it on?"

"No, but I'm sure you can see why I'm leaning in that direction, given what happened to me and my consultant today. May I ask why you wanted to see me?"

When she had walked into the spacious foyer of Cliff House a short time ago, she had been struck by an eerie sense of emptiness. It wasn't that there weren't people around. In addition to the house-keeper who had greeted her at the door, there was a team of florists and a number of workers engaged in various tasks that appeared related to preparations for the upcoming birthday reception.

But somehow the big house felt empty. And dark. And cold.

Jack had driven her through the gates of the Webster family compound. He had escorted her to the door and waited until the house-keeper had appeared. Then he had returned to the SUV, which he had made a point of parking in the front drive where everyone in the vicinity would be aware of his presence. The message was plain. She had not entered the lion's den alone.

"Do the police have any idea of what caused the explosion and fire out at Aurora Point?" Louisa asked.

"Not yet," Madeline said. "It's still under investigation."

"Rumor has it that a woman claiming to be Tom Lomax's grand-daughter was present at the scene."

"I'm impressed that you know so much about the incident," Madeline said. "It only happened a few hours ago."

"You know how it is in a small town." Louisa folded her hands on top of her desk. Her expensive rings sparkled with a hard, cold light. "Is it true?"

"Oh, yes, there was a woman at the scene. And she did claim to be Tom's granddaughter."

"That is difficult to believe." Louisa's mouth tightened at the corners. "Tom Lomax was such an eccentric loner."

"We all have stories in our pasts, don't we?"

To her surprise, Louisa looked unnerved. The strange air of shock lasted only a second or two. She recovered immediately.

"Why would Tom Lomax's granddaughter want to kill you?" she asked finally.

"Good question. But then, I'm not at all sure I was the target. Perhaps it was Mr. Rayner who was the intended victim." Madeline got to her feet. "If the only reason you asked me to come here today was to question me about what happened out at the Aurora Point this morning, you could have just phoned. I'll be leaving now."

"No," Louisa said, an edge of panic in the word. "I want to talk to you about a business matter. Sit down. Please."

Concluding that she would learn more by staying than by leaving, Madeline sat down again.

"I understand that you came here to get the Aurora Point Hotel ready to put on the market," Louisa said. "That is an excellent plan. We never understood why your grandmother held on to it for so long. I suppose she hoped that the property would one day increase markedly in value."

Louisa paused expectantly, waiting for confirmation or denial of her theory. Madeline smiled politely.

Louisa abandoned the attempt to gain more information.

"Unfortunately, land prices around here have been stable for years," she said. "In fact, they've actually gone lower in some cases. I'm afraid Cooper Island will never be a major vacation destination here in the Pacific Northwest."

"Doesn't look like it," Madeline said.

Louisa tapped one finger on the desk. Her rings glinted again in the glare of the lamp.

"The hotel buildings and cottages are worthless, of course, but the property has some long-term potential," she continued. "Egan and I believe that it can be transformed into a community recreational area.

With that in mind, we would like to purchase it. I'll write the check today."

"I will certainly consider your offer," Madeline said. "But I'm not ready to make a decision yet."

Louisa's jaw jerked twice. "This is about what happened today, isn't it? You think that because of the incident at the Crab Shack involving my son Xavier and your Mr. Rayner, Xavier is somehow responsible for the explosion and fire."

"Those are your words, not mine."

Louisa came up out of her chair. "I will not allow you to make unfounded accusations against a member of my family."

"I haven't made any accusations, Louisa. You were the one who brought up Xavier's name."

Louisa's face got tight. Her eyes glittered with the same hard light that infused the stones in her rings.

"I think it would be best if you and your so-called consultant left Cooper Island immediately."

"So now we get to the real reason you asked me to come here today. You're trying to run my consultant and me out of town."

"Don't be ridiculous. I'm suggesting that the two of you leave before there is any more trouble."

"Why would there be more trouble?"

"You're an intelligent woman, Madeline. I'm hoping that you will also demonstrate that you have a sense of responsibility."

"Does this mean my consultant and I are no longer invited to your husband's birthday reception?"

Rage flashed in Louisa's eyes. "I'm trying to deal with you as a mature adult."

"You're terrified because you know that Xavier was humiliated at the Crab Shack. You're afraid that he might go to extreme lengths to get even."

Louisa turned to stone. "That is utter nonsense. But I will tell you this, Madeline Chase: Your presence here and the presence of your so-called consultant is stirring up trouble. It would be better for all concerned if you left immediately. Never say that you weren't warned."

"Don't worry, Louisa, I won't say that." Madeline got to her feet again and hitched the strap of her bag over her shoulder. "It looks like we're finished here. If you'll excuse me, my consultant is waiting for me."

She turned and started toward the door.

"Damn it, don't you understand? I'm trying to do what's best for all of us."

Madeline paused, one hand on the doorknob. "You mean you're trying to do what you think is best for your family. I do understand. Believe it or not, you have my sympathy."

"Get out of here. Now."

Madeline opened the door and went out into the hall. There was no one waiting to escort her back to the entrance. She would have to find her own way.

In the unnatural stillness that gripped Cliff House, she thought she heard soft sounds coming from the study. Louisa was sobbing.

Madeline hurried toward the far end of the hall. When she reached the foyer, the housekeeper appeared.

"I'm so sorry," the woman said. "Mrs. Webster didn't ring to let me know that you were ready to leave."

"Not a problem," Madeline said.

A sense of relief that bordered on euphoria shot through her when she saw Jack lounging against the fender of the SUV. The dark mirrors of his sunglasses glinted in the silvery daylight. It took an enormous effort of willpower to walk, not run, down the steps.

He opened the passenger-side door for her. "How did it go?"

She climbed into the vehicle. "Let's just say we won't be going to the ball, after all."

CHAPTER TWENTY-NINE

When the dark memories came, they usually came late at night. Jack awoke from a troubled dream and lay quietly for a time, thinking about the past . . .

> The metallic thud of the fishing spear striking his aluminum dive tank was the first indication he had that Victor Ingram meant to murder him.
>
> The impact of the blow caused him to lose his grip on the guide line that marked the route through the underwater cave. He turned quickly, trying to believe that Victor had discharged the spear gun by accident. But some part of him—the part that was now focused on survival—was already dealing with the knowledge that Victor wanted him dead.
>
> Victor's eyes widened behind the faceplate of his mask. He had not planned on missing the shot. Panic set in fast. He dropped the empty spear gun and grabbed his dive knife. Kicking furiously, he propelled himself forward, the blade extended for a slashing strike . . .

He pushed back the covers, sat up on the edge of the bed, and checked the time. One nineteen. From long experience he knew he would not be going back to sleep anytime before dawn. He listened to the big house for a moment. Outside, the storm was still lashing the windows and pounding on doors, but nothing sounded unduly alarming.

He checked his phone. No pings from the motion sensors he had installed that afternoon.

He didn't think the killer would make another move so soon, but he had been wrong before.

He pulled on jeans and a T-shirt, picked up the holstered gun, and went out into the hallway.

The door to Madeline's room stood slightly ajar, just as it had when she had turned out the lights a few hours ago. He paused, listening again. There was no sound from her room.

Between the trauma of the explosion and the unpleasant interview with Louisa Webster, she had been exhausted. She needed sleep. She had been living on adrenaline and disturbing memories for the past several days now. That combination was hard on the body, the nerves, and most of all the mind. It got in the way of sound judgment and clear thinking.

Just who was he lecturing here, he wondered, Madeline or himself?

He went downstairs, sat at the kitchen table, and opened his computer. There was an email from Abe.

> Thought you might find the attached interesting. The brokerage firm is the one where Webster worked before moving to Bellevue, WA.

The attached document was from a San Diego newspaper. It was dated a little more than twenty years earlier.

The bodies of two people believed murdered in the course of a home invasion were discovered by police this morning. The male victim was identified as Carl Seavers, a stockbroker who worked for a firm in La Jolla. The woman who was found dead at the scene was identified as Sharon Richards, also an employee of the brokerage business. Neighbors reported that they heard nothing alarming during the night.

According to his co-workers, Seavers enjoyed considerable success as a broker. "He had a golden gut when it came to picking stocks," one noted. Authorities are investigating the possibility that drugs may have been involved.

Jack unclipped his phone. Abe answered on the fourth or fifth ring. He sounded groggy and short-tempered.

"It's one thirty in the morning," he snarled.

"Tell me about the home invasion robbery," Jack said.

"I can't tell you anything more yet. I don't know anything more. The guy we interviewed today mentioned it when he talked about the old days at the firm. Evidently Webster left town to fire up his hedge fund about a month after the deaths of Seavers and the woman. Now leave me alone. You may not need sleep, but I do."

The connection went dead. Jack looked at the device for a while but finally decided not to hit *redial*.

He got up and went into the living room to contemplate the view from the windows. The fractured moonlight painted the cold water in icy shades of silver.

Memories drifted at the edges of his consciousness. During the day he could ignore the ghostly images, but at night that was a lot harder to do.

Two years ago he had accepted the fact that for the rest of his life he would likely get visits from the ghost of Victor Ingram. There had been a price to pay.

But it was not until he met Madeline that he had understood the true enormity of the cost.

He heard her footsteps on the stairs, but he did not turn around until she spoke.

"Jack?"

He did turn then, and saw her in the doorway, a wraithlike figure silhouetted by the soft glow of a night-light.

"Sorry," he said. "Didn't mean to wake you. Just checking email. Abe sent a newspaper clipping. It seems that two colleagues of Webster's from the La Jolla days died in a home invasion a little more than twenty years ago."

"Yes, I know. I got a message from Daphne. Weird."

"Very weird."

"But what does it mean?"

"I don't know yet. Abe and Daphne are going to talk to someone else from Webster's old brokerage firm tomorrow."

Madeline smiled briefly. "Between you and me, I think Daphne is rather enjoying the role of private investigator."

"Glad someone is. Nearly getting you killed today certainly took the thrill out of the business for me."

"You didn't nearly get me killed. You saved my life."

"That's not how I remember it."

She walked through the doorway and stopped in front of him. She was so close, only inches away. So close he could feel the warmth of her body. So close her scent stirred his blood. So close he could see the invitation in her eyes.

"That's exactly how I remember it," she said. "If I tell you that I want you to kiss me, will you tell me to go back to bed?"

"If you want to kiss me because you think I saved your life, I'll take a rain check."

"I don't do rain checks. This is a take-it-or-leave-it offer. And for the record, it's got nothing to do with the fact that you saved my life. I will remind you that I wanted to kiss you before today happened."

"You were feeling emotional that first night here on the island. You were vulnerable."

"That does it, I've had enough." She took a decisive step back toward the door. "For the record, I am not too emotionally vulnerable to make an informed decision tonight. In spite of appearances to the contrary, I do know what I'm doing—or at least what I wanted to do before you so rudely implied otherwise."

"Damn it, Madeline—"

She was already on the stairs, heading back to her bedroom.

"Forget it," she called down to him. "I don't want to hear any more excuses. If you don't want to go to bed with me, just say so. I promise to stop bothering you."

"Madeline, wait."

He broke through the trance and started after her.

He made it to the top of the stairs in time to see her disappear into the shadows of the bedroom.

The door slammed shut just as he reached it. He pushed it open again before she could lock it. She stood her ground, very fierce and proud. And incredibly exciting.

He stopped abruptly. "You don't understand."

"What, exactly, do I fail to grasp about this situation?"

"The future."

"What about the future?"

"I can't offer you one."

She went utterly still, visibly shocked. "Jack, please tell me, do you have some terrible disease?"

"No, nothing like that." He winced. "Sorry. Didn't mean to go down that road. Look, this is complicated."

"How complicated? Are you gay?"

"*No.*"

"Are you going to tell me that you've got a wife and kids stashed away somewhere?"

"No. What I'm going to tell you is that I've got a lousy track record when it comes to relationships. They never last long. My fault every time. Don't you understand? I don't want any misunderstandings between us. I can't make any promises."

"Ah. Commitment issues."

"Something like that."

She considered briefly and then nodded once. "Okay."

"Okay? That's all you can say?"

"I'm good with your issues if you're good with mine."

"Your issues don't begin to compare to mine," he warned.

"Now we're comparing issues?"

"You think running background checks on the guys you date constitutes a serious issue?"

She frowned. "Of course not. Paying someone to run background checks on my dates is just common sense. My issues are a lot more personal. I do not intend to discuss them with a man who isn't interested in having a relationship with me. Good night, Jack. Again."

"Wait. You're saying you're okay with my commitment issues?"

"Right. Now, if you're done with this conversation—"

"We're not having a conversation, we're conducting a damn negotiation."

She raised her brows. "Is that right?"

"Just to be clear—you'd be okay with a relationship based on the understanding that I've got a lousy track record in the relationship department?"

"I'll put my lousy track record up against yours anytime." She folded her arms. "However, I do insist on monogamy on both sides while we are involved in this uncommitted relationship."

Her voice was as tight as that of a gambler who was doubling down on a desperate bet.

"Agreed," he said. He did not want to think about her with another man. "Anything else you want to negotiate?"

"Can't think of anything offhand," she said. "You?"

"Nothing comes to mind."

"Then it looks like we have established the terms and conditions of a relationship."

"Are you going to whip out a contract for me to sign?"

Her brows snapped together. "What?"

"Talk about taking the romance out of things."

She stared at him for a beat. Then she went off like a volcano.

"You started it," she said.

Her voice was harsh with indignation, anger, and—maybe—pain. Or maybe—just maybe—those were the emotions tearing through him.

"Me?" he shot back. "You're the one who wanted to compare issues."

"I can't believe you're trying to make this my fault."

He moved closer to her. "Damned if I'll let you stick me with the blame for this fiasco."

"First you accuse me of taking all the romance out of our relationship and then you call it a fiasco. You're right. Whatever happens between us probably won't last very long, not at the rate we're going, so I suggest we get started before it fizzles out completely."

She closed the short distance between them, clamped her hands around his shoulders, stood on tiptoe, and kissed him.

It was a kiss fueled by the energy that had been charging the atmosphere between them for almost three months; a kiss powered by the emotional fallout from the explosion in the garage; a kiss that carried the fire of adrenaline and frustration and anger.

And it acted like a powerful accelerant for the hunger that had been simmering deep inside him since the day he met her.

"To hell with our issues and the future," he said against her mouth. "All I care about right now is tonight."

"Tonight works for me."

CHAPTER THIRTY

The rush of desire caught Madeline by surprise. She should have been prepared, she thought. She had, after all, kissed Jack on one other occasion. The heat had been intense that time, too. But he had been in charge that time, deciding what she needed and just how far things should be allowed to go.

Tonight was different. She had started the brush fire this time. She was in control.

She took great fistfuls of his T-shirt in both hands and wrenched her mouth away from his.

"Last time we stopped because you claimed you didn't think I knew what I was doing," she said. "Tonight you can't use that excuse. Do you understand that?"

He trapped her face between his hands. "It wasn't an excuse."

"It was as far as I'm concerned. So, one more thing you need to know—if you want to stop tonight, you're going to have to flat-out tell me you don't want me. No more pretending you're trying to do what's right for me. Got that?"

He looked at her with eyes that were a little savage. "Damn, woman. Do you always talk this much before you get into bed?"

He didn't wait for a response, which was a good thing because she had no ready answer to the question.

He captured her mouth in a kiss that told her all she needed to know. This time he would not be calling a halt. Only she could stop this, and that was the last thing she wanted to do.

She wound her arms around his neck and opened her mouth for him. There was nothing practiced or deliberately seductive about the kiss because the simple truth was that she had never kissed anyone else in this way—with such excitement and need and anticipation.

This was a kiss that crossed all the lines that she had drawn for herself eighteen years before; a kiss that pushed back her personal boundaries in ways she had never imagined possible. It was a kiss that broke the rules.

Jack's response was equally primal, devoid of the artistry and finesse of the skilled lover. It was raw and elemental and it told her more clearly than words that tonight was different for him, too.

That was reason enough to break the rules.

They fumbled their way to the bed. By the time they reached it she was unnerved and shivering and taking in oxygen as though it were a rare and fleeting commodity.

Jack released her long enough to get out of his T-shirt, pants, and briefs. When he turned back to face her, she sensed his subtle hesitation and knew that he was waiting for her to reaffirm her decision. It dawned on her that she was not the only one in the room who was in uncharted territory. Jack needed to know that she still wanted him now that he stood naked before her.

She moved closer and once again stood on tiptoe to kiss him. His rigid erection pushed against her thigh. She reached down and took him gently in her hand.

He groaned and pulled her closer. She realized they were about to fall together onto the tumbled sheets. Panic flared for an instant. She opened her mouth to tell him that she had to be on top.

But there was no need for explanations. As if he had received the message via psychic intercept, he landed flat on his back and steered her descent so that she landed on top of him. Exactly where she needed to be.

The flash of fear vanished in the next instant. She was flying now, lost in a glorious haze of pure desire. Some part of her knew it was irrational. It would no doubt end the way it usually did——with a whimper, not a bang. Nevertheless, in that moment she dared to believe that she was normal, that she could respond like any other normal woman would respond when she was in the arms of a sexy man who seemed to want her as much as she wanted him.

And she did not doubt that Jack wanted her——his rigid erection and the achingly tender way he touched her intoxicated and seduced her. He handled her as if she were the most valuable, most amazing, most exquisite creation that he had ever encountered.

She raised her head briefly to look down at him, an unfamiliar sense of profound certainty rushing through her.

"It's all right," she said. "I won't shatter."

"I know that. You're strong." He wrapped one big hand around the back of her head and drew her mouth down to his. "But I sure as hell will fracture into a million little pieces if I screw this up."

"But you're not screwing it up," she whispered.

She wanted to add more reassurances, but there was no chance because he was kissing her again. His free hand moved down her body to her thigh and then he was tugging the hem of her nightgown upward, crushing the soft fabric gently around her waist. His fingers sank into the curve of her buttocks and then he began to explore her even more intimately.

She took a quick, sharp breath when she felt his fingers on the inside of her leg. He went utterly still beneath her. When she opened her eyes partway, she saw that he was watching her with an intensity that told her just how hard he was working to maintain his control.

She kissed his throat and then his chest and then she reached down and stroked him intimately, trying to tell him without words that she liked his touch.

No, she *craved* his touch. She did not want any other man to touch her ever again. Just Jack.

His hips moved against her, encouraging her to part her legs for him. When she accepted the invitation, he touched her more deeply still, drawing forth a response that stunned her. A great urgency tightened her insides.

"Yes," she whispered. "Yes. Now."

But he continued to stroke her as though she were a fragile flower. He did not seem to realize that she needed more—so much more.

Galvanized by the spiraling tension building within her, she levered herself up so that she could ride him astride. He groaned when she guided him slowly, carefully into her. His fingers gripped her thighs. He watched her as though in that moment she were the only thing that mattered in his world.

He groaned. His jaw was as rigid as the rest of him. He pushed upward, slowly, deliberately; filling her completely, astonishing her.

He added one more element to the volatile mix of sensations. He moved his thumb against her clitoris, and with that she was lost. The waves of a release unlike anything she had ever experienced crashed through her and she was truly breathless.

He surged upward one last time, going impossibly deep. His climax thundered through him. A low, husky roar of satisfaction ripped through the night. She had given him that gift, she thought, elated. She had fully and completely satisfied this man.

And he had given her something even more wondrous in return. Tonight, for the first time, she had responded in a way that, until now, she had never believed possible—a way that felt normal. Real.

All she needed was the right man—Jack—a man who was anything but normal.

CHAPTER THIRTY-ONE

Egan did not bother to switch on the lights in the great room. The drapes were open. The cold, bright moon and the outdoor security lamps combined to illuminate the path to the liquor cabinet. He could have made the trek blindfolded. He'd had a lot of practice over the decades.

He had always been a restless sleeper. His doctors had prescribed meds from time to time, but in the end he always returned to his standby drug of choice—a few large shots of good scotch. On the bad nights nothing else would do.

This was one of the bad nights.

He picked up the bottle and splashed the first generous dose into a glass. For a time he stood at the window, sipping the scotch and watching the moonlight glaze the dark waters of the cove. He had been consumed more and more with thoughts of the past lately. It made him uneasy. He wondered if that was the price of getting old. Age was supposed to bring wisdom, but he woke up too often in the middle of the night thinking of what might have been if he had taken another path back at the start. Maybe nothing would have changed. Maybe he would still be in the same place.

The door opened quietly.

"Egan?" Louisa walked into the room and closed the door. "Is something wrong?"

He did not turn around. "I'm fine."

"Another bad night."

It was not a question. He heard her cross the room to the liquor cabinet. Glass clinked on glass. He knew she was pouring herself a drink. She preferred the orange-scented liqueur.

She came to join him at the window. They sipped their drinks in silence for a while. It was not the first time they had gone through the ritual together. It had been years since they had been lovers, but he was certain that as long as both of them were alive they would be partners. Their strengths and weaknesses complemented each other.

"I made Madeline Chase an offer for the hotel today," Louisa said.

"I assume she refused."

"Yes. I also advised her to leave Cooper Island."

"Did you tell her why it would be in her best interests?"

"There was no need to spell it out. She understood exactly why I was warning her to go away. She suspects who was behind the explosion."

"And still she refused to leave." Egan drank some scotch. "The question is why, after all this time, is she suddenly spending time here?"

"You know why. Her grandmother is dead and now Tom Lomax has been killed. She no longer believes that Edith Chase's death was an accident, assuming she ever did believe it, and I'm sure she thinks Lomax's death is somehow connected. Madeline Chase is investigating every option, Egan, and that is going to be dangerous."

Egan swirled the liquor in his glass. "I talked to Dunbar earlier this evening. Still no sign of the woman Madeline Chase and Rayner claim was at the scene of the explosion."

"We both know there are plenty of empty summer cottages where she could have holed up for the night."

"There's another possibility. Someone might have had a boat waiting in case things went wrong."

Neither of them spoke. There was no need to spell out who might have provided a getaway vessel. Xavier's name seared the atmosphere of the darkened room as surely as if it had been written in neon blood. Xavier had been piloting boats of all kinds since he was old enough to take the wheel.

"There's nothing we can do until he goes too far," Louisa said.

"It's very likely that he went too far today."

"There's no proof," Louisa said.

"Don't you understand? If Xavier gets arrested for murder, Travis's candidacy will be destroyed. Every politician carries some baggage, but there are limits. Having a mentally ill brother who turns out to be a murderer would be more than enough to sink Travis's campaign."

"Xavier hasn't killed anyone."

"Yet." Egan swallowed some more scotch. "At least not that we know of. He's smart, Lou. If he did kill someone, he would be very careful not to leave any evidence."

Louisa stilled. "You're thinking of Tom Lomax and Edith Chase, aren't you? But that makes no sense. Xavier had no reason to do harm to either of them."

"I said he was smart, but he's also crazy. He doesn't need a logical reason to do anything."

In most circumstances, Louisa could be relied on to think pragmatically and strategically. But when it came to her younger son, she had a blind spot. He couldn't blame her, Egan thought. There had been a time when he'd had the same blind spot. Xavier had been the golden boy—the strong, brilliant son who possessed the charisma, the intelligence, and the ruthless edge it took to acquire real power.

But Xavier had proven to be fatally flawed. That meant the future of the family empire was now in the hands of the weaker son.

"Xavier is obsessing on Rayner because of the incident at the café," Louisa said. "It . . . disturbs him to see Rayner here in town. If we can convince Rayner to leave and take Madeline with him, I think Xavier will refocus."

Egan considered that for a time. "I could try talking to Rayner. He's a businessman. Maybe I can get him to see that leaving town would be in his financial interest as well as in the best interests of his client."

"Don't waste your time. Rayner won't leave without Madeline Chase, and you can't get rid of her by offering her cash," Louisa said. "I tried to buy her out, remember? She threw my offer back in my face."

"We can't go on like this indefinitely. Something must be done and it must be done soon, before the damage is irreparable."

"I know," Louisa said.

She sounded unutterably weary, but she was also resigned.

They stood in front of the window for a while longer, finishing their drinks. There was no need for further conversation. When it came to the difficult decisions involving the future of the family, they were always in agreement.

CHAPTER THIRTY-TWO

"For the record," Madeline said. "You didn't screw up."

He had been drifting, happily lethargic and more relaxed than he had been in what seemed like forever, but her words startled him into a crack of laughter.

He opened his eyes partway and watched her stretch. The action made him think of a cat. Everything about her was sleek and feline.

Her hair was tangled and tumbled on the pillow. At some point in the proceedings he had managed to get rid of the prim cotton nightgown. She had pulled the sheet up to cover her breasts, but he could see her bare shoulders. They were elegant and gracefully curved. He could not recall ever being so fascinated by that part of a woman's anatomy. But then, everything about Madeline fascinated him.

"Good to know I didn't screw up," he said. "Because toward the end there I lost track of events. In fact, it's all a blur. A very nice blur, but there's no getting around the fact that it's a blur. We should probably do it again, and soon, so that I can make sure I get a clear understanding of exactly what happened."

She had been smiling, a lazy, sultry, rather smug and deeply feminine smile, but without warning she turned serious. She rolled toward him onto her side, levered herself up on one elbow, and watched him with a pensive expression.

"It was a very nice blur for me, too," she said. "And that's the first time that's happened."

He tried to decipher the meaning of the comment for a few seconds and finally abandoned the effort.

"Is that good news or bad news?" he asked.

She smiled again and his world shifted on its axis.

"It's good news, at least for me," she said.

"Yeah?"

"I've always had a few issues in this department."

He tensed. "Are we back to the issues thing?"

"I freak out if I'm not on top. I usually go straight into a panic attack."

He tried to grasp the enormity of her issue. And failed.

Instead he shrugged. "Given what happened to you all those years ago, it's understandable that you'd have a problem with being pinned down. Seems logical to me. Wouldn't call it an issue."

Her brows snapped together. "Of course it's an issue. I've had full-blown panic attacks at some very awkward moments in my life. My *issue* has ruined more than one relationship."

"Yeah?"

"I've learned the hard way that a lot of men start out thinking that the position is sexy, but sooner or later one of two things happens. Either it turns out they're looking for a dominatrix, in which case I lose interest, or they decide I'm way too controlling, in which case they lose interest."

He wanted to tell her that her so-called issues were nothing compared to his own, but that would require an explanation, and any explanation would mean asking her to carry another heavy secret. He had no right to do that to her.

"You don't have an issue, sweetheart," he said instead. "What you've got is a preference."

Her brows rose. "A preference?"

He smiled, pleased with his uncharacteristically smooth diplomacy.

"Everyone is entitled to preferences when it comes to sex," he said. "Or anything else, for that matter."

"That is . . . very understanding of you. But what about your preferences?"

He reached out and pulled her to him so that she sprawled across his chest.

"At the moment, my preference is to do whatever it takes to make things a blur for you," he said.

Her smile was a little misty. "That is very generous of you."

"That's me," he said. "Generous to a fault."

She laughed. The sound was light and feminine and real. It warmed all the empty places inside him. For a time he could make believe that he didn't have a few issues of his own.

CHAPTER THIRTY-THREE

Daphne was pretty sure that Gillian Burns had once been slim and sexy, and her surgically enhanced breasts had probably looked great in a tight-fitting, low-cut top. But she was closing in on seventy now. Her figure had been transformed into a gaunt, unnaturally proportioned caricature of a Hollywood starlet. The too-short, too-snug dress, the high heels, and her strawlike blond hair added to the overall sense of wrongness.

The smoking certainly hadn't helped, Daphne thought. Gillian's face had a hollow cast and an unhealthy color that no amount of cosmetic surgery could conceal.

"Sure, I remember Carl Seavers," Gillian said. She snorted. "He was the office star. A young hotshot. The other brokers hated his guts because he always picked the winners. Made everyone else look bad, y'know? But he died a long time ago. Murdered along with a woman who worked in the office. Sharon something. Why are you two interested in him?"

Daphne looked at Abe and waited for him to take the lead. They had agreed on their cover story before arriving at the restaurant to interview Gillian. She had been cautious during the introductions, but once they had been seated at a table, curiosity and a martini had overcome her initial wariness.

Daphne thought there might be another factor at work, as well. Gillian bore all the earmarks of a woman who had lived hard and fast in her younger days and had no doubt had a lot of male friends. She was the kind of woman who had probably once viewed other women as rivals.

But now the men were gone, and because Gillian had not bothered to form close friendships with any of her female acquaintances along the way, she found herself alone. A conversation with strangers probably went a long way toward filling an otherwise empty afternoon.

"A family member has asked us to look into the circumstances of Carl Seavers's death," Abe said. He adjusted his glasses and cleared his throat. "Some patent issues have come up. That, in turn, impacts the inheritance."

"Huh." Gillian shrugged. "Didn't know Carl had any family. He never mentioned his relatives."

"You know how it is when there's money involved," Daphne said. "Turns out there is always family, however distant."

"You got that right." Gillian munched the olive that had graced the martini. "If you've got money, there will be plenty of people around at your bedside when it's your time, and each and every one of them will be only too happy to pull the plug. Die broke and you don't even get a phone call at the end."

Daphne exchanged glances with Abe. Neither of them spoke.

Gillian grunted. "Well, I can't tell you much. I was the receptionist at the brokerage firm where Carl and Sharon worked until they were killed. I lost my job when the company was bought up by one of the big national chains. That was my last halfway decent job. Do you know how hard it is to get a good-paying job after you turn forty-five or fifty?"

"The murder of the brokerage firm's star stock picker must have come as a shock to you and your colleagues," Abe said.

"Oh, yeah." Gillian gulped some more of her martini. "The rest of the brokers pretended to be horrified by the news, but if you ask me, none of them cared about him. In fact, I think they were all happy that he was gone. He was their competition, you see."

"What about Sharon Richards?" Daphne said.

Gillian made a face. "She was one of the brokers. Good-looking, young, and sexy as hell. She knew how to work it, too. She'd sleep with anyone who could do her a favor. She and Carl were an item. Guess she figured that if she gave him what he wanted in bed he'd share some of his stock picks with her. But if that was the plan, it sure as hell didn't work out well."

"No," Abe said. He made a note on his computer. "You and your colleagues must have had some theory about the murders."

"Most people figured it was a drug thing," Gillian said. "Pretty sure the police thought so, too. It was no secret that a lot of brokers used—cocaine mostly in those days."

"Do you think that Carl Seavers was using drugs?" Abe asked.

"That's the weird part." Gillian pursed her hard mouth and shook her head. "I would have sworn that he was the one guy in the office who was clean. Didn't even drink much. He was obsessed with his computer, though. When he wasn't working on it, he carried it around like it was made of solid gold."

Daphne knew without looking at him that Abe had gone on high alert. But when he spoke his voice was calm and professional—just a busy investigator trying to cover a lot of ground.

"Was Seavers a gamer?" he asked. "Did he get obsessed with computer games?"

"No, at least I don't think so," Gillian said. "I teased him sometimes. Asked him if he was using his computer to watch Internet porn because he was always so intense when he was on the damned thing. He said no. Told me that what he was doing was a lot more fun because it was going to make him rich."

Daphne folded her arms on the table. "Any idea what he was doing on the computer?"

Gillian shrugged and waved one heavily veined hand in a vague gesture. "Computer stuff. Symbols. Weird words. You know what I mean. There's a name for it."

"Do you think," Abe said carefully, "that Carl Seavers might have been writing code?"

"Yeah, that's it, code. See, I don't think he was a gamer, but I figured he might be trying to invent one or maybe a program or something. I hear there's plenty of money in that business."

"You've been very helpful, Gillian." Abe turned a page in his notebook and contemplated a name as though it were unfamiliar to him. "Just a couple more questions. There was another man working in the office at the time that Carl Seavers and Sharon Richards were murdered. Egan Webster."

"That prick?" Gillian rolled her eyes. "Oh, yeah, I remember him. The son of a bitch was married with a couple of kids, but he'd sleep with anything that wore high heels and a skirt. He came on to me a few times, but I always told him to get lost."

There was bitter pride in her voice.

"Did you refuse him because he was married and had a couple of kids?" Daphne asked.

Gillian snorted again. "I suppose I could lie and tell you that was the reason. But the truth is, there was something about the guy— something real cold and a little scary. Never could put my finger on it. He was good-looking, I'll give him that. And he had a vibe that brought in the business. You should have seen his client list. It was filled with old people who turned over their life savings to him to invest. Amazing. Heard he moved to Washington State and set up his own hedge fund. Made a damned fortune. Which, between you and me, is very hard to believe."

"Why do you find it hard to believe that Webster was so successful?" Abe asked.

"Never saw all that moneymaking brilliance on display when I knew him," Gillian said. "I'd say he was just average when it came to picking stocks. As often as not, he sold whatever Carl was pitching. Hell, everyone in the office tried to sell whatever Carl was pitching. But I guess Webster must have had some hidden talent. Of all the guys in the office, he was the only one who went on to the big time."

"Thank you very much, Gillian," Abe said. He took out his wallet and removed some large bills. "This should cover your tab at the bar today."

Gillian looked at the money on the table. Her tattooed brows rose. "Hell, that'll cover my tab for the whole damn month. Thanks."

Abe gathered up his notes and his computer and got to his feet. Daphne followed him out of the booth.

Gillian looked out the window at the view of the La Jolla street scene.

"Got to tell you, this is damn strange," she said.

"What is?" Daphne asked.

"Haven't thought much about Webster and Seavers for a couple of decades. Then, out of the blue, I get people coming around wanting to talk about the past."

Daphne held her breath. She did not dare to look at Abe.

"Someone else inquired about the Seavers murder?" he asked.

"Yeah. A young woman came around a few months ago. Pretty. Real sweet. Bought me drinks, just like you. Said she was a journalist doing background research on Egan Webster on account of his son was getting set to run for office in Washington State. Forget the name of the son."

"Travis Webster?" Abe asked in the same disinterested manner.

Gillian's head jerked in a quick, pleased nod. "That's it. You know how reporters like to dig up dirt on politicians. Not that the pols don't deserve it, if you ask me. Anyhow, this gal wanted to know all about Egan."

Abe set his computer back down on the table, opened it, and brought up the photo of Ramona Owens that Tom Lomax had taken. Without a word he turned the screen so that Gillian could see it. She squinted.

"Yeah, that's her," Gillian said. "Can't remember her name."

Daphne cleared her throat. "What did you tell her?"

"Pretty much the same thing I told you." Gillian downed the last of her cocktail. "Like I said, sort of strange that I'd get so many people coming around asking about Webster after all these years. But I guess that's how it goes when someone runs for office."

CHAPTER THIRTY-FOUR

"Okay," Abe said. "I think we may just possibly have the first, faint glimmering of a full-on conspiracy theory."

"What, exactly, are you thinking?" Daphne asked.

They were sitting on the bench that she had come to think of as their bench. The parade of dogs, joggers, and bicyclists looked the same as it had earlier—same high-end athletic gear, same high-end and not-so-high-end dogs. The only difference this time was that she was eating popcorn and Abe was drinking a caffeine-charged soda.

"I'm thinking that maybe the young and very talented Mr. Seavers developed a sharp stock-picking program," Abe said. "And I'm thinking that maybe, just maybe, Egan Webster murdered him and stole the computer that contained the program."

Daphne exhaled all the way to her toes. She hovered there at the bottom of the breath for a beat and then inhaled.

"That's quite a theory you're working on," she said.

"I know, but it ties things together."

"Well, it would explain why Webster's financial talents blossomed in the years following his departure from his old brokerage firm," she admitted.

"Yes."

Daphne munched some popcorn while she thought about that. "The thing is, we're talking about not just one, but two murders. There was a woman killed at the scene, too."

"Maybe just collateral damage as far as Webster was concerned."

"If you're right, that's a pretty serious accusation. And one we probably could never prove."

"Keep in mind that this whole thing started with a secret so dangerous that Edith Chase was afraid it could get you and your mom and Madeline killed. A secret that made her afraid to go to the Cooper Island police. It was so dangerous that she sent you and your mother away from Cooper Island, and then she quietly shut down the resort and took Madeline out of state."

Daphne stopped munching popcorn. She watched the bright sun spark on the water. "Webster was a very powerful man. At the time, he more or less owned Cooper Island. He probably owned the police chief."

"Webster had a hedge fund empire to protect and maybe a couple of murders to conceal."

"And now he's got a son who is about to go into the big leagues of politics," Daphne said. "As the father of a U.S. senator, Egan Webster will have even more access to power than he had as the head of a successful hedge fund. Even more to protect."

"If any of this is even close to the truth, then we have to assume that whatever was in that briefcase would be enough to implicate Webster in the murders of Carl Seavers and Sharon Richards."

"Madeline's grandmother called it insurance," Daphne whispered.

"What?"

"The contents of the briefcase," Daphne said. "Edith Chase referred to it as insurance."

They meditated on that in silence for a time.

"Are you thinking what I'm thinking?" Daphne asked eventually.

"Depends. Are you thinking about the very attractive journalist who interviewed Gillian a few months ago?"

"Uh-huh. Ramona Owens. Where does she fit into this thing?"

"I have no idea," Abe said.

He took out his phone. Jack Rayner must have answered on the first ping because Abe started talking almost immediately. Daphne watched the parade on the jogging path while she listened to the one-sided conversation.

Abe rattled off the facts and followed up with his own speculations. The call ended abruptly.

"Well?" Daphne said.

"He likes my theory," Abe said. "But he pointed out that it leaves us with a couple of real big questions: Who has the briefcase now and what do they plan to do with the contents."

"So what happens next?"

"We go back to Cooper Island and await developments."

"Is Jack sure there will be developments?"

"Oh, yeah."

"Is he always right about that kind of thing?"

"Always. Remember, he used to consult for the FBI."

"What kind of consulting?"

"Profiling. He was very, very good at it. People said he had a knack for predicting what the bad guys would do next."

She sank against the back of the bench and stretched her legs out in front of her. "You like doing this kind of work, don't you?"

He shrugged. "Probably appeals to the old gamer in me. In some ways it's the ultimate game."

She shook her head, very certain now. "More like the ultimate art. Get it right and you pull a little truth out of chaos. You're an artist, Abe. That's what you are. And what's more, you're a very good artist."

CHAPTER THIRTY-FIVE

"I printed out your media schedule." Xavier pulled a sheaf of papers out of his briefcase and set it on the desk. The pages were neatly stapled in the upper left-hand corner. "It's on your smart phone as well, but I know you prefer hard copy when it comes to this kind of stuff."

"Thanks." Travis leaned forward in his chair and picked up the schedule. He leafed through the list of interviews. "Looks like you pulled in a lot of coverage. Nice mix."

"There's a bunch of small, local, and regional stuff in the morning—radio and TV. I even threw in the Cooper Island High School newspaper. Sorry about that. But you know the rule."

"Never neglect the hometown media."

Xavier went to stand at the window. "The locals can make or break you, especially at the beginning. The kids will probably be thrilled. Even if they're not, their parents will be, and it's the parents who vote."

"Right." Travis set the schedule on the desk. "Anything else I need to know?"

"That's it, at least for now. I gave Patricia her schedule a few minutes ago. I think you're both up to speed, but I'll be following around right behind you like a faithful puppy dog in case there's a glitch."

"What about Mom and Dad?"

"I see them next. I've got their talking points. The trick will be to make sure Dad doesn't go off-message. He's used to being the star of the show, you know. It's not going to be easy for him to step back and let you go into the spotlight."

"I know. Thanks, you've done a hell of a job, Xavier. I appreciate it."

Xavier turned around to face him. His blue eyes were alight with enthusiasm and anticipation. "Hey, we're just getting started. This is just one step on the way to the White House. We're going to change the world, remember?"

"I remember," Travis said.

After all these years he was still in awe of Xavier's ability to counterfeit human emotions. Xavier could project whatever he wanted you to see. At the moment he was doing an excellent job of portraying the loyal younger brother who wanted nothing more than to help his big brother fulfill a grand destiny. He was so good in the role that there were times when Travis found himself wanting to buy the act.

But he had learned long ago that with Xavier, it was all an act. Sometimes he wondered if he was the only one who could see the cold-blooded snake just beneath the surface.

"Well, that's it for now." Xavier turned to go toward the door. "Let me know if you have any questions."

"One more thing before you go," Travis said. "Any word on what caused the explosion out at the old hotel yesterday?"

Xavier paused, one hand on the doorknob. "Dad talked to Chief Dunbar and the fire chief. The blast and the fire have been labeled suspicious, but that's mostly because Madeline Chase and Rayner insist that there was someone else at the scene—a woman who told them that she was Tom Lomax's granddaughter."

"Yeah, I heard that much. Mom doesn't believe Lomax had a granddaughter, but that doesn't mean someone isn't pretending to be related to him. The question is, why? Lomax didn't have anything worth stealing. Everyone around here knows that. And why try to kill Madeline Chase and Jack Rayner?"

"Beats me." Xavier got the door open. "You'll have to ask them."

Travis leaned back in his chair and steepled his fingers. "Speaking of Rayner, everyone on the island is aware of the confrontation that took place between the two of you at the Crab Shack. What, exactly, happened?"

"There was no confrontation." Xavier's jaw tightened almost imperceptibly. "I stopped to say hello to Madeline. Rayner got up suddenly and crashed into me. The clumsy bastard knocked me on my butt. It was a little embarrassing but no harm done."

That was bullshit. Anything that knocked Xavier on his butt in front of an audience constituted a serious affront—one that warranted revenge.

"Be careful, Xavier. You said Rayner was in the security business."

"Trust me, I've got everything under control. I had Mom invite him and Madeline Chase to the reception for the old man. I figure Rayner and I can take a little walk along the cliffs and have a chat. Get a few things straightened out."

And maybe Rayner would suffer a fatal fall from the top of the cliffs, Travis thought. He didn't see any way that fire could be involved in such an accident, but that didn't mean that Xavier wouldn't improvise something.

Xavier went out the door. Travis sat quietly for a while.

Xavier was a dangerous sociopath, but he was one very smart sociopath. There was no way to know what he had planned in the way of revenge, but he was in the red zone now. Something had to be done.

CHAPTER THIRTY-SIX

She should have run, Ramona thought. She gripped the steering wheel very tightly and drove fast through the rainy night. The instant she found out that Madeline Chase and Jack Rayner had survived the explosion, she should have run.

Instead, she'd told herself she had time. It had been easy enough to get off the island in the boat. With luck it would be weeks or even months before the right storm or tide conditions exposed the rental car in the water at the foot of the cliffs.

She would run tonight, just as soon as she got the last payment. She would drive back to Seattle and destroy every scrap of evidence that connected her to the Ramona Owens identity. She would pick up her carefully concealed go-bag and head for the airport. Everything she needed for a new identity was inside. There was something else in the go-bag as well—copies of every single bit of damning evidence that she had found inside the briefcase. It always paid to take out insurance when you did business with dangerous people.

The rain was getting heavier. She began to worry that she had missed the sign. Relief swept through her when it finally appeared out of the darkness, glowing neon-bright. The roadside restaurant advertised twenty-four-hour food and drink to the weary traveler.

It's almost over, she thought. Finally, the project was about to conclude. She was about to collect the biggest payday of her career. She smiled at the thought. The money was unbelievable. So much money— enough to finance a new life in a place far, far away. Enough to live the way she had always dreamed of living.

She had been working penny-ante scams her whole life, but the Cooper Island project was the big score she had dreamed about. After tonight everything would be different.

The restaurant was located just off the highway. The lights were on inside, although it was one o'clock in the morning and the parking lot was mostly empty. Ramona decided that the two cars in front probably belonged to the late-night staff. When she looked through the windows she could not see anyone seated at the tables or the counter.

She drove slowly around to the rear of the restaurant, following instructions. The weak yellow glare of a lone streetlamp illuminated a small portion of the parking area, but it waged a losing battle against the darkness.

There were two vehicles parked side by side in the shadows. A man and a woman were in the front seat of one of the cars. The window on the passenger side was down.

Another man sat behind the wheel of the second vehicle. His window was also down. There was a negotiation going on. Someone was selling and someone was buying. Drugs or sex, Ramona thought. She'd been there at various times in her life. But never again.

When her headlights speared the scene, the meeting broke up abruptly. Both cars roared out of the parking lot and disappeared in the rain.

She brought her vehicle to a stop but left the engine running.

Tonight it would be finished. The only part she regretted was conning the old man. She had developed an unexpected fondness for him. Maybe in some way he really had become the grandfather she'd never known. He had been so thrilled to discover that he had a long-lost granddaughter. She hadn't realized that he was going to die. For a time she had told herself that maybe his death had been caused by an intruder, just as the police said.

But when she had been instructed to lure Chase and Rayner into the maintenance building and lock them inside, she had finally acknowledged the reality of her situation. She was working for a cold-blooded killer.

She opened the console and took out the gun she had stashed inside. Just in case.

Another set of headlights lanced the shadows of the parking lot. She watched the dark car in her rearview mirror. It parked directly behind her. The driver got out, a briefcase in one hand. Ramona relaxed a little. A briefcase full of money, as promised.

She lowered her window but kept her hand on the gun, holding it just out of sight alongside her thigh.

"It's about time you got here," she said.

She let go of the gun so that she could get a good grip on the heavy briefcase. She turned to put it on the passenger seat.

She caught a glimpse of the gun out of the corner of her eye, but by then it was far too late to pick up her own weapon.

Should have run, she thought.

And then it was over.

The shot echoed loudly in the darkness, but the night shift working in the roadside café were not fools. They did not go outside to investigate the events in the rear parking lot. They locked the doors and called the police.

By the time the cops arrived, the killer was several miles away.

CHAPTER THIRTY-SEVEN

"Somehow, everything looked bigger when we lived here as kids," Daphne said. "The hotel, the town, the cottage where Mom and I lived. Even this beach. Now it all seems so much smaller. How does that happen?"

"I suppose it's a change of perspective," Madeline said. "When we were growing up, Cooper Island was our whole world."

"And then we went out into a much bigger world, so the island and everything on it now seem smaller in comparison."

Madeline studied the opposite end of the rocky beach and thought about how far away it had seemed when she and Daphne had come here in the old days. They had sought the privacy of the beach to share the secrets and mysteries of the girl-into-woman metamorphosis they were undergoing.

Today when they had felt the need to get some fresh air, they had both instinctively turned toward the cliff path. There had been no need for words. The beach had called them when they were young, and it called them now.

The day had dawned crisp and sunny. If you were in the sun, as she and Daphne were, it was surprisingly warm. But in the shade there was a chill.

"I think that's how it works," she said. "We have a different perspective, a different frame of reference now."

Daphne glanced at her, sunlight glinting on her dark glasses. "So if the past looks smaller in hindsight, why does it bear a striking resemblance to a very large asteroid on a collision course with us?"

"You know the old safety warning—*objects in the rearview mirror are closer than they appear.*"

"You and I should have done something about our particular asteroid a long time ago. We should have opened up that wall in room two-oh-nine and taken a good look at whatever was in that briefcase. At least we'd have known what we're dealing with."

"I thought about doing that once in a while," Madeline said. "But for some reason I never felt like I had the right. The secret always seemed to belong to the adults—my grandmother and Tom. I was just a kid."

"But now we are the adults."

"Yes."

They walked in silence for a while. It seemed they had almost never shared long silences as girls. There had always been so much to talk about—boys, school, boys, clothes, boys, the doings of movie stars, boys. Sister travelers on the great journey to adulthood, they could not wait to reach their destination.

And then had come the night of blood and violence, the night that had changed everything. The journey to adulthood had been just as relentless in the wake of that shattering night, but Madeline knew that neither of them had traveled it in the protective cloak of innocence. The man named Porter had given them a glimpse of the darkness that was always just below the surface of the world. Once viewed, it could never be forgotten.

"You and Jack seem to have crossed a bridge while Abe and I were in La Jolla," Daphne said.

"I suppose it is sort of obvious."

"The fact that you two are now sharing the same bedroom was definitely a clue. But I knew from the start that there was something serious going on between you and Jack. The electricity in the atmosphere is off the charts."

"We've been circling each other for about three months now. Grandma hired him just before she died. I inherited him."

Daphne smiled. "That's certainly an interesting way to start a relationship."

"Saves hanging out in bars or filling in questionnaires at the online matchmaking sites."

"True. Think there's a future with Jack?"

"No. He made it very clear that he's not interested in a future. As Grandma would have said, he's not the marrying kind."

"Has Jack actually said that?"

"He went to great pains to make sure I got the point before we wound up in the same bed."

"Ouch. Well, at least he was honest about it. Unlike some people I could mention—my lying, cheating husband, for example."

"Oh, yeah," Madeline said. "Jack was very up-front about his lack of interest in marriage."

"He used those words? *Lack of interest?*"

"Well, no, not exactly. He just said something about not being able to offer a future."

"Good heavens." Daphne halted and turned quickly. "Is he ill?"

"No, nothing so dramatic."

Daphne relaxed and started walking again. "I can't believe that he's got a secret wife and family tucked away somewhere. I'm sure Abe would have mentioned it."

"I'm pretty sure there's no secret family."

"So what's wrong with our picture of Jack Rayner?"

"I don't know," Madeline admitted. "I suppose I could hire a private investigator to do a background check on him. It would be sort of strange, though."

Daphne chuckled. "Who do you hire to investigate the man you hired to conduct investigations?"

"Exactly. But in this case I don't think there's any reason to push it. Odds are good that whatever Jack and I have going won't last long."

"I thought you executive types liked to think positive."

"I'm trying to be realistic," Madeline said. "That way there's less of a shock when things go south."

"Why are you so sure your relationship with Jack is doomed?"

"For the same reasons all my previous relationships have been doomed."

"Your intimacy issues."

"Uh-huh."

"Jack knows about your issues?"

"Yep. We had a lengthy conversation about his issues and mine before we—you know."

"Before you fell into bed together," Daphne concluded.

"Mm."

"Sounds romantic."

"I sense sarcasm."

"Do you always have conversations like that before you go to bed with someone?" Daphne asked with what sounded like clinical curiosity.

"I try to be honest about my issues."

"Does it work?"

"No. At the start, men always think I'm going to be the perfect date——a bit of the woman-in-leather thing spiced with commitment-free sex."

"A real wet dream for a lot of guys."

"At first."

"What goes wrong?"

"You mean, aside from the fact that I don't actually wear leather in bed?"

"Aside from that," Daphne said.

"What usually goes wrong is that I make a few demands. I take my time deciding if I want to have sex with a man. I want a companion, not just someone to fall into bed with."

"You want a relationship. Perfectly natural."

"I admit that I like to date men who are willing to engage in extended conversations about a variety of subjects," Madeline said.

"You were always interested in anything and everything."

"While I'm having those conversations with a man, I run a background check on him. If all goes well, I'm willing to get into bed. But I do tend to drag my feet during the getting-to-know-you phase because the sex phase is always the beginning of the end."

"Maybe you should rethink the whole leather-in-bed thing. Spark up your wardrobe. Get a nice little whip. Might make your relationships last longer."

Madeline felt the giggles rise up out of nowhere. And suddenly she was laughing.

"You know, you haven't changed, Daphne. Always there with the helpful styling tips. You should write a column."

"One thing I've learned over the years is that nobody really wants my good advice. They just pretend to listen to it."

"Probably because most people just want to whine about their problems. They don't want to actually take the hard actions that will fix those problems."

"You haven't changed much, either," Daphne said. "You're still the pragmatist you were when you were twelve. You look at something that you're pretty sure won't work and you cut your losses."

"Go ahead, say it, I'm a boring business executive."

"No, you're a very fine hotel executive who knows how to create a warm and welcoming environment for travelers."

"Thank you. But I suspect that I'm also a very boring hotel executive."

"You have recently survived an attempt on your life, you faced down Louisa Webster, you are trying to solve an eighteen-year-old mystery, and you are sleeping with a man who carries a gun. I think we can say with absolute certainty that, whatever else you may be, you are not boring."

Madeline thought about that for a beat. "You're right. At the moment my life is not the least bit boring."

"Abe said that Jack was a lot like a freight train once he made a decision. Anyone standing in the path had two options—get out of the way or get on board."

"So?"

"So I'm thinking that if Jack ever did make a commitment, you could take it to the bank," Daphne said.

"I think you're right."

"Present circumstances aside, how do you feel about taking over your grandmother's hotel chain?" Daphne asked.

Madeline thought about that for a few steps. "I've never even asked myself that question. I always knew where I was going. Never considered doing anything else. Grandma made me start out in housekeeping and work in every department and at every skill level in the business until I made it into upper management. I loved all of it. So yes, I'm fine with the job. I've been in training for it my whole life."

"You were born into the family business."

"Yes. But I still miss Grandma terribly. We argued over a lot of things. She could be so damn stubborn. But she loved me and I loved her."

"You were family," Daphne said. "I understand. My mom and I are close, too. She's been worried about me since Brandon died."

"Did you ever tell her about the other woman?"

"No. I was afraid it would just make things worse. She liked Brandon so much and was so happy that I had found my soul mate, as she put it. She was looking forward to grandchildren."

"You should tell her the truth."

"Think so?"

"Yes. Who are you trying to protect by keeping the secret? You or your mom?"

"Good question. I hadn't thought of it that way." Daphne paused. "Me, probably. I didn't want to admit to anyone, including Mom, that I had been such a trusting fool."

"You were not a fool. You are an honorable person who made a commitment in good faith. The bastard who asked you for that commitment lacked honor and integrity. He was not worthy of you, but that does not make you weak or foolish. I've got a hunch that sooner or later, all decent, honorable people make the mistake of trusting the wrong person. All we can do is move on."

"Who are you lecturing? Me? Or yourself?"

"Both of us, I guess," Madeline said.

"Sounds like good advice."

For a time they walked in silence.

"Say you could go back in time," Madeline said after a while. "Right back to the moment when your husband got his diagnosis. Say you found out that same week that he'd been having an affair. Do you really think you would have walked out and left him on his own?"

"In a heartbeat," Daphne said, grimly cheerful and defiant.

"No," Madeline said. "I don't think so. You would have been

crushed and you would have been angry, but you wouldn't have left him alone."

"What makes you so sure?"

"I know you."

"You knew me when I was a girl," Daphne said.

"You were a very kind, very brave girl. Grandma always said that people don't change, at least not way down deep inside where it counts. You wouldn't leave anyone to die alone, not even a husband who had cheated on you."

"But at least I would have been able to tell him to his face that I knew that he was a lying, cheating bastard."

"Oh, yeah," Madeline said. "At least you would have been able to tell him that."

She looked down at a tide pool where tiny creatures were going about the business of survival. The little crabs and the small fish darting here and there in the shallow water lived out their lives in a world that was only a couple of yards across. Within the confines of that world they did what all living things did. They searched for food, reproduced, and tried to hide from the predators in the shadows.

Perspective was everything. And yet nothing. The predators were out there, regardless of the size of your world, Madeline thought. But so was friendship. You just had to reach out and make it happen.

Maybe, just maybe, it was the same with love.

CHAPTER THIRTY-EIGHT

Abe snapped the stem off the last spear of asparagus and gestured proudly at the heap on the cutting board. "What do you say, boss? Do I get an A?"

Jack looked up from the salmon fillets he was rubbing with a mix of spices. He glanced at the large pile of asparagus.

"Looks good," Jack said. "Now blot 'em dry with some paper towels, put them in a bowl, and toss them with a little olive oil and salt and lemon juice."

"Whoa, whoa, whoa." Abe held up both hands, palms out. "Easy for you to say. How much oil? How much salt?"

"Just eyeball it."

"No way. I'm not screwing this up and taking the blame for any ensuing disaster."

"Okay, step aside, grasshopper," Jack said. "I'll handle the olive oil."

He washed his hands, dried them, and moved to the cutting board. He scooped up the asparagus and dumped it into a bowl. He drizzled the spears with olive oil, added some flaked salt, and squeezed half a lemon over the top.

"Okay, they're all yours," he announced. "Line the baking sheet with parchment paper and spread the spears out on the sheet."

"Then what?"

"Then I will get started on the hollandaise sauce."

"Wow. We're trying to impress the ladies tonight, aren't we?"

"Got a problem with that?"

"No, sir," Abe said. "Got one more question for you, though."

Jack took the eggs and some butter out of the refrigerator. "What?"

"Does this cooking thing make it easy to meet women?"

"Not that I've noticed."

"Come on, women must find it romantic."

"Sometimes," Jack said. He put the butter into a pan and set it on the stove to melt. "At the start. But the effect doesn't last long. Sooner or later other stuff gets in the way, and then my ability to cook dinner loses its attraction. Turns out women are smart. They figure out right away that they can order in."

"The other stuff that gets in the way being your issues."

"Yeah."

"I'm no expert on relationships, but for what it's worth, I don't think Ms. Chase has a problem with you or your issues."

"She will." Jack sliced open another lemon and squeezed the juice into a measuring cup. "Eventually. Why don't you stop standing around doing nothing and slice up that loaf of sourdough bread I picked up today."

"That's one of the things I admire about you, boss."

"What?"

"Your sunny, optimistic outlook. It's downright inspirational."

"I live to inspire my staff."

"Speaking for all two of us—Becky and me—we appreciate that."

Jack's phone pinged just as he finished separating the third egg. He wiped his hands on the towel and unclipped the device.

"Becky. About time you checked in. What have you got for me?"

"Nothing that you can take to the police and certainly nothing that would stand up in court, but it looks like Edith Chase may have had a visitor on the night of the fire," Becky said.

Jack felt the old, familiar spike of adrenaline. "Go on."

"After the alarms sounded, the situation was the usual controlled chaos that you get in a major evacuation, but the safety procedures were in place and they worked." Becky paused. "Well, except for the one fatality."

"Mrs. Chase. Go on."

"I finally managed to track down almost every member of the staff. One of the bellmen said that when the alarm went off, he was tasked with going door-to-door on the floor just below Mrs. Chase's floor. He was busy getting people out of their rooms and into the stairwell. He had a list and he was counting heads to make sure he hadn't missed a room. He was concentrating on his floor but when I asked him about the floor above, he said something interesting."

"I'm waiting for the other shoe to drop here."

"Right. By the time he arrived at his floor there were several guests already descending the emergency stairs. But just before he opened the fire door to go into the hall, he heard the stairwell door on the floor above open and close. He's sure there was someone on the landing."

"Huh."

"He didn't pay much attention because he was focused on his assigned floor. But at the time he assumed the person coming down the stairs was Mrs. Chase or whoever had been sent to make sure she got out safely. As you know, the penthouse occupies the whole top floor of that hotel. She was the only guest in that room."

"Did he see the person on the floor above?"

"No. The bellman had a job to do and he did it. He went down his assigned hall and started banging on doors. I asked him if he thought the person he had heard on the landing above his floor was male or female. He said he just didn't know. He assumed female because——"

"Because he assumed it was Mrs. Chase."

"Exactly. Like I said, he didn't stick around to make sure because he had his own responsibilities that night. After he found out that Mrs. Chase hadn't made it out of the building, he told the investigators that he had heard someone in the stairwell, but from what I can tell, nothing was done with the information. Got a hunch no one thought it was important."

"The investigators probably assumed that, what with all the people and noise in the stairwell, the bellman had not heard correctly."

"You know how sound carries in an emergency stairwell," Becky said. "It's all the hard surfaces. In most stairwells you can hear people talking several floors above or below wherever you're standing."

"Thanks, Becky. You've done some good work on this."

"That means a raise, right? And a company car?"

"How about a gold star to stick on your computer?"

"Self-sticking or do I have to lick it?"

"If you're going to get picky, you can forget the gold star."

"I'll take whatever I can get," Becky said. "Anything else I can do on this end?"

"You said you've been able to track down almost every member of the hotel staff. Who's still missing?"

"The housekeeper who was assigned to the penthouse that day. She had to leave town shortly after the fire to take care of her elderly parents."

"Find her."

Jack ended the call and glanced up to see Madeline and Daphne standing in the doorway of the big kitchen. Madeline looked amused. Daphne's brows were slightly elevated. Abe was focused on arranging the asparagus in a neat row on the baking sheet, but the corner of his mouth was twitching a little.

Jack looked at Madeline. "Am I missing something here?"

"Have you ever actually said good-bye before you ended a call?" Madeline asked as though she were genuinely curious.

"I don't like good-byes," Jack said.

"Because they're a waste of time?" Madeline asked.

"No," he said. "Because they sound so damn final. I only say good-bye when I really mean good-bye. As in, I won't be seeing that person again or at least I hope like hell I won't be seeing him or her again."

They were all gazing at him now, evidently speechless.

He put the egg yolks, lemon juice, salt, and a dash of cayenne into the blender and hit the on switch. Very slowly he drizzled in the melted butter. It wasn't the classic way to make hollandaise sauce, but it was practically foolproof. He didn't want any screwups tonight.

"Dinner will be ready in twenty minutes," he said over the roar of the blender. "Anyone else want another beer or a glass of wine?"

CHAPTER THIRTY-NINE

Madeline ate the last bite of asparagus and put down her fork with a deep sense of satisfaction.

"That was the best meal I've had in a very long time," she said. "Possibly in forever."

"Fantastic," Daphne declared. "Absolutely incredible. I want the hollandaise recipe."

Jack's face was as unreadable as ever, but Madeline was pretty sure she detected a flicker of something that might have been gratification in his usually enigmatic eyes.

Abe looked at Daphne. "Just to be clear, I did the roasted asparagus."

"Really?" Daphne looked impressed. "I'd love to have that recipe, too."

Abe beamed. "I'll email it to you."

Jack got to his feet. "Let's clear the table. We need to talk about a few things."

"What about dessert?" Abe asked, suddenly anxious.

"It can wait a bit," Jack said.

Abe was clearly downcast by that news, but he did not argue. He rose and picked up Daphne's plate.

The dishes disappeared from the table. The men disappeared into the kitchen.

Daphne looked at Madeline across the width of the table.

"I could get used to this kind of service," she whispered.

"You and me both," Madeline said.

Jack and Abe emerged from the kitchen a short time later. Jack wiped his hands on a dish towel, sat down, and took out his notebook.

Abe pulled out his phone and glanced at the screen. "Huh."

"What?" Jack asked.

"Got a hit on that alert you had me set up," Abe said. "The one about recent deaths within twenty miles of the ferry dock over on the mainland. There was a murder in the parking lot of an all-night diner eight miles from the dock. A woman was shot in the head. Looks like a drug deal gone bad."

Madeline got a chill on the back of her neck. When she looked at Jack she saw that he was sitting very, very still.

"Did they ID the victim?" he asked.

"She was carrying a driver's license issued to an Anna Stokes," Abe said. "Age thirty-two. Seattle address. Hang on, there's a picture." He whistled softly. "Say hello to Ramona Owens."

Abe put his phone down on the table so that they could all see the image on the screen.

"That's her," Madeline said. "That's the woman who claimed to be Tom's granddaughter. The one who suckered us into going inside the maintenance building just before the explosion."

"You were right, boss." Abe picked up his phone. "She was probably hired talent. Someone used her and, when she was no longer needed, got rid of her."

The chill that Madeline had sensed on the nape of her neck was now affecting the whole room. She was amazed that there were no icicles dripping from the tabletop.

The atmosphere around Jack was the coldest place of all.

"Find out everything you can about her," Jack said. His tone lacked any vestige of emotion. He got to his feet and headed for the kitchen. "I'll make some coffee. We're going to be up late tonight."

He disappeared through the kitchen doorway. A moment later Madeline heard water running in the sink.

A peculiar silence descended on the table. Daphne watched the empty doorway.

"Is he okay?" she whispered.

Abe frowned, glanced toward the doorway, and then leaned toward Madeline and lowered his voice.

"He gets like that sometimes," Abe said. "It just means he's thinking about some aspect of the case that isn't coming together the way he thinks it should."

Jack was certainly deep into his own thoughts, Madeline mused. But she was not at all certain that he was assessing facts and running scenarios—not just then, at any rate.

She crumpled her napkin on the table, got to her feet, and went into the kitchen. Jack was at the sink, filling the glass coffeepot. He spoke to her without turning around.

"The coffee will be ready in a few minutes," he said.

"Ramona, or whatever her name was, helped someone try to kill us," Madeline said. "She may have been the person who killed Tom Lomax."

Jack poured water into the reservoir of the coffeemaker and stuck the empty pot on the hot plate. He pressed the on button.

"It's possible, but I doubt it," he said. "I think we're going to find out that the fake Ramona Owens was a low-level con artist who got in over her head."

"What does that tell us?"

Jack turned around and lounged against the edge of the old tile counter. He folded his arms. "I don't know yet, but this may be the break I've been looking for. The killer made a huge mistake."

"Why do you say that? It seems to me that whoever killed Ramona went out of their way to be careful. After all, she wasn't murdered on the island. She was killed several miles inland in a scenario that made the cops think it was a drug deal gone bad. Furthermore, it sounds like she wasn't carrying any Ramona Owens ID."

"The killer would have made sure of that," Jack said. "But the problem for whoever is behind this is that you and I can identify the dead woman as the fake Ramona Owens. And now we find out that she was killed way too close to the epicenter of this thing. It was a mistake."

"Why?"

"Because it spells out in a very large, very bold font that there has to be a connection between the woman who posed as Lomax's granddaughter and someone on this island."

Madeline thought about that. "Xavier Webster?"

"That would fit. Beautiful con artist gets manipulated by charismatic sociopath who is an even more talented con. Definitely one possible scenario. But I've made mistakes in the past when I've tried to narrow down the list of scenarios before I've had enough information."

"Abe will get more information. Daphne says he's an artist with a computer."

Jack's mouth twitched at the corner. "An artist, huh? Wonder how he feels about that. His goal is to be the white-hat, hard-core code writer who cracks the cold cases with his brilliant gaming programs."

Madeline thought about the way Abe's eyes got a little warmer and a lot more intense when he looked at Daphne.

"I think Abe's okay with being called an artist," she said.

Jack turned and looked out over the top of the yellowed kitchen curtains and contemplated the night as though surprised to see that darkness had fallen hours earlier.

"I'm going to get a little fresh air," he said. "I'll be back in a few minutes."

He turned away from the window, opened the door, and went outside into the shadows of the wraparound porch. Chilled currents of night air whispered into the room.

Madeline watched through the window for a while, unsure of her next move. She was still struggling to categorize her relationship with Jack. For all that they had been through together in recent days, she was well aware that there was an invisible wall between them.

Jack walked around the corner of the porch and was lost in the shadows.

She wondered when he had become a loner. He evidently had a family that cared about him, but it was clear that Abe and the others had not been able to reach through the crystalline barrier that separated Jack from the rest of the world.

Maybe the real problem was that Jack did not want to be rescued.

She went to the arched doorway that separated the kitchen from the dining room. Abe and Daphne were sitting close together at the big table, studying whatever was on the screen of Abe's laptop.

They both looked up when she appeared in the opening. She knew they had heard the kitchen door open and close. Abe glanced behind her into the empty kitchen. His jaw tightened a little. He turned back to the computer.

Daphne's eyes filled with sympathy, but she asked no questions.

Madeline made up her mind.

"I'll be right back," she said.

She turned around, crossed the kitchen, and opened the back door.

Closing it quietly, she wrapped her arms around herself to ward off the chill and made her way to the far end of the porch.

Jack was braced against the darkness, his big hands gripping the railing. He did not turn around.

She stopped about a yard away from him.

"You knew that the woman calling herself Ramona Owens would probably wind up dead, didn't you?" she asked.

For a time she wasn't sure that he would answer. She told herself that she probably should have stayed inside and let him deal with his own demons in his own way. But they had shared too much. There was a bond of some kind between them. She could not leave him to battle on alone, not tonight. So she waited, aware that she was trying to coerce an answer out of him with the unsubtle tactic of silence.

"It seemed like the most likely scenario," Jack said. "Her role as Lomax's granddaughter had all the hallmarks of a carefully scripted, professional con. She was no amateur. She was hired to do a job. But she wasn't the one behind this thing, so yeah, once her role was finished, her services were no longer required."

"I'm going to take a flying leap here," Madeline said. "It occurs to me that predicting someone's death—knowing there was nothing you could do to prevent it—would give a person a very cold feeling."

Jack looked at her for the first time. He did not speak.

"I should have said that it would give any *decent* person that kind of feeling," Madeline added. "It might make such a person wonder if the ability to put yourself in the mind of a killer means you might be capable of the act. Maybe it even makes you wonder if you're somehow not the person you believed yourself to be."

He didn't say anything. He just looked at her.

"Is this the kind of work you did when you consulted for the FBI? Profile killers and make terrible predictions about who might be the next victim to die a violent death?"

"It gets old," Jack said. He sounded unutterably weary. "Very, very old."

"No shit."

Jack said nothing.

"I'm so very sorry that I dragged you back into a world that you tried to leave behind," she whispered.

"No." He moved abruptly, crossed the small distance between them, and wrapped his arms around her. "That's not the problem, Madeline. The problem is that I'm terrified that this time I might screw up."

"Just remember that you're not alone in this."

She hugged him very close and very tight. After a while some of the cold seeped out of him.

"Madeline," he said.

That was all he said, but he said it very quietly, as if it were all that needed saying in that moment.

They stood together in the shadows for a very long time.

CHAPTER FORTY

Daphne glanced uneasily toward the kitchen doorway. "They've been out there quite a while."

"I know." Abe did not look up from the screen of his computer. "You know, I'm starting to think that she's good for Jack. He's different when he's with her."

"Is that so?"

"I told you, the family has been worried about him for a while now."

"Because of his problems with relationships?" she asked.

"It's partly that. All he cares about these days is his business. Like I said, Mom is afraid he's given up on marriage."

Daphne looked at the kitchen doorway again. "What's your theory of why Jack never married?"

Abe hesitated. She got the feeling that he was reminding himself that he needed to be a little more cautious now.

"He's been busy building Rayner Risk Management," Abe said. "Takes energy to get a business off the ground, especially when you're starting over from scratch."

"That's what Jack had to do?"

"His first company, the one he co-founded with a friend from his FBI days, went bust after the friend was killed in a diving accident. So yes, it's been a lot of hard work getting RRM up and running."

"What about you?" she said. "Think you'll remarry someday?"

Abe went very still. He did not take his eyes off the screen. "Probably. It's what we do in our family."

"Get married?"

"Yeah."

"But next time you'll be more careful, right?"

"I'll try to be more careful. But let's face it, there are no guarantees when it comes to marriage. I messed up the first time. I'd just as soon not make the same mistake again."

She shuddered. "I know where you're coming from. I feel the same way."

"You're still grieving," Abe said, very serious now. "You need to give yourself time."

"I stopped grieving the day I found out that Brandon was having an affair with another woman throughout most of our marriage."

"Oh, shit." Abe sat back in his chair and exhaled heavily. "Sorry. Didn't realize."

She looked at him for a few seconds, and then she smiled. "Just to be clear, I've been really pissed off this past year. Not grief stricken."

He pondered that for a moment. "So the reason you haven't been eating well isn't because you're in mourning?"

"I just lost my appetite somewhere along the line. Maybe it was a form of depression or something."

"You looked like you enjoyed dinner tonight."

"I did." She paused. "Especially the asparagus."

Abe looked pleased. "You're feeling better, then?"

"Much better. Talking to Maddie about Brandon was very . . . therapeutic."

"What did she tell you?"

"She reminded me that I outlived the bastard and that, as revenge scenarios go, it doesn't get any better."

Abe whistled appreciatively. "Cold."

"Uh-huh."

"I like it. No wonder Madeline and Jack get along together. They have a lot in common. Both of them get to the bottom line in a hurry. So how's that revenge scenario working out for you?"

"Very well, thank you. It was just a matter of changing my perspective."

"Good. That's great." Abe cleared his throat. "So if you're no longer in mourning and your appetite has returned, does that mean you're ready to move on?"

Daphne smiled. "I believe it does."

CHAPTER FORTY-ONE

Jack came awake to the rumble of his cell phone. He opened his eyes, momentarily disoriented by the realization that he was not alone in the bed. He had gotten used to sleeping alone in the past two years. He was not accustomed to the feel of a warm, soft body lying next to him. But he could definitely get used to sharing a bed with this particular warm, soft body, he concluded.

The phone rumbled again. Madeline stirred.

"Your phone," she mumbled. "Not mine."

"I knew that."

Reluctantly he disentangled himself and sat up on the side of the bed. He reached for the phone and grunted when he saw the code on the screen.

"Is this some kind of joke, Abe? I'm in the same house, remember? Right down the hall from you."

"I was trying to be polite," Abe said. "I didn't want to barge in unannounced. Thought I'd call first."

Jack looked at Madeline, who was watching him from the shadows. He couldn't see her expression, but he knew she was wide-awake and listening. He turned his attention back to the phone.

"Good thinking," he said. "What the hell is so important you had to wake me up at one o'clock in the morning?"

"I just got an interesting ping. Woke me up. You know that search you had me run on the recent travel records of everyone involved in this case?"

The edgy vibe in Abe's voice would have been amusing under other circumstances, Jack thought. Abe was jacked up on adrenaline.

"You got something?"

"I think so. I did a search for Ramona Owens using the Anna Stokes ID. I got a very interesting hit."

"Talk to me, Abe. You know I'm not into the melodrama."

"She made a trip to Denver about three weeks ago while Daphne was on the cruise. She stayed one night. What do you want to bet she was the one who tossed Daphne's apartment and stole her computer?"

"Huh."

"Yeah, that's pretty much the same thing I said. Think that means I might be executive material, after all?"

"I doubt it. It's all in the nuance."

"I lack nuance?" Abe said, offended.

"Forget nuance. Have you got anything else?"

"Not yet."

"Have you told Daphne that we may know who tossed her place?"

There was a short pause on the other end of the connection.

"As a matter of fact, I did mention it to her," Abe said.

This time his voice sounded oddly strained.

"Before you called me?" Jack asked.

"I figured Daphne had a right to know first. After all, it was her apartment. Well, that's all I've got for now. See you in the morning. Get some sleep, boss."

"Wait, don't hang up—"

The line went dead.

Jack glared at the device. Madeline giggled. He glared at her. She had levered herself up to a sitting position and wrapped her arms around her knees.

"What's so funny?" he asked.

"You," she said. "Confused and disoriented because someone hung up on you before you could hang up first."

He set the phone down on the night table. "You know, keen detective that I am, I'm starting to suspect that Daphne and Abe are getting very . . . friendly."

"I've noticed that, too," Madeline said. "Forget Daphne and Abe. Did Abe just tell you that Ramona Owens was the person who searched Daphne's condo?"

"Looks like it, yeah. Now all we have to do is figure out who she was working with."

"Someone who was willing to murder her."

"Yes," Jack said. "Someone who was willing to use her and then kill her."

"Xavier?"

"He's certainly at the top of the list of possible suspects."

"There's a list? I thought Xavier was our only viable suspect."

"One thing you learn early in my business—there is always a list until you get all the answers."

CHAPTER FORTY-TWO

"Xavier is out of control," Travis said. "He's been under too much stress lately and he's going to snap. This time he could do some real damage. You know that as well as I do."

Egan was standing at the window of Louisa's study. He did not turn around, but he closed one hand into a fist.

Louisa, seated at her desk, reached for a tissue. "The doctors at the Institute were so sure that this time they had found the right balance of medications."

"Maybe they did," Travis said. "But that doesn't mean that Xavier is taking the drugs that were prescribed. We all know he very nearly murdered Madeline Chase and her consultant, Rayner."

"No, we don't know that," Louisa said. "There's no proof. No one saw Xavier. Madeline and Rayner claim there was a woman on the scene."

At that Egan did turn his head to look at her. "Louisa."

She subsided. "When he was a boy they told me it was just anger management issues."

She said it as though there were still some hope for a simple diagnosis. The word *management*, after all, implied that the impulsive rages could be controlled with counseling and meds. But there was no hope of a good outcome, Travis thought. He had to make his parents understand. They were the only ones who could deal with Xavier when he went over the edge. And the former golden boy of the Webster clan was right on the brink.

"We need to get him out of the way until after the election," Travis said.

"That's over a year from now," Louisa said. "He'll never consent to return to the Institute for an entire year. He calls it a prison."

"It's for his own good, as well as the good of the family," Travis said.

"If we could just make Xavier understand," Louisa whispered.

She was pleading now, Travis thought, just as she had always pleaded Xavier's case.

"If we don't do something, he's going to kill someone," Travis said quietly.

"No," Louisa whispered. "No, he would never go that far."

"Or maybe get himself killed," Travis added deliberately. "Rayner is in the security business, remember? For all we know he's carrying a gun."

Louisa's mouth opened. Shock widened her eyes.

"No," she said. "Oh, no. Rayner wouldn't dare—"

"Don't be so sure," Travis said. "Rayner isn't the kind of man who is easily intimidated by people like Dad."

Egan turned his head, eyes narrowing. "What the hell is that supposed to mean?"

"It means," Travis said deliberately, "that you can't buy off Rayner and you won't be able to scare him away."

"This is all Madeline Chase's fault," Louisa said. "I don't understand why she's here in the first place. She doesn't want that old hotel. No one wants it. If she leaves, Rayner will leave. Why does she insist on hanging around?"

Travis started to pace the small space. "She made it clear that she thinks Tom Lomax was murdered. She wants answers."

"That's the job of the police," Louisa said. "They're convinced the killing was the work of a transient who no doubt left the island immediately."

"Enough." Egan held up one hand. "Travis is right. We can't control Madeline Chase and Jack Rayner. But we can exert some influence over Xavier."

"He won't go back to the Institute for a whole year," Louisa warned. "Not willingly. He's not a boy any longer, Egan. We can't just pack him up and ship him off. Not this time."

"I've got one tool left in my tool kit," Egan said quietly. "I can make Xavier's greatest wish come true. I'll give him what he needs to set up his own hedge fund—access to his inheritance. I'll tell him that he can have the money but he has to establish the headquarters offshore."

Travis raised his brows. "That's not a bad idea."

Louisa dried her eyes and turned thoughtful. "It might work. At least for a while."

Travis stopped in the middle of the room and looked at Egan. "In other words, you're going to bribe him."

Egan turned back to the window. "For the good of the family."

"I just hope it works," Louisa whispered.

The despair in her eyes was too much. Travis went to the door and let himself out into the hall.

Confronting his parents had been a gamble. He had talked it over with Patricia first, just as he did all of the important decisions now. She had agreed it was the only available option. Egan and Louisa had always been able to exert some control over Xavier through a combination of bribes and threats. Xavier was amenable to both. He was, after all, a very talented survivor. In the end, he would not do anything that might jeopardize his income and future inheritance.

Travis went down the hall and turned in to the foyer, eager to escape his parents' house.

Xavier was lounging in the arched entranceway, one shoulder propped gracefully against the wall, arms folded across his chest. He smiled his sorcerer's smile.

"Have a nice chat with Mom and Dad?" he asked.

Travis stopped. "It was a chat. Not sure I would characterize it as nice."

"Did my name come up?"

"We discussed the plans for the trip to Europe that everyone seems to think is vital to add some foreign policy cred to my candidacy."

"Is that right?"

"Can we talk later, Xavier? I have to work on my announcement speech with Patricia."

"Sure. I'm available anytime for you, brother."

Travis started to open the front door, but he stopped when he saw the hot, jealous rage that burned in Xavier's eyes.

He'd seen that look before at various times in the past. Xavier's eyes burned with a hellish fire just before he lost control. Everyone in the family knew the look. It wasn't the first time they had been forced to deal with the problem of the golden boy.

Keep your enemies close.

Travis stopped and glanced at his watch. "You know what? That damned speech can wait. I'm sick of it already and I haven't even finished the final draft. What do you say we go and grab a beer at the Crab Shack?"

Xavier thought about that for a few beats. Then he shrugged and pushed himself away from the wall.

"Why not?" he said. "I've always got time for a beer with the next senator from the great state of Washington."

CHAPTER FORTY-THREE

Madeline dreamed . . .

. . . She walked through the scorched ruins of the burned-out hotel, searching each room for Daphne. The hallway on the second floor was endless. Each door she passed was marked with the same number—209.

The dreamscape was rendered in the colors of midnight. Icy moonlight slanted through empty windows. A terrible urgency drove her, but she could not move any more quickly. She had to open each door. She could not miss a single room.

It was her fault that her secret sister was trapped somewhere in the ghost hotel . . .

Somewhere in the endless gray of the dream world a clock struck the time . . .

The dreamscape shifted and blurred . . .

She came awake on a surge of adrenaline. Her eyes snapped open. She saw Jack silhouetted against the window. He was looking out into the darkness. His cell phone glowed in his hand.

She realized that the shifting sensation she had sensed a few seconds earlier had been the movement of the mattress as Jack got out of bed.

"The motion sensor app just pinged," he said.

"There's someone out there?"

"Maybe. Could have been a large animal or a falling tree branch. The sensors aren't foolproof." He turned away from the window and picked up his trousers. "I'm going to wake Abe. Whatever you do, don't make a target of yourself by turning on the lights. Understand?"

"Yes."

She pushed aside the covers and got to her feet, barely aware of the cold floor.

Jack took the holstered gun out of the bedside drawer. Fear zinged through her, icing her blood.

"Jack—"

"I'm going to take a look outside. You and Daphne will stay here with Abe. Understood?"

She wanted to argue. She thought about saying something intelligent such as *let's call the cops*, but it would take a while for help to arrive. She reminded herself that Jack knew what he was doing. *Let the man do his job,* she thought.

She stepped into her slippers, grabbed her robe, and followed Jack out into the dimly lit hall. Abe, clad in only a pair of briefs, was standing in the doorway of his bedroom. He and Jack were talking quietly. When Abe saw Madeline, he ducked back behind the door and peered around the edge, embarrassed.

"Get some clothes on," Jack said to him. "Make sure Madeline and Daphne put on their shoes in case you have to get out of the house in a hurry. This guy likes to set fires. Wait downstairs in the main hall. That will give you plenty of options for getting out of the house. Once you're in place, everyone stays silent. The idea is to make him think we're all still asleep."

"Got it," Abe said.

He disappeared back into his room.

Jack glanced at Madeline. "Remember what I said. Stay away from windows."

She clutched the lapels of her robe, fighting the urge to beg him to stay inside, behind locked doors. But locked doors offered no protection from a crazy person who liked to start fires. Her grandmother had died behind a locked door.

"Jack, be careful," she said instead.

"That's the plan," Jack said.

He did not wait for a response.

Madeline went past Abe's room, intent on knocking on Daphne's door.

"Never mind," Daphne said behind her. "I'm awake."

Madeline turned around. Daphne emerged from Abe's room, pulling a robe around herself. She was flushed. Her short hair was wildly tousled.

"Oh," Madeline said. She stopped with that because she could not think of anything else to say.

Daphne smiled. "Turns out Abe is also a night person."

"Oh," Madeline said again.

Abe emerged from the bedroom strapping on a holster. He was dressed in his cargo pants and an unbuttoned flannel shirt. He had his glasses on now, and he peered at Madeline and Daphne in turn with an air of calm authority that caught Madeline by surprise. She noticed that Daphne blinked a couple of times, too.

"You heard the boss," Abe said. "Grab your shoes, ladies, in case we have to make a run for it. We'll wait for Jack downstairs."

Madeline looked at Daphne and knew that they were both experiencing the same unnatural sensation of intense focus. It was as if the world had narrowed down to encompass only the old house and the four of them.

Without a word, she went back into her bedroom. Daphne disappeared through the doorway of her own room.

CHAPTER FORTY-FOUR

You learned a lot about people when you went into the business of stopping bad guys before they repeated their crimes, Jack thought. One of the things you figured out right away was that people who liked to do bad things were surprisingly predictable. Over time, human predators tended to stick with the classic *if it ain't broke, don't fix it* approach. They used whatever strategy had worked on previous occasions. The trick was to figure out the pattern.

Xavier liked fire. But there was one major technical problem with his style—at some point in the process he had to get very close to his target without being observed. If he was the one who had triggered the alarm tonight, it meant that he had required a car to make the five-mile drive from Cooper Cove and carry whatever fire-starting equipment he planned to use.

He probably hadn't taken the main road around the island because of the likelihood that someone would notice the familiar vehicle. That left only one other approach—the back road that dead-ended at the thick stand of trees behind the rental house.

The moon was out, but it didn't penetrate far into the woods.

Whoever had tripped the alarm had no choice but to use a flashlight to work his way through the trees to the back of the house.

When the intruder reached his objective, he would confront the problem of the porch lights. No arsonist wanted to work under a spotlight. As it happened, there was one empty light fixture above the back porch steps.

The empty fixture was not an oversight. It was a beacon intended to invite the intruder to take advantage of the dark path it provided.

Jack waited in the shadows beside the woodshed, a few feet away from the back steps. Madeline, Daphne, and Abe were all on the first floor now. The house seemed unnaturally silent, as though it were holding its breath.

He heard the intruder before he saw the narrow beam of a flashlight snaking through the woods. It was next to impossible to prowl through heavy undergrowth without making noise. A storm would have masked the small sounds, but tonight there was only an unnatural stillness. The small creatures of the night had gone silent in response to the presence of a human predator.

Twigs and dead leaves snapped and crunched underfoot. Tree limbs rustled when they came into contact with the sleeve of a jacket. Pebbles scattered. The flashlight beam drew closer.

Abruptly it disappeared. Whoever was approaching had concluded that he could use the porch lights to navigate the rest of the way.

It was amazing how many decisions got made based on the arrangement of light and shadow, Jack thought. If you knew which one your quarry wanted or needed, all you had to do was set the stage properly to guide the way.

A thud followed by a low grunt emanated from the woods. The intruder had either run into an object or managed to slam something he was carrying into one. A can of accelerant, most likely.

A dark figure emerged from the trees. For a moment he stood silhouetted in the moonlight. He was dressed for the night's work in black clothing and a billed cap. He carried a five-gallon fuel can in one hand.

He homed in on the shadowy path that led to the porch with the unerring instinct of an insect seeking to escape the light.

The intruder made it to the steps and quickly reached down to start removing the cap on the fuel can.

Jack stepped partway out from behind the woodshed into a position that would allow him a decent shot if he needed it. The thick logs stacked in the shed offered cover if that proved necessary.

He switched on the heavy-duty flashlight, aiming the fierce beam squarely at Xavier's face.

"It stops here, tonight, Webster," he said.

He spoke quietly. In such dense silence there was no need to raise his voice. He was dealing with a man who might well be flirting with insanity. The goal was to keep the situation under control. Sometimes you could do it with voice alone.

Sometimes that did not work.

"*You fucking bastard.*" Xavier's voice was hoarse with rage. "You can't stop me, Rayner. No one can stop me. I'm Xavier Webster. My father owns this island."

He straightened and reached into the pocket of his dark jacket. The white-hot beam of the flashlight glinted on the gun that appeared in his hand.

He fired wildly, the way people always did in a firefight. The odds of striking your target on purpose were stunningly small under such conditions. But the chances of getting hit by sheer accident were uncomfortably high.

Jack crouched behind the woodshed and waited out the volley of gunfire. When it stopped, he leaned around the far end of the shed and fired a single shot, aiming for a spot on the ground several yards away from the house—going for effect, not a hit.

Xavier screamed again, his fury and disbelief piercing the night. He dropped the gun, ran down the side of the porch, and vaulted from the top step to the ground.

He fled toward the road. His thudding footsteps echoed for a time in the night.

After a moment Jack holstered his gun and took out his phone.

The kitchen door cracked open.

"All clear, boss?" Abe asked quietly.

"He's gone." Jack aimed the flashlight at the container of accelerant. "Careful. Don't touch anything. With luck Xavier's fingerprints will be all over that can."

Abe came out onto the porch. Madeline and Daphne followed. They all looked at the can of accelerant.

"That bastard was going to torch the place with all of us in it," Daphne said. "Did he really think he'd get away with it?"

"Yes," Madeline said. She glanced at the container and then looked at Jack. "He assumed he would get away with it. You heard what he screamed there at the end. '*I'm Xavier Webster. My father owns this island.*'"

"If his plan had worked, there wouldn't have been any witnesses," Daphne said. "He probably would have gotten away with it."

Abe glanced toward the road. "He's on the run."

He spoke in a neutral tone, but Jack knew what he was thinking; what they were all thinking.

The 911 operator answered.

"*. . . the nature of your emergency . . .*"

"Attempted arson," Jack said. "Shots fired. Suspect fleeing south on Loop Road."

"*. . . Do you know the identity of the suspect?*"

"Xavier Webster. Lots of witnesses this time. He'll either head for his family's compound or try to get off the island in a boat."

He ended the connection before the operator could demand more details.

"What now?" Madeline asked.

"I don't think that Xavier Webster will be a problem for much longer," Jack said. "His family can no longer afford to keep him around. He's causing too much damage."

"Do you think they'll force him to go to a psychiatric institution?" Madeline asked.

"It would seem to be the obvious solution," Jack said. "But there is another, simpler way out of this if someone wants to take it."

Madeline looked at him. "You're predicting again, aren't you?"

"Can't help it," he said. "It's what I do."

He looked at Madeline because he did not want to look anywhere else.

Without a word she came down the steps and wrapped her arms around him, holding on as though afraid he might try to leave.

But he had no intention of going anywhere without her. Not tonight.

The four of them stood quietly, listening to the distant wail of sirens on Loop Road.

"I really don't like this island," Madeline said.

CHAPTER FORTY-FIVE

Xavier huddled in the shadows of the boathouse, struggling to control the racking chills that swept over him in waves. Part of him wondered if he was coming down with the flu. But the other part—the part that spoke to him from the fringes of his mind—had concluded that this was what real fear felt like. Maybe this was the kind of terror that he sometimes saw in the eyes of others who came to know him too well.

He'd had occasional brushes with the spiderweb strands of fear in the past. He'd felt real panic the first time his parents had shipped him off to the Institute. But he had soon discovered that the doctors and therapists were as easy to deceive as everyone else. Nevertheless, each time he had been sent back to the Institute, he had known some anxiety. There was always the chance that *this* time would be different— *this* time he would not be able to pull off the illusion.

But in the end, he was always successful in the role of The Healed Patient because the doctors and therapists were so eager to believe that they could work magic. They were also very enthusiastic about collecting the huge sums that Egan and Louisa paid for each miraculous recovery. *Should have gotten a commission from the Institute every time*

I allowed myself to get cured, he thought. After all, he was the one who had to do all the hard acting work.

He had experienced a few other anxiety-inducing situations over the years, but in the end his father had always come to the rescue. The folks Egan could not intimidate were invariably happy to accept money in exchange for their silence.

What no one understood was that he didn't have an anger-management problem. Other people *provoked* him. Other people caused him to lose it once in a while. None of the incidents had been his fault.

Over the years he had met a few individuals who could see his true nature, but they were rarely a problem because most of them had the common sense to fear him.

The only people he had ever really worried about were the bastards who did not fear him; did not respect him; did not realize how powerful he was—the ones who could not be scared off or bought off.

Bastards like Jack Rayner.

The memories of the debacle that night seared him. He would find a way to even the score. Rayner was a walking dead man. Just a matter of time.

The low rumble of the boat engines interrupted his fevered imaginings. He scrambled to his feet. Help was here. In a few minutes he would be safely away from the damned island.

Once he was clear, his father would take care of any legal problems that came out of the incident tonight. He was, after all, the golden boy, Egan's true son and heir.

The high-powered boat cruised almost silently out of the darkness. It glided to a halt at the dock. Xavier grabbed the rope.

"What took you so long? The cops will be searching for me by now."

He stepped into the boat and took over the wheel. His rescuer climbed out onto the dock.

Xavier eased the boat away from shore and headed toward open water. He had been piloting boats since he was a kid.

Elation slammed through him, driving out the last vestiges of fear. Within minutes he would be lost in the jumble of islands, large and small, that constituted the San Juans. He would spend the night in a sheltered bay off one of the uninhabited chunks of rock. At dawn he would head for the mainland. There were plenty of places where he could ditch the boat.

He would survive the incident tonight. That was what he was, a survivor.

He would take his time preparing his revenge.

He was still within sight of Cooper Island when the boat exploded into flames. The blast could be heard in town. The fireball lit up the night with a dazzling display of hellish light.

The watcher onshore waited until all that was left was the burning hulk of the boat.

CHAPTER FORTY-SIX

Madeline was at the kitchen table with Daphne and Jack, drinking orange juice because they had run out of coffee and checking the latest news reports on her computer, when Abe banged into the kitchen. He carried a large sack of groceries in his arms. His expression said he had news.

"Well?" she asked before anyone else could speak. "Inquiring minds and all that. What are the locals saying?"

"They pulled the body out of the water this morning," Abe said. He set the bag of groceries on the kitchen table and adjusted his glasses on his nose. "No question but that it was Xavier Webster. There are currently three working theories about the cause of the explosion. Number one is the theory being pushed by the Webster family. And I quote, *It was a terrible accident.*"

"Don't tell me, let me guess," Jack said. "A leak in the fuel tank, maybe?"

"Yep." Abe took a package of coffee out of the sack. "Turns out there are a lot of ways that a boat can go up in flames. All that fuel on board, you know. And so many things that can ignite it, including an electrical failure, signal flares that are unintentionally ignited, et cetera, et cetera."

Daphne leaned back in her chair and looked thoughtful. "What are some of the other theories?"

"Theory number two is being spoken in what you might call hushed tones," Abe said. "A few brave souls are wondering if someone did the world a favor and murdered the golden boy of the Webster clan. But no one is speculating very loudly about that possibility because there are way too many suspects."

Madeline drummed her fingers on the table. "Starting with most of the longtime residents of Cooper Island."

"I suppose the four of us are on that list," Daphne said. "Talk about motive. It was this house that Xavier tried to torch last night."

Jack picked up the coffee and went to the counter. "Don't worry. We are the only ones they can't put on the suspect list, at least not with any degree of credibility."

They all looked at him.

"The four of us were right here, explaining the situation to the cops, when the boat explosion occurred, remember?" he said. "And there are all those spent shell casings in the woodpile that will be shown to have come from the gun that will have Xavier's fingerprints on it. It's very likely there will be some of his fingerprints on the can of accelerant, too."

"Assuming some or all of those items don't disappear from the evidence locker of the local police department," Daphne said.

"Assuming that," Jack agreed. "But I think Chief Dunbar will do his job. I got the impression that he is as relieved as everyone else to know that Xavier will no longer be a problem."

Madeline looked at Abe. "Any other theories?"

"One more," Abe said. "Suicide."

Daphne stared at him. "*By boat explosion?* Don't tell me anyone actually believes that."

"I doubt it," Abe said. "Hey, don't look at me. I just report the news. I don't make it."

"The accident theory will prevail," Jack said quietly. "Xavier Webster, a man who, it turns out, had a history of mental illness, suffered a complete breakdown last night. For reasons that are unclear, he set out to torch a local house. When he was discovered in the act, he fled the scene, took one of the family boats, and tried to escape. The boat exploded by accident. Xavier was killed. His brother, an aspiring senatorial candidate, will make a statement about how he intends to seek better funding for mental health issues when he gets to the other Washington."

Madeline watched him measure heaping scoops of coffee into the machine.

"Someone killed Xavier."

"Oh, yeah," Jack said. He ran water into the coffeepot. "Xavier was set up last night. I think he was the intended victim all along. The only question is, who involved in this thing had the technical expertise to pull off two rather sophisticated explosions?"

"Two explosions?" Madeline frowned. "You mean, it wasn't Xavier who tried to kill us in the maintenance building?"

"I doubt it," Jack said. "Got a feeling that whoever set that trap wanted Xavier to get the blame." He finished pouring water into the coffeemaker and hit the on switch. "Several birds with one stone, I think. Someone is trying to clean up the Webster family history."

"So that it won't come back to haunt the bright, shiny candidate," Daphne said. Her eyes widened. "Step one, find the briefcase and whatever it is inside that is dangerous. Step two, get rid of the people who know about the briefcase. Step three, get rid of the psycho on the family tree."

"Whoa." Madeline held up one hand. "You and I and your mother didn't know what was in that briefcase. Only my grandmother and Tom Lomax were aware of the contents."

"But the killer has no way to know that," Jack pointed out. "Probably figures it's better to make a clean sweep and get rid of all possible witnesses."

"There is one person in the Webster family we suspect may have committed cold-blooded murder in the past," Abe said. "Egan Webster."

"All I know is that my grandmother was so afraid of his reach eighteen years ago that she closed down the Aurora Point and let it rot into the ground rather than take the risk of going to the local cops," Madeline said.

"It's the timing that bothers me," Jack said. "Why clean up the family history now?"

"That's obvious," Madeline said. "It's because Travis Webster is getting set to run for office."

"If Egan was aware that there was evidence that could link him to the murder of an old colleague, why didn't he do something about it twenty years ago?" Jack asked.

Abe looked at him. "Maybe it was only recently brought to his attention."

"By whom?" Madeline asked.

Jack tapped one finger against the tile counter. "By someone hoping to blackmail the Websters, maybe."

"Someone outside the family, then," Madeline said. "The fake Ramona Owens? Do you suppose she ignited this firestorm by somehow stumbling onto the secret of the briefcase?"

"But why would she or anyone else just happen to stumble into this thing after years of silence?" Abe asked.

"I think someone went looking for dirt on a rising political star and found it," Jack said. "The woman who called herself Ramona Owens is one of the keys to this thing. We need more data on her."

"She might still be able to talk to us from beyond the grave." Abe glanced at the screen of his computer. His eyes heated with excitement. "An address for a woman using one of Ramona's four identities popped up this morning while I was out picking up coffee and doing detective stuff in town. For once it's not a vacant lot."

Jack stilled, very focused now. "Where?"

"Seattle," Abe said. He started tapping keys. "She rented the apartment several months ago. Evidently her landlord hasn't heard that she's dead because Ramona is still listed as the tenant."

"If she was there for several months, she would have settled in," Daphne said. "It was her personal space. She would have felt safe there under her other identity. You're right, Abe, she might be able to tell us a great deal."

"Assuming no one else has gotten to her apartment to clean it out," Jack said. "You need to move fast on this."

"Me?" Abe asked.

"That would be you and Daphne," Jack said. "You, because you know what to look for if you get lucky and find some of her tech— phones, computers, anything that might tell us who she talked to and communicated with during the past year."

"And me?" Daphne prompted.

"You go with Abe because you're the one who knows how to get a read on people based on their living spaces."

"Oh, wow," Daphne said. "I get to play forensic designer."

"I see a book and possibly a TV reality show in this," Madeline said.

"Stick with me, kid." Daphne pushed herself up from the table. "I'm headed for the big time."

"Get moving, both of you," Jack said. "You've got time to make the early ferry."

"What about you and Madeline?" Abe asked. "If someone did try to take out all four of us last night using Xavier as a weapon, he knows he failed. He may decide to make another pass."

"We've got some time," Jack said. "Whoever it is, he won't risk making another move here on the island because it would be too damn obvious. Can't blame Xavier for any more mysterious fires or explosions."

Daphne shuddered. "It's horrible to think of someone using another person as a weapon. But that's what happened, isn't it? Someone aimed Xavier and pulled the trigger. And then got rid of him. That is stone cold."

"You'd be amazed at what people will do when they think they're doing it for the good of the family," Jack said.

CHAPTER FORTY-SEVEN

"Thank you for seeing me today, Madeline." Louisa sank slowly into a chair and clasped her hands in her lap. "I know you and your friends have been through a very difficult experience. I should have called first. But given what has happened, I was afraid that you would not agree to talk with me. So I took a chance and drove out here, instead."

"What is it you want to say to me?" Madeline asked.

Louisa's car was parked in the driveway. She had arrived shortly after the early ferry had departed, taking Daphne and Abe to the mainland in Abe's rented car.

Louisa was as cold and composed as usual, but it seemed to Madeline that her eyes were bleak with a grim mix of resignation, pain, and the kind of grief only a mother could know. But there was also something quite fierce and determined about her. It occurred to Madeline that a woman caught up in such a maelstrom of emotion was a very dangerous creature.

"It's about Xavier," Louisa said.

Madeline waited. She knew she probably ought to say something along the lines of *I'm sorry for your loss*, but the truth was she was not sorry that Xavier was gone. In addition, her intuition warned her not to trust Louisa any farther than she could spit, so there didn't seem to be much point in going with the polite social niceties. She wondered if Jack's approach to such things was starting to rub off on her.

Louisa had asked to speak to her alone, but Jack had quietly shaken his head, indicating that was a nonstarter. Louisa had witnessed the low-key signal. Her mouth had narrowed to a very tight line, but she had obviously realized that she did not have any bargaining power. She had accepted his presence without further comment. He stood at the window now, his back to the glary gray daylight. He was wearing his leather jacket. It was unfastened to reveal a glimpse of the holster underneath. He did not take his eyes off Louisa.

"My son had a mental breakdown last night," Louisa said. "The police believe he came here with the intention of setting fire to this house while you and your friends were sleeping. I am not here to defend his actions. Please believe me when I tell you that my entire family has been devastated by what has happened. We are in shock. Xavier's nerves have always been somewhat fragile. But I swear we had no reason to think that he would go over the edge the way he did."

"I understand, Mrs. Webster," Madeline said. "What, exactly, do you want from me?"

"My son is dead. There is nothing more he can do to harm you. I would take it as a great kindness if you and your companions——" She paused to glance uneasily at Jack. "If you and your friends would let things rest."

"What do you mean by 'rest'?" Madeline asked.

"By now I'm sure the local media have contacted you, asking for your version of events."

There was the faintest of question marks at the end of the sentence. Louisa paused and waited.

"We are not giving any statements to the media, if that is what is worrying you," Madeline said. "The police advised us that there is an ongoing investigation."

"Of course." Louisa looked faintly relieved. "Thank you. But I'm afraid it won't be long before the national media pick up the story. We all know they have the power to destroy lives, not to mention careers."

She stopped speaking again. This time Madeline did not try to fill in the silence. After a few seconds, Louisa continued.

"As I'm sure you know, my son Travis is preparing to run for office. He feels a calling to public service, but if his brother's breakdown is cast in the wrong light, Travis's future could be ruined before he even has a chance to prove himself."

"What do you see as the right light?" Madeline asked.

"The family has discussed the situation in great detail. We feel that the best way to handle things is to simply tell the truth."

"Always an interesting approach," Madeline said.

Louisa bristled. "I'm not asking you to lie. Xavier suffered a mental breakdown. He stole a boat, took it out into open water, and killed himself by setting the vessel on fire. All I'm asking is that you let the Webster campaign public relations people handle the media."

"In other words, you want us to let the Webster campaign put its spin on the story. They plan to just skip over the part where Xavier came here to torch this house and then fired a number of shots at my consultant."

Louisa clenched her handbag. "My son was the only victim and he's dead. There is no point airing the details of the incident in the press. The campaign spokesperson knows how to deal with this sort of thing. She will stress that Travis intends to make accessible, affordable mental health care a major issue once he is elected."

"If it helps, I can assure you that I have no interest in giving interviews to the media," Madeline said. "But I'm not going to cover up what happened here last night. Nor am I going to stop asking questions about Tom Lomax's death."

"I'm sure I don't have to point out that the members of my family are not the only ones who have a vested interest in trying to keep this situation under control."

There was a new, steely chill in the oddly hushed atmosphere. Madeline did not have to glance at Jack to know that he had felt it, too. They were now coming to the real reason Louisa had driven out to the cottage.

"I beg your pardon?" Madeline said.

"I didn't want to bring this up, but you leave me no choice," Louisa said. "In exchange for your cooperation in this matter, I am prepared to make sure that the media do not learn that Sanctuary Creek Inns is experiencing serious financial difficulties."

Anger flashed through Madeline. She controlled it with an effort of will.

"Sanctuary Creek Inns is not in financial trouble," she said.

"Let me be clear, Madeline, my husband is a very powerful man in financial circles. If he expresses concern for the financial stability of your hotel chain, the rumors will be picked up immediately. Among other things, it will make financing for renovations and new properties extremely difficult to obtain."

"Louisa, are you threatening me? Because I do not respond well to threats."

"Perhaps you should reconsider your response. Rumors of financial problems will cause you a great deal of trouble, but you may feel you can survive them."

"I will survive them."

"Do you think you can survive rumors that your hotel chain may be the target of an arsonist?"

"What is that supposed to mean?"

"There has already been one fire at a Chase property—the Aurora Point Hotel. Three months ago your grandmother was killed in a hotel fire. If the traveling public is convinced that some demented individual might strike a Sanctuary Creek Inn at some point in the near future, the results could be quite devastating for your chain. No one will want to book a room in a hotel that might have been targeted by a madman."

Madeline went cold.

"I don't think there is any need for further clarification, Louisa," she said. She was amazed by the unnatural state of calm that had settled on her. "That is definitely a threat. Do you agree with me, Jack?"

"No doubt about it," Jack said.

He reached inside his jacket. Panic tightened Louisa's face for an instant. But she relaxed somewhat when she realized that he was not going for his gun.

He removed a digital voice recorder and hit *rewind* and then *play*. Louisa listened in stunned shock when her own voice came out of the machine, sharp and clear.

"Do you think you can survive rumors that your hotel chain may be the target of an arsonist?"

"Bastard," Louisa whispered. She bolted to her feet and looked at Madeline. "You are a very foolish woman. You don't know what you're up against."

Clutching her bag, Louisa made for the door without another word. Madeline followed more slowly and stood in the entrance, watching Louisa get into her car.

Jack moved to stand behind Madeline. Together they watched Louisa's car speed down the drive toward Loop Road.

"Now what do we do?" she asked softly.

"We fight fire with fire," Jack said.

"Dear heaven."

"Unfortunately, it's the only thing some people understand."

"You mean it's the only thing thugs understand."

"Yeah, that's what I mean."

CHAPTER FORTY-EIGHT

"We're too late," Abe said. "Someone else got here first." He surveyed the apartment, his face grim with disappointment. "Damn. Jack isn't going to like this."

The Seattle address for the woman they knew as Ramona Owens had proven to be a two-story apartment complex in a quiet neighborhood. There was no on-site manager, no cameras, and no serious security.

Abe had experienced no trouble with the main entry door or the door of apartment six. But he was right, they were too late, Daphne thought. Until that moment she had been both excited at the prospect of discovering Ramona's secrets and terrified at the possibility of getting caught. But at the sight of the chaotic scene in the living room, she was overwhelmed with disappointment and a simmering anger. Ramona had very likely killed Tom, and she had, at the very least, been an accessory to the attempted murder of Madeline and Jack. But it looked as if she had gone to the grave with her secrets.

Abe took out his phone. "Jack. Yeah, we're at the address, but someone else has already been here and gone. Whoever it was tossed the place. Sure. We'll take a look around, but the guy who did this job was pretty damn thorough. What?" Abe glanced at Daphne's plastic-sheathed hands. "Of course we're both wearing gloves. Give me a little credit. I watch TV. Okay. Later."

Daphne studied the living room. The space was in chaos. The furniture had been overturned. Cushions had been ripped open. The television had been removed from the wall.

"This is pretty much how my apartment looked the day I got home from the cruise," she said.

"Someone came here looking for something."

"Whoever it was must have been desperate," Daphne said.

"Jack says to take a fast look around and then get the hell out of Dodge."

"I'll take the bedroom," Daphne said.

She went down the hall and stopped short when she saw the expensive lingerie and the array of sex toys that littered the floor.

"Oh, my," she said very softly.

She checked the bathroom and then went back down the hall.

"I know this probably isn't too useful," she said, "but I can tell you with a fair degree of certainty that Ramona had a lover."

Abe looked at her across the top of the kitchen counter. "How do you know?"

"Little things," Daphne said. "An interesting assortment of sex toys, for example. Also some very pricey lingerie. Investment pieces, I think. The kind of stuff you buy to wear for someone else."

Abe gave that some thought. "Was she entertaining a man or a woman?"

"Judging by the nature of the sex gadgets, I'd guess that her visitor was male, but that's sheer speculation."

"Maybe one of the neighbors can give us a description."

"I wouldn't count on it. Looks like the kind of apartment complex where people mind their own business. Short-term stays. That means high turnover."

"You never know," Abe said. "Let's go. There's one more thing we need to check."

"What?"

"Her mailbox in the lobby. You'd be surprised how frequently people forget to check the U.S. mail."

Ten minutes later they were back in the car, heading for the interstate. Daphne made the phone call to Madeline and Jack.

"Ramona was paying monthly rent on a storage locker. We lucked out. Next month's bill was in her mailbox. We're on our way to the facility."

The storage locker facility was located in a semirural area about a mile off the interstate. It was protected by a chain-link fence and a gate that was standing wide open when Abe and Daphne arrived. The attendant was sitting in a small office, watching videos on his computer. He barely looked up when Abe drove through the gate.

Daphne had been holding her breath while they approached the gate. She exhaled after they drove through.

"Okay, that was easier than I had expected," she said. "What would you have done if he had asked for your ID?"

"Showed it to him. All he would have cared about was whether I knew where I was going. We've got a locker number. That's all you usually need to get into one of these places. So long as the rent gets paid, no one asks too many questions."

"I guess a storage locker in a place like this is about as anonymous as a person can get in this day and age."

"Simple and low-tech works every time."

Abe brought the car to a halt in front of locker number 435, the number on the invoice they had found in Ramona's mailbox. It was a small locker, secured with a padlock. Abe got the bolt cutters he had purchased at a hardware store and snapped the lock. The door rolled up into the ceiling with an aluminum clatter.

There was only one item in the locker—a small roll-aboard suitcase.

"This looks interesting," Daphne said.

Abe moved forward. "Let's see what we've got."

He unzipped the suitcase.

"You were right," Daphne said. "This was her version of a safe house, the place she planned to retreat to if the con went south. She intended to grab that suitcase and run, maybe to the airport or maybe hit the road."

"But she never made it back here," Abe said. "Whoever searched her apartment didn't know about this locker. That means she didn't trust him."

"Or her," Daphne said. "This was Ramona's secret."

"Like Jack always says, a secret is only a secret as long as only one person knows it. Stands to reason that a professional con would probably have a few trust issues."

"I'm beginning to think that a lot of people have trust issues."

Abe started to rummage through the contents of the suitcase. "I trust you."

He said it so matter-of-factly, so casually, so calmly, that for a second or two she didn't think she had heard him correctly. Such a statement should have been a very big deal, she thought. In fact, it *was* a very big deal, but he had said it as though it were a simple fact of life as far as he was concerned.

"Thank you," she said, oddly rattled and uncertain how to proceed. "I am . . . honored. Not sure that's the right word."

He flashed her a quick grin. "Neither am I, but I guess it will have to do for now."

"No," she said, suddenly very sure. "No, it doesn't have to do for now. I trust you, Abe."

Abe smiled, satisfied, and went back to the suitcase.

It was neatly packed with the bare essentials a woman on the move might need: a change of underwear; a couple of sets of dark, nondescript clothes; a few travel-sized cosmetics; a pair of studious, black-framed glasses; a dark-haired wig; a bucket hat designed to shield the face—and a large, thick envelope.

"I think," Abe said, "that we should get out of here before we open that envelope. There is always the possibility that someone else might find this place. Be better if we weren't inside if that happens."

"Good plan."

Abe stowed the suitcase in the trunk of the car, tossed the envelope to Daphne, and then closed the locker.

They drove sedately back through the front gate and turned onto the road that would take them to the interstate.

Daphne opened the envelope very carefully. Her fingers shivered a little.

"You do realize this could be construed as tampering with evidence," she said.

"Someone used a crazy person to try to torch all of us in our beds last night," Abe said. "The police on Cooper Island do not inspire confidence. I think we've got a good reason to try to figure out what the hell is going on."

"This is true."

Very carefully she removed the contents of the envelope. There was another, smaller envelope inside and another set of IDs featuring Ramona's picture. In the driver's license photo her hair was cut short. She wore the black-framed glasses and the wig that had been packed in the suitcase.

Daphne set the ID aside and opened the second envelope. Several photographs fell out. The pictures looked as if they had been taken with a long-range camera lens. There were also three printouts of newspaper articles dated just over twenty years earlier and photocopies of several pages from a small notebook. The writing on the lined pages was cramped and sloppy.

Last but by no means least, there was a photocopy of a California driver's license issued to Norman Purvis.

Daphne stared at the items, hardly daring to believe what she was seeing. Then she glanced at the headlines on the newspaper articles.

"What have we got?" Abe asked.

"You'd better find a place to get off the interstate," Daphne said. "You need to see these."

A short time later Abe parked in a strip mall lot, shut down the engine, and picked up the pictures and photocopies.

"Well, hell," he said softly.

Daphne handed him the photocopy of Purvis's driver's license.

"I think we're looking at copies of the contents of that damned briefcase," she said. "Ramona knew she was involved in something dangerous. She probably kept a copy of everything she found, thinking it would be insurance."

"Same mistake Tom Lomax and Edith Chase made." Abe took out his phone.

"Jack, it looks like we found copies of the contents of that briefcase that got sealed up in a certain wall eighteen years ago. They were in a getaway suitcase that Ramona stashed in the storage locker. You need to see this stuff. I'm going to scan in everything we found and email it to you."

CHAPTER FORTY-NINE

Madeline stared at the image on the private investigator's license that had just come up on Jack's computer screen. A moment ago she had been standing at the kitchen table, but when Norman Purvis's picture appeared, she was once again struck with a disturbing sense of vertigo. She could feel his overwhelming bulk crushing her into the sacks of garden loam. His hand across her mouth, threatening to suffocate her. His voice grating in her ear. *Be quiet, you stupid little bitch, or I'll kill you. I swear I will.* She wanted to scream her rage to the uncaring universe, but she couldn't breathe.

She collapsed into the nearest chair. *He's dead. Dead and buried under the gazebo. He can't hurt you.* But the mantra was no longer a source of comfort because his ghost was staring up at her from the license, haunting her. From beyond the grave the bastard had managed to turn her world upside down again.

Jack was still on the phone, but he was watching her closely. She tried to concentrate on listening to his side of the conversation, but she could not look away from the monster in the picture.

"Hang on," Jack said into the phone. He reached out and gripped Madeline's hand.

His touch broke the nightmarish trance. She looked up from the computer screen and into Jack's eyes.

"He's dead," Jack said.

She nodded, unable to speak. Jack took his hand off hers and did something fast on the keyboard. The license disappeared. A newspaper clipping about the murders of Carl Seavers and Sharon Richards took its place. She read it, oddly numb now.

. . . A stockbroker and a female companion were found dead from gunshot wounds in a suburban neighborhood . . . Police speculate that drugs may have been involved . . .

"No," Jack said. He was once again focusing on the scanned images open on his computer. "You and Daphne are not coming back here to the island. You're going to Arizona. Don't worry, Madeline and I are going with you. We'll leave the island on the late ferry. Meet you at Sea-Tac. Buy four tickets to Phoenix."

Madeline looked up from the screen. It was the first time Jack had said anything about leaving the island.

". . . As soon as I end this call I'll get in touch with my contact in the FBI and make sure he sees this material," he continued. "What do you mean, how will I explain the stuff coming into my possession? I'll tell Joe we came across the items in the course of what we assumed was an unrelated investigation that we are conducting for a client. No, he won't push it. I'll cite client confidentiality and the fact that he owes me a couple of favors. Not the first time this has happened. Joe and I have an understanding . . ."

The first of the scanned photographs came up on the screen. Madeline stared at it, stunned.

Jack ended the connection in his customary fashion—he tapped a button and put the phone aside. He continued to focus intently on the screen. "So this is what was in the damn briefcase. Incredible. No wonder your grandmother and Tom were afraid to go to the police."

The photos had all been shot just after dark on what appeared to be a summer evening in a quiet residential neighborhood. There was still a little light in the sky. In addition, the photographer had been aided by a fair amount of ambient light from streetlamps and nearby houses.

"If Egan Webster knew that Grandma and Tom had seen these pictures, I don't doubt for a second that he would have arranged for them to suffer fatal accidents," Madeline said. "And he probably would have gotten rid of Daphne and me and Daphne's mom, as well."

"Your grandmother made an executive decision," Jack said. "She looked at the bottom line and made the hard call."

Madeline continued clicking slowly through the images. The camera had been a very good one. In spite of the low lighting, there was no difficulty making out a male figure dressed for a twilight jog. In the first few images it was impossible to make out his features because the hood of a black windbreaker had been pulled up to conceal much of his face. Nevertheless, she could tell that the man was tall, with a slender, athletic build.

The next series of photos showed the subject standing on the front steps of a bungalow-style house. The door of the house was open. Another man was silhouetted against the interior lights. In two of the photos a woman could be seen in the background.

"The victims," Jack said. "Carl Seavers and the woman who was with him that night—Sharon Richards. She was probably collateral damage. Wrong place, wrong time."

More pictures followed, several of which had obviously been taken at much closer range through a living room window. The venetian blinds were only partially closed. The camera had been aimed through the cracks.

In the living room shots, the face of the visitor was visible. He had pushed back the hood of his jacket. His silver-blond hair and distinctive, sharp-boned profile was unmistakable——Egan Webster as he had looked two decades earlier.

In the next photo Egan was shown with a gun in his hand, bending over two bodies. Even though she had steeled herself for what she knew was coming, Madeline was shocked in spite of herself.

"My God," she whispered. "Egan Webster shot them in cold blood."

"Norman Purvis must have been stunned when he realized what he had photographed," Jack said. "He was probably scared as hell. But he also must have realized that what he had was worth a fortune in blackmail money."

"The gun looks strange."

"Silencer," Jack said.

"Webster planned the killings."

"You don't take a silencer out jogging if your only reason for having a gun is for self-protection."

Madeline clicked to another photo. It had been shot from a more discreet distance, but it was a fairly clear image of Webster exiting through the rear door of the bungalow. In the scene he was illuminated by a bright porch light. It was possible to make out an old-fashioned laptop in his gloved hand.

Madeline shuddered and turned away from the screen.

"We were right," she said. "Egan Webster murdered Carl Seavers and stole the computer that must have contained the stock-picking program. But how could Porter-Purvis have known that Webster planned to murder Carl Seavers that night?"

"I doubt if he had any clue about what was going to happen that night. I think we can assume that Porter-Purvis was hired to follow Webster for some other reason. Purvis had probably been tailing Webster for days, stalling as much as possible so that he could pad the bill. He just got lucky with the photos of the killings."

"Lucky."

Jack moved one hand impatiently. "You know what I mean."

"Yes, I know what you mean. Okay, we know that Porter-Purvis was a private investigator. Who would have hired him to follow Egan Webster?"

"No way to know for sure yet, but offhand I can think of one very common reason why PIs get hired to follow married men around."

"Damn. Even at the age of twelve Daphne and I were aware of the rumors about Egan Webster's womanizing. Everyone on the island knew he had a reputation. I'll bet Louisa Webster hired a PI to get some proof."

"The PI got something that was a lot more valuable," Jack said. "He must have come here to the island that night to make a big trade—maybe one last payoff. Webster was very rich by that time. The PI used a different name when he checked into the Aurora Point Hotel. Trying to be careful."

"Webster must have gone crazy for a while, wondering why the blackmailer just disappeared," Madeline said. "He must have wondered why the demands stopped."

Jack lounged deeper into his chair, brooding on something only he could see. "Maybe he tried to search for the blackmailer from time to time. But he would have had almost nothing to go on."

"Unless he concluded that Louisa had hired someone to follow him and confronted her. Then he could have gotten the name of the PI from her."

"That information may not have led him to the anonymous Mr. Porter," Jack said. "And even if he did connect the two names, he still had a problem because Porter-Purvis had vanished. You know, it's interesting to think that Louisa and Egan Webster have probably both been sweating this mystery for years, wondering if and when the blackmail material would come out into the open."

"And now it has."

Jack smiled a thin, humorless, utterly unnerving smile.

"Yes," he said. "It has come back to haunt them. In fact, it's now online in the form of a couple of email attachments and it's about to go to the FBI. There's no way this can be hushed up."

Madeline looked out the kitchen window and thought about the gazebo.

"What about the part of the past that is connected to Daphne and me and Daphne's mom?" she asked.

"The rest of the story will come out once the FBI and the San Diego police get involved. You and Daphne and Daphne's mother will probably have to give statements, but I think that will be the end of it. Daphne's mother acted as she did because she feared for her daughter's life as well as her own. The sooner it comes out, the safer you and Daphne will be."

Madeline thought about that. "You may be right. In any case, there's no going back to the way things were."

Jack smiled. "That's what I like about you, Madeline. You go straight—"

"—to the bottom line." Madeline bared her teeth. "You know, I'm really getting tired of having people tell me that's what they admire about me."

"It's not the only thing I admire about you," Jack said.

She eyed him with some suspicion. "You're sure?"

"Positive."

"Name a few other things."

"I'll be happy to go through the list point by point." Jack got to his feet. "But not right now. There's something else we need to do first."

"What?"

"We're going to have a little chat with Egan Webster."

She shot to her feet. "Hold on, bad idea. You're turning this problem over to the FBI, remember? Let them handle Egan Webster. He's a cold-blooded killer. We know that for a fact. You just said I'm good with the bottom-line thing, remember? Well, that's the bottom line here."

"Not quite. There's only one strong emotion that a man like Webster comprehends. Fear."

"Fine. I get that. But soon he'll have the FBI breathing down his neck, not to mention the local cops. Let them make him feel fear."

"I don't think that's going to be enough to neutralize Webster. He's got platoons of lawyers to throw at the forces of law and order. He may not win in the end, but his legal team can probably keep him out of jail, at least long enough for him to get to some no-name island or a country that doesn't have an extradition treaty."

Madeline wanted to argue, but there was no point. Jack was right.

"All right," she said.

He raised his brows, amused. "Just like that?"

She gave him a warning look. "It's not like I've got a better idea."

"If you do happen to think of one, please let me know."

"I'll do that." She paused to make sure she had his full attention. "I'm going with you when you talk to Egan."

"No."

"This is not open for debate."

He watched her, not speaking. She smiled.

"Forget the gunslinger stare," she said. "I'm in charge here, remember?"

Jack's expression hardened but he did not respond. Instead he did a quick staccato on the table with his fingers. "There is one really big question left to answer here."

"Who decided to tidy up the Webster family history?"

"Right, that question. But first things first. Let's go talk to Egan Webster."

CHAPTER FIFTY

"I must admit that you and Ms. Chase are among the very last people I expected to come here today," Egan said. "Please, sit down."

"We won't be staying long," Jack said.

He was pleased to see that Madeline picked up the cue. She made no move to take a chair. She had excellent intuition, Jack reflected. There were times when you made sure to sit in the presence of the enemy because it demonstrated confidence and hinted at superior fire-power. But there were other occasions when common sense dictated that it was more prudent to stay on your feet—occasions when you might have to pull out a gun. He did not think that would be necessary today, but with a guy like Webster it seemed wise to take precautions.

When they had arrived at the Webster compound a short time ago, it had come as no surprise to see that the household had been plunged into shock and mourning. The shock was real enough, Jack thought. But he wasn't so sure about the cloud of mourning. He suspected that most of it was a thin cover-up for what everyone else on the island felt—relief. As far as he could tell, no one—with the possible exception of Louisa—had been fond of Xavier Webster.

The housekeeper had announced in low tones that Egan was in seclusion with the rest of the family, but when Jack had pushed her, she had disappeared to let her employer know who was at the front door. When she had returned, she had immediately escorted the visitors into the study. Egan had received them with an air appropriate to a grieving father.

"Well, then, what was it you wanted to say to me?" Egan asked. He made a show of looking at his watch. "My wife and I have an appointment with a funeral director this afternoon."

"Louisa came to see me earlier today," Madeline said. "Threats were made."

"I know." Egan closed his eyes briefly. He looked at Madeline with an imploring expression. "I apologize on her behalf. I hope you will understand that she is distraught at the moment. She never lost hope that Xavier's mental health issues would respond to therapy, you see. Between you and me, we spent a great deal of money on doctors and counselors and cutting-edge treatments over the years. But in the end, we failed to find a cure."

"Yeah, that much was obvious last night," Jack said.

Egan flashed him a reproachful look. "I'm trying to explain that my son had some problems."

"You no longer need to concern yourself with Xavier's problems," Jack said. He walked to the desk and set his computer down in front of Egan. "You've got more than enough of your own. The photos on this computer were emailed to the FBI and the San Diego police this afternoon. What happens next is up to the authorities."

Egan stared at the computer and then looked up. For the first time he appeared wary. "What the hell are you talking about?"

"In addition to reopening the case involving the murder of Carl Seavers and Sharon Richards, I'm going to make sure that the FBI takes another look at the hotel fire that killed Edith Chase. We've been assuming that it was Xavier's work, but in light of this new evidence, it seems you had plenty of motive."

Egan turned a violent shade of red. "I have no idea what this is about, but I do know you're acting crazier than my son." He reached for the phone. "I'm calling the police."

"Show him the pictures, Madeline," Jack said. "And don't forget the notes."

She moved to the desk and, without a word, brought up the first of the incriminating photos.

Egan scowled at the image, clearly bewildered. In the next instant he realized what he was looking at.

"No," Egan hissed. "It's not possible."

Madeline clicked through a few more pictures. When she got to one of the pages in the old notebook, Egan looked stunned.

"That's enough," Jack said quietly.

Madeline picked up the computer and stepped back.

"They're fakes," Egan said. Everything about him was tight with rage and something that looked a lot like panic. "Everyone knows it's possible to doctor photographs and documents online."

"In addition to the photos, the private investigator left very detailed notes," Jack said. "He saw you buy the gun, Webster. And the silencer. It gets better—he got a picture of you ditching both off a pier near La Jolla."

"Lies," Egan whispered. "All lies. Where did you get these?"

"Long story. No reason to go into it now. The FBI has the details. Those are just scanned copies of the originals. Not sure who has those. You, maybe? Are you the one who hired the woman who posed as Ramona Owens to help you clean up the Webster family tree?"

"Get out of here." Egan started to open the top drawer of his desk.

"Don't," Jack said. He had his gun in his hand now. "Get up and move away from the desk."

Egan stared at the weapon. Slowly he got to his feet. He took a couple of reluctant steps to one side.

"You don't know who you're fucking with, Rayner." He looked at Madeline. "You are a very foolish woman."

"You murdered my grandmother, didn't you?" Madeline asked. "You killed her, you bastard."

The dangerous edge on her voice worried Jack. He had been afraid that it might be a mistake to let her accompany him today. The kind of mutually assured destruction strategy that he had employed with Webster did not allow for stray fireworks and emotional outbursts. Success relied on maintaining absolute control.

"Time for us to leave," Jack said quietly. He spoke to Madeline, but he did not take his attention off Webster.

"You're the reason Tom Lomax is dead," Madeline said. "Were you the one who murdered him and then tried to hunt me down at the hotel that day, or was that Ramona? Either way, you're responsible for his murder. And you set your own son up to take the fall when things started to go wrong."

Webster shook his head. "You stupid little bitch. You should have sold the hotel when you had the chance. Before this is over I'll see Sanctuary Creek Inns destroyed. Do you hear me?"

"Madeline," Jack said. "The door."

He did not raise his voice, but Madeline finally got the message. She turned and walked to the door. Jack kept his focus on Webster.

"Whatever happens next is between you and the authorities," he said. "But you're smart. I'm betting you'll be safe on some no-name island before the guys with the badges knock on your door. But just so we're clear, if for any reason I have cause to believe that either Madeline or Daphne is in danger at any time, I will come after you myself."

"Get out of my house, you son of a bitch," Egan roared. "You'll pay for what you've done to me. I promise you that. You have my fucking *promise*."

Madeline had the door open. She was out in the hall. Jack picked up his computer and followed her, never turning his back on his target. He closed the door on Webster and looked at Madeline.

"We're leaving now," he said.

"Okay."

He kept the gun in his hand and instructed Madeline to get behind the wheel of the SUV so that his hands were free. Just in case.

Madeline drove straight to the ferry dock, where her own car was waiting in line.

The ferry sailed on time.

CHAPTER FIFTY-ONE

Madeline stood at the rail and watched Cooper Island slide out of sight. The hood of her jacket was pulled up around her face. Jack stood beside her, his big frame blocking some of the chilled wind coming off the dark water.

"You went too far," she said quietly. "You made yourself a human target when you threatened Webster personally."

"Had to be done," Jack said.

That was all he said.

She looked at him through the lenses of her sunglasses. She couldn't see his eyes because he, too, was wearing dark glasses. But she had learned a lot about Jack in recent days. He had retreated into his own personal no-go zone. She wanted to force her way past the invisible barrier, but she had no clue how to go about it. No clue if it was even possible. And no clue about how Jack would react if she was successful.

In the past she had always stopped at the invisible barricade because she knew she had no right to intrude.

But this time was different. He was her lover now.

"Why did you do it?" she asked. "Why not just let the authorities handle Webster? I never asked you to put yourself in his sights."

"You hired me to deal with the problem. I told you at the start of this thing that I would use my best judgment. Until now you've been reasonable about most of my tactics. But today you insisted on going with me to see Webster. You changed the dynamic."

Understanding slammed through her, leaving her momentarily stunned.

"You made that last threat because of me, didn't you?" she said. "Because I'm the one who lost control and accused him of murdering Grandma and Tom."

"It didn't make any difference in the end."

"If I had kept my mouth shut, you could have stopped the brinks-manship game with the evidence and the news that the authorities were in possession of those photos. Webster would have focused on the problem of dealing with the FBI. Instead, he's going to target you now."

"Maybe not."

"What do you mean, maybe not? You saw him. He'll do whatever he can to get at you."

"He's going to have his hands full for a while," Jack said. "I'm sure his first thought will be to get out of the country. He's a survivor. He won't hang around to take his chances with the authorities. He may hate my guts, but he won't risk arrest just to get revenge against me. He'll tell himself he should go to ground now."

"I see what you mean." She took a deep breath, aware of a tiny frisson of relief. "His first consideration will be his own survival."

"Right now he's probably giving orders to get the yacht fueled and readied for an ocean voyage. If Webster makes it on board he'll be in international waters within hours. He'll be untouchable as long as he stays out of the country. He knows that. I'm sure he made contingency plans long ago."

"Offshore accounts?"

"He would have been a fool not to make arrangements for a quick retreat."

"Good point." She thought about that. "I don't know whether to hope he gets arrested or that he escapes to some country or island that doesn't have an extradition treaty. If he gets picked up by the authorities, he'll probably make bail within hours."

"In which case he might still be able to get to the yacht."

"So, either way, the odds are he won't go to prison."

"I doubt it."

"Then what?"

"One thing I've learned in my business, Madeline. Sometimes it's a mistake to look too far down the road. There are times in life when you can't be sure of the pattern. You have to meet circumstances as they are."

She used one hand to hold her wind-tangled hair away from her face.

"That sounds like the same approach you take to your personal relationships," she said.

He smiled. "Saves me having to pay a private investigator to do a background check on all of my dates."

"That," she said, "was a low blow."

"Yes, it was. I apologize."

She turned toward him. "Jack, sometimes you scare me."

"I apologize for that, too."

"Not because I'm afraid you'll hurt me."

"Never."

She finished the sentence in her head. *You scare me because I'm afraid I'm falling in love with you.*

This wasn't the time or the place for words. Jack wasn't ready for words. She reached out and took his hand, instead. For an instant she thought she had pushed too far.

But his powerful fingers closed very carefully, very firmly around hers.

She did not feel trapped or crushed or pinned like a butterfly. Instead she experienced an exhilarating rush of *rightness*. *We are stronger together,* she thought. *When will you realize that, Jack?*

Together they watched Cooper Island slide into the mist.

After a while a stray thought jolted through her.

"What did you mean when you said *if* Webster makes it on board the yacht?" she asked.

"I'm not sure yet. What I know is that we're witnessing the implosion of an entire family. It's like watching a volcano that is starting to erupt. You want to be sure you're not standing too close to the scene. That's why we're going home to Arizona."

"Home sounds good."

"Yes, it does."

CHAPTER FIFTY-TWO

Egan carried a pile of shirts across the bedroom and dumped them into the suitcase. He shot Louisa a savage look and went back to the closet for more clothes. He realized that he hated her now as much as he hated Jack Rayner. They would both pay, he thought.

"This is all your doing, you stupid, crazy bitch," he said. "Everything, including the death of your precious Xavier. You had me followed that night in San Diego, didn't you? *Didn't you?* The PI who took the photos had your initials and your old phone number in his damn notebook."

Louisa stood near the door, clutching her purse.

"What photos?" she said, her voice very tight.

"Pictures of me in the house with Seavers and that little slut he was sleeping with. Pictures of pages from a notebook. Pictures that could send me to prison for the rest of my life."

She took a breath. "So you did murder them for the stock-picking program, didn't you? I always wondered, but I told myself you wouldn't have gone that far. I told myself that not even you would have crossed that line. But I knew. Deep down inside, I knew."

Egan looked at her with disgust. "We were partners every step of the way, Louisa. Remember?"

"In those days I was still hoping that you loved me, at least a little." Louisa's voice steadied. "Yes, I hired a private investigator to follow you around on your visits to your whores. I never got his final report. Norman Purvis billed me on a weekly basis for nearly two months and then he just disappeared. I assumed I had been scammed."

"That bastard you hired was the one who started blackmailing me twenty years ago."

"You told me that someone was trying to blackmail you, but you implied that it had to do with some insider trading issue."

"Bullshit. You knew it was Purvis, didn't you? The PI you hired goes missing and the next thing you know I'm being blackmailed. You must have guessed that Purvis had found something and was using it against me. But you never said a word."

She ignored that. "What happened to Purvis?"

"How the hell should I know? For the first two years it was just a slow bleed. I kept telling myself that one day I would find him and get rid of him. Then my fund took off and Purvis got greedy. He demanded a couple of million to be transferred into an offshore account. I agreed to pay it but only if I got the photos. I had it all arranged. I got him to agree to make the transfer here on the island. Figured once I knew he was here I would be able to control the situation. *But he never showed.*"

"And you never heard from him again."

"At first I told myself that he'd lost his nerve. After time went by with no word from him I decided that maybe one of his other blackmail victims had taken him out. That's probably what did happen."

"But why would the pictures and his notebook turn up now?"

"I don't have all the answers, damn it."

Louisa had a death grip on her handbag. "Where are you going, Egan?"

"Isn't it obvious?" He zipped the suitcase shut. "I'm getting as far away as possible."

"You're going to abandon this family?"

He wanted to scream at her, but at the last second he remembered that he had other, more effective weapons at his command. He had always been able to charm his targets.

"It's best if I leave, Louisa," he said, gentling his voice. "Don't you see? It's the only way to deflect the attention of the authorities and the media. This way it will be all about me—the evil financier who murdered a colleague for a stock-picking program nearly two decades ago, deceived his family, friends, and business associates for years, made a fortune, and vanished when the truth came to light."

"That's an interesting narrative. But what about Travis and the campaign? You can't just leave him here to pick up the pieces."

"It won't do him any good if I stay. He'll be in a much better position to manage the fallout if I disappear. Don't worry about Travis. He'll land on his feet. Took me long enough to realize that he's the one who got my talent for surviving."

"What do you mean?"

"Get real, Louisa. Hasn't it dawned on you that Travis will be the last one standing when this is all over? Don't you see? He was the one who got rid of Xavier last night. It must have been him."

"No. Xavier was his brother."

"Ever heard the story of Cain and Abel? Think about it. Xavier was always a problem for Travis. It was only a matter of time before Xavier did something that would have ruined the campaign. Travis must have realized that he had no choice but to get rid of his brother. The only surprising thing is that he had the guts to do it. Should have given him more credit."

"You don't know that he murdered Xavier. You can't possibly know that."

"It's the only logical explanation for what happened to Xavier last night." Egan hoisted the suitcase off the bed. "I don't care what the campaign people are saying, we both know he wasn't a suicide. And I sure as hell didn't rig that boat to blow sky-high. It must have been Travis. Now get out of my way."

"No," Louisa said. "I won't let you abandon this family. Not after everything you've done. I've worked too hard. Put up with too much for too long. It almost drove me crazy, you know—your affairs, the realization that you were incapable of loving anyone, not even your own sons. Knowing that you routinely cheated and lied."

"And made a hell of a lot of money. Don't forget that part. You liked the money, didn't you? You liked the things it bought you, right up to and including Travis's campaign."

"Which you have now destroyed."

"You're the one who had me followed that night, remember? If it hadn't been for you, the past would have stayed buried. You brought this disaster down on all of us."

From out of nowhere a disturbing calm settled on Louisa. Egan's intuition suddenly kicked in. He needed to get out of the house. Now.

"You're right," Louisa said. "What is happening to this family is my fault. I'm the one who must do what I can to repair the damage."

She reached into the handbag and took out a gun. *His* gun. He stared at her, incredulous.

"You think killing yourself will solve all of Travis's problems?" he asked. "Fine. Go for it."

"You don't understand," Louisa said. Her voice was very calm and steady now. "I'm not going to kill myself."

CHAPTER FIFTY-THREE

Breaking . . . Egan Webster, founder of a hedge fund empire and father of a potential congressional candidate, was found dead in the family compound on Cooper Island, Washington, earlier today. According to the police, cause of death was multiple gunshot wounds. The victim's wife, Louisa Webster, has been taken into custody. Sources report that she has confessed to the killing.

In the wake of Webster's death, rumors of past improprieties related to the operations of his hedge fund and questions concerning its current financial status have begun to surface. The FBI has opened an investigation.

There is also speculation that a murder investigation into the unsolved deaths of two of Webster's former colleagues will be reopened . . .

Madeline looked up from the computer screen. "I can't believe it. Louisa shot Egan right after we left on the ferry."

Daphne and Abe had been waiting for them at Sea-Tac Airport. The four of them were gathered around a small table in the first-class lounge, waiting for the flight to Phoenix. Abe had collected a small mountain of free snacks on a plate that he had placed in the center of the table—little plastic-wrapped packets of white and yellow cheese and crackers, small packages of carrots, some hummus dip, and cookies. They were all drinking coffee.

"Are you really shocked?" Jack asked. "She probably found him packing to take off in the yacht. It was the last straw."

"He was going to leave her and Travis and Travis's wife to deal with the wreckage," Madeline said.

"Webster pushed Louisa one step too far," Daphne said. "So she shot him."

"When you look at it from that angle, I suppose it isn't surprising," Madeline said. She sat back in her chair. "Maybe the real question is, why did it take her so long to do it?"

"She had probably made her peace with her marriage," Daphne said. "After all their years together they had formed an alliance. Webster provided a financial empire and, in turn, she gave him a son who was on the road to a seat in Congress and, eventually, maybe even the White House."

"But it was all built on lies and murder," Abe said. "Someone discovered the truth about the past and set out to clean it up and, as a side benefit, get rid of the rather nasty problem of Xavier at the same time."

"My money's on Travis," Jack said.

Madeline looked at him. "You think he's the one who set events in motion?"

"I think," Jack said, "that Travis Webster is a chip off the old block— Egan Webster's true son and heir. When he decided to go into politics he did some serious opposition research on his own family and came up with the same troublesome anomaly that we did when we went looking—his father's sudden, meteoric rise in the investment world."

"He must have stumbled across the mystery of Carl Seavers's murder and started looking under rocks," Madeline said. "I wonder how he got as far as Porter, or, rather, Norman Purvis."

Jack helped himself to a packet of cheese. "Remember, Travis had an inside source of information—his mother."

"If Travis confronted Louisa with questions about the past, she might have confided that once upon a time she hired a private investigator to follow Egan. And maybe she happened to mention that she never got the results of that investigation because Purvis disappeared."

"With that much background information, Travis would have been on his way to piecing together the whole story," Jack said. "He must have figured out that Purvis headed for Cooper Island and vanished shortly after arriving there. I'll bet his initial conclusion was that his father had killed Purvis and dumped the body."

"It would have been a logical assumption," Abe said.

"How did he figure out that wasn't what happened?" Daphne asked. "Assuming we're right, what led Travis to conclude that Purvis made it as far as the hotel before he disappeared?"

"It's not like there would have been a lot of options when it came to places to stay on Cooper Island," Madeline pointed out. "Eighteen years ago, the Aurora Point Hotel was the only large inn on the island. The rest of the places were small B-and-Bs. It's impossible to remain anonymous at a B-and-B."

"So Travis concluded that Porter-Purvis had checked into the Aurora Point eighteen years ago but never checked out?" Jack shook his head. "Maybe. But it seems like a stretch. I'll bet he turned up something much more conclusive."

"The dead sister." Abe straightened abruptly in his chair, put aside a cracker, wiped his fingers, and started tapping very fast on his computer. "The one who died from an overdose a few months ago. Remember her? It was her car that Porter-Purvis was driving the night he checked in at the Aurora Point. Here we go. Sandra Purvis."

"That's it," Jack said. He looked satisfied. "Travis Webster tracked down the sister and got enough information to convince him that Purvis had made it to the Aurora Point before he disappeared. He then realized that the only person around who might know what happened eighteen years earlier was the eccentric caretaker."

"Travis used Ramona to cozy up to Tom Lomax and pump him for information about Porter-Purvis," Madeline said. "She hit the mother lode when Tom told her about the briefcase in the wall, the one that contained an insurance policy."

"But why would he do that?" Daphne asked.

"I'm just winging it here," Jack said. "But I can envision a scenario in which Tom thought he could use the contents of the briefcase to blackmail Egan Webster."

Abe paused in midbite. "Why would Lomax suddenly decide to blackmail Webster?"

"Because he thought he could get money out of Webster," Jack said patiently. "A lot of money."

"Again, why?" Abe said. "By all accounts Lomax didn't give a damn about money."

Madeline picked up her coffee cup. "Tom had discovered a long-lost granddaughter. Maybe he wanted to do what a lot of grandparents try to do for their offspring—provide an inheritance."

They sat quietly for a time, absorbing the story.

"Can't prove some of it, not yet," Jack said. "But most of the pieces fit."

"It's so sad," Daphne whispered. "Poor Tom. He must have been so thrilled to discover a granddaughter."

"A secret isn't a secret if more than one person knows it," Jack said.

"Yeah, yeah, we know," Abe said. "You need a new slogan, boss. That one is getting old."

"It's not a slogan, just a fact," Jack said. "I think we've got a pretty good handle on the case, but there are a few loose ends to tidy up."

"Such as?" Daphne asked.

Madeline tapped the side of her coffee cup a couple of times. "The mysterious Ramona Owens."

"Right." Jack drank some of his coffee. "I'd sure like to know where she came from and how she hooked up with Travis Webster."

"Well, I'm not an ace detective like some people at this table," Madeline said. "But maybe—just maybe—Travis inherited other aspects of his father's less-than-sterling character."

Daphne leaned back in her chair and shoved her fingers into the front pockets of her jeans. "You mean, maybe Travis is a womanizer, too?"

"Just like dear old Dad," Madeline said. She shuddered. "If we're right, he seduced her into playing the role of accomplice and then murdered her when she was no longer of any use to him."

"The Websters are one vicious clan," Abe observed. He unwrapped a packet of cookies and put them on Daphne's plate. "Marrying into it must be a lot like marrying into a mob family."

"It's starting to look like Travis is the meanest one of the bunch," Jack said.

"If we're right about any of this, there's a very good reason to believe he's a murderer several times over," Madeline said. "Think the FBI will figure it out?"

"My buddy Joe has enough to run with now," Jack said. "It may take him a while to sort it all out, but I know him. He won't stop until he gets to the end."

"If Travis is not just the meanest but also the smartest member of the Webster family, he's probably already on board the family yacht, headed for some convenient island," Madeline said.

Jack unwrapped another packet of cheese. "Maybe."

Madeline decided that was all they were going to get out of him for now. She smiled at Daphne.

"It will be good to go home. You can stay with me until all the loose ends are snipped off. We've got a lot of catching up to do."

Daphne smiled. "That sounds like a most excellent plan."

"You two can spend all the time you want catching up," Jack said around a mouthful of cheese. "But you're not going home, Madeline. At least not to spend the night. You and Daphne will stay at my folks' house until I get the all-clear from Joe."

Madeline looked at him. "Why can't we stay at my place?"

"Better security at my parents' house," Jack said.

Daphne frowned. "You're really concerned about the loose ends?"

"It's always the loose ends that cause the most trouble," Jack said.

CHAPTER FIFTY-FOUR

The late-afternoon temperature had hit eighty degrees, but the desert cooled down rapidly after dark. Still, Madeline was comfortable lounging on the patio in trousers and a lightweight pullover. The outdoor heaters kept the slight chill at bay.

The home of Jack and Abe's parents was a graceful combination of modern and traditional Southwestern design that looked as if it had been sculpted out of desert rock. It was located on a hillside overlooking the town of Sanctuary Creek and commanded sweeping views of the valley and the mountains beyond.

Not everyone appreciated having unexpected houseguests thrust upon them, but Charlotte and Garrett Rayner could not have been more welcoming.

Spring nights in the desert were very different from nights in the Pacific Northwest, Madeline thought. The vast evening sky; the scents of the wild, rugged landscape that was never far away, even in an urban area; the calls of the creatures that buzzed, chirped, and howled into the darkness: It all made for a different world—her world. She was home, even if she was going to be spending the night in someone else's house, and it felt good.

She was not alone on the patio. Charlotte and Daphne were with her. It occurred to her that neither she nor Daphne had been alone at all since Jack had arrived on Cooper Island to take charge of the investigation.

Jack, Abe, and Garrett were in the kitchen, working on dinner. From time to time masculine laughter spilled out onto the patio. Max, the friendly beast of a dog, had joined them. Something told Madeline that Max was no fool. He had obviously figured out that the kitchen was the source of his next snack.

Garrett Rayner had proven to be a man straight out of the Old West. One glance at him and it had been obvious that Jack had inherited his lean, tough build, his edgy profile, and his hard-to-read eyes from his father.

Charlotte was a vivacious woman with a flair for the dramatic. Tonight she wore a long sweep of a maxi dress in the brilliant, bold colors of a Southwestern sunset. Her black hair was shot with silver. She wore it tied back at the nape. Gold and silver bangles clashed musically whenever she moved one of her graceful hands to underscore a comment.

Two bottles of white wine on ice sat on a nearby table. One bottle was empty. Madeline was pretty sure that no other wine had ever tasted so good. She knew it was the knowledge that Cooper Island was far away and that she and Daphne were safe among newfound friends that made the difference.

She met Daphne's eyes and realized they were both thinking the same thing. It was so easy to read each other's thoughts, just as they had done when they were girls. She raised her glass a couple of inches in a wry toast.

"To the end of a very, very long day," she said. She smiled at Charlotte. "And to the very, very kind people who have welcomed a couple of strangers into their home."

"I'll drink to that," Daphne said. She raised her own glass and downed a healthy swallow.

"Thank you," Charlotte said. "But rest assured, we are all delighted to meet you. From what Jack and Abe have told us, you have all been through some extremely exciting times in the past few days. Fires. Explosions. Murders. It must have been downright horrible. Who knew the hotel business could be so dangerous?"

"I promise you, our problems are not the norm in the field," Madeline said.

"You know, when Jack told us that he was going to quit the FBI profiling work and start a high-tech security firm with his friend, we all figured he'd be bored to tears within months," Charlotte said. "But that didn't happen. Then his friend was killed in a diving accident and the business went bankrupt. Garrett and I were sure Jack would go back to the profiling work at that point. Instead he told us he was going out on his own. It's been a struggle, and he has refused to let us help him out financially. That's why he was so elated to get the Sanctuary Creek Inns account. You are his first major client."

"So I've been told," Madeline said. "The good news is that we don't get a lot of serial killers checking in to Sanctuary Creek Inns, but as my grandmother liked to say, running a hotel is like operating a version of Fantasy Island. Every time the plane lands, a bunch of strangers arrive to spend the night. You never know what you're going to get."

Daphne nodded. "It's true that when you stay in a hotel you have an expectation of anonymity. There's a sense of having entered another world, a place where no one knows who you really are."

Charlotte chuckled. "I suppose that sense of anonymity is why so many people go to hotels to meet prostitutes, sleep with other people's spouses, and make shady financial deals."

"Okay, there is that aspect of the business," Madeline said. "But I assure you Sanctuary Creek Inns does not cater to those markets."

Charlotte laughed.

"On the bright side, there is a lot of fun in the fantasy business," Madeline continued. "We get to help make dreams come true with weddings, honeymoons, anniversaries, birthdays, and other kinds of celebrations." She paused to clear her throat. "Not to mention the occasional boring corporate seminars, drunken fraternity reunions, and wild bachelorette parties."

Charlotte looked intrigued. "How often do you find a guest dead in bed in one of your hotels?"

"Okay," Madeline admitted. "It happens. But usually from natural causes, I swear it."

"We'll take your word for it," Charlotte said. She gave Madeline a considering look. "You love it, don't you?"

"The innkeeping business? Yep. Guess it's in the blood."

"What do you think? Will Jack be satisfied with the hotel security business?"

"You'll have to ask Jack. But yes, I think it will suit him in the long run."

Charlotte watched her with rapt attention. "Why do you say that?"

"I don't know this for certain," Madeline said carefully, "because Jack and I have never actually discussed it, at least not in so many words. But I think that he's had enough of the horrors and the nightmares that must go with criminal profiling work. He still needs to do what he does best—protect others from the bad guys—but he knows that he needs to do that in a way that will allow him to have a more normal life."

She took another sip of wine and reached into the bowl for a tortilla chip. She paused with the chip halfway to her mouth when she realized that Charlotte was gazing at her, mute.

Madeline lowered the chip. "I'm sorry, I shouldn't have speculated about Jack's motives. I had no right to try to guess his intentions."

"It's fine." Charlotte's smile was a bit wobbly. There was a sheen of moisture in her eyes and a slight crack in her voice. "It's just that I found your observations on my son's career move very—insightful. Now, if you'll excuse me, I'd better see how dinner is coming along."

She came up off the lounger, bangles clashing, the skirt of her brilliant dress swirling around her. She had a paper napkin in one hand. She used it to surreptitiously blot her eyes as she went through the open slider door.

Chagrined, Madeline looked at Daphne. "I shouldn't have opened my mouth."

"Don't worry about it," Daphne said. "Abe told me that Jack's family was very concerned about him for a time after his business partner died. They were afraid that Jack blamed himself for not being able to rescue his friend. Survivor's guilt and all that. Evidently the friend's wife and family made it clear that they held him responsible for the death, as well. Jack's fiancée dumped him. Then it turned out the business was on the verge of bankruptcy. Jack lost everything he had put into it. There was a lot of bad press. It was a huge mess all the way around."

"And Jack took responsibility for all of it."

"Yes, according to Abe."

"He was protecting someone," Madeline said.

Daphne started to answer, but she stopped abruptly, lips parted, and looked past Madeline.

"How do you know that my son was protecting someone?" Charlotte asked quietly.

Madeline froze. But it was too late to turn back.

"It's what Jack does," she said.

There was a tense silence before Charlotte spoke again.

"Yes," she said, "that is exactly what Jack does. Not everyone understands that. I'm very glad that you do, Madeline."

CHAPTER FIFTY-FIVE

"I'm going to take the afternoon ferry," Patricia said. "I'll stay in a hotel in Seattle tonight."

She put the carefully folded designer dress that she had bought for the birthday reception into the suitcase. She wasn't sure why she was bothering to take it with her. It wasn't like she would have another opportunity to wear it, at least not in the foreseeable future. She had chosen the dress because it was the perfect dress for the Candidate's Wife. It was just the right shade of blue, decorously cut to show a discreet amount of bosom and leg; expensive but not exorbitantly so. Classy but not high-class.

The Candidate's Wife had to walk the fine line between being subtly glamorous and in-your-face flamboyant. She had to appear to be a person in her own right and at the same time exhibit absolute belief in her husband's ability to change the world.

She had spent the last year immersing herself in that role, and she knew that she had been brilliant. She had dedicated herself to her part because she had envisioned a glorious future as the wife of one of the most powerful men in the country. From that point on, doors would open.

But the curtain had fallen on act one of the play. It was time to cut her losses and find another role. She would not have her looks forever.

No, she would not need the Candidate's Wife dress. She yanked it out of the suitcase and tossed it into the little trash bin beside the dresser. The blue fabric billowed over the top of the container and spilled onto the floor.

The good news was that there was now more room in the suitcase. She went back to the closet to ponder the issue of shoes.

Travis watched her from the bedroom doorway. "Will you at least show up at my father's funeral?"

"I don't think that will be necessary or useful." She picked up a pair of black pumps and studied them critically. Candidate's Wife shoes. She tossed them on top of the dress. "Under the circumstances, I'm sure it will be a small, private affair. I doubt if anyone will notice if I'm not there."

"The media will notice."

There was a raw edge in Travis's voice. For a moment it almost sounded as if he might miss her. But this was Travis Webster. The only person he cared about was himself and his climb to the top.

Still, the Websters could be dangerous when provoked. She had certainly learned that lesson recently. She turned toward him and managed a sad, wistful smile.

"Of course I'll come back for the funeral if you think it will help," she lied. "But right now I want to be alone for a while. I need time to think."

"Time to find a divorce lawyer, you mean."

"No. Travis, I'm not leaving you, I swear it. I'm going to the lake house. You can join me there at any time. We can talk about our future when the immediate crisis is past."

"I do have a future, damn it. The media frenzy will die down in a few weeks if not sooner. I talked to my mother's lawyer this morning. He's working on a self-defense angle. He thinks he can get Louisa off entirely."

"Are you serious?"

"Dead serious. Keep in mind that my father evidently murdered two people some twenty years ago. When Louisa confronted him about the killings he went into a rage and tried to choke her. She shot him to protect herself."

Patricia thought about that. She smiled and shook her head. "It just might work."

"It will work," Travis vowed.

"The thing is, I'm not sure that will make it possible for you to run for office, at least not in the upcoming election. The public will need time to forget."

"So I'll spend the next year cleaning up the mess my family made. Eventually I can make it all go away."

You're crazy if you think it will all go away, she thought. But she did not say it out loud. It was clear now that every member of the Webster family was capable of murder. She might as well have married into a mafia family. She had to look after herself now. She had to escape the island and try to disappear.

She pretended to be intrigued by the possibility that they would survive the disaster.

"If the campaign people can manage to put the right spin on the situation—make it look like your father was the source of all the trouble—you just might be able to turn this around."

"That's the plan," Travis said.

Everything about him seemed to get a little brighter, almost radiant. He was once again The Ideal Candidate. The charisma thing was amazing, Patricia thought. And Travis could literally turn it on and off at will. He probably would find a way to get back into politics—assuming someone didn't kill him first. But right now her goal was to get off the damned island.

"I believe you," she said. "In time you will be able to get back into the game. And for the sake of the country you should do just that. We need strong leadership. But right now, it's important that I go into seclusion. I need to get away from the stress."

He narrowed his eyes. "Why?"

Inspiration struck. Very deliberately she put her hand on her belly. "Because I think I'm pregnant."

Travis stared at her, stunned. "Are you sure?"

"No, but it's a real possibility. Now do you see why I need to get out of the line of media fire? I don't want to lose our baby because of stress."

"A baby would go a long way toward building a new image," Travis mused.

"Yes, it would. The fact that I'm pregnant would also provide you with a reasonable excuse for my absence for a while."

He looked at her for a long time. "You want to go to the lake house?"

"It's always been a safe retreat for us. The media doesn't know about it."

"Good idea." Travis started to turn away and then paused. "I'll join you there just as soon as I get things under control here. It wouldn't hurt for both of us to disappear for a while."

"No," she said.

"I'll send someone to help you with your luggage."

"Thank you."

She waited until he was gone before she allowed herself to take a deep breath and turn back to the packing. She had lied. There was no baby. She had taken care to make certain there wouldn't be one, at least not until Travis had won his first big election.

It wasn't the first time she had lied to Travis. But he had lied to her, as well.

The Websters were very dangerous people.

She had to get off the island.

CHAPTER FIFTY-SIX

Madeline waited until she was almost certain that Daphne was asleep in the adjacent bed before she pushed the covers aside and got to her feet.

"Going somewhere?" Daphne mumbled.

"Sorry. Didn't mean to wake you. I can't sleep. I'm going to go into the front room and work on some email."

"Give my regards to Jack."

"I am not heading for a secret rendezvous with Jack."

"Why not?"

"Go back to sleep."

"Okay. Have fun."

Daphne turned on her side and pulled the covers up over her shoulder.

The curtains were open, allowing the light of the desert moon into the room. Madeline pulled on her robe, stepped into her slippers, and crossed the space to the small desk. She picked up her computer and headed for the door.

She and Daphne had been given the guest suite, a gracious bedroom with two beds and a private bath. Jack and Abe had been assigned a room at the other end of the house.

Night-lights lit the way down a corridor to the glass-walled great room. She sat down on a low, rust-colored sofa, curled one leg under her, and cranked up the computer. The dog, Max, padded into the room and stretched out on the rug. She reached down and scratched his ears.

And then she started searching.

It did not take long to find the information she was looking for. None of it was new information, but tonight she considered it from a different perspective. She knew a lot more about Jack than she had a few months ago when she had looked into his past.

The body of Victor Ingram, president and CEO of a high-tech security firm in San Jose, California, was recovered late yesterday in the waters off a popular Mexican resort town. Local authorities announced that Ingram was the victim of a diving accident. He had gone spearfishing with his friend and business partner, Jack Rayner, but the two became separated while exploring an underwater cave system.

Ingram is survived by his wife and two children. In the wake of his death, rumors have begun circulating that the security firm Ingram co-founded with Rayner is experiencing serious financial difficulty.

CHAPTER FIFTY-SEVEN

The desert nightscape looked and felt good after the dark, claustrophobic world of Cooper Island.

Jack braced one foot on the bottom rail of the fence that enclosed his mother's cactus garden and immersed himself in the night. Something inside him relaxed a little. He had been running in a state of heightened awareness since the call from Madeline that had taken him to Cooper Island. But tonight she was safe in his parents' house and he could let down his guard, at least for a while.

He heard the crunch of shoe leather on the gravel path that wound through the garden, but he did not turn around. He recognized his father's stride.

Garrett came to stand beside him. He, too, propped one foot on the low rail and looked out at the sparkling lights of the houses scattered across the valley.

"Thought I heard you come out here," Garrett said. "Still worried about your clients?"

"They're safe here."

"That's a fact. We've got damn good security, thanks to that over-paid expert we hired."

"The overpaid expert may have been a bit obsessive about it, but tonight he's glad you bought the upgraded package."

"We've also got a dog."

"A loud, barking dog beats high-tech every time."

"Cheaper, too." Garrett leaned on the top rail. "So what's wor-rying you?"

"A few loose ends. I can monitor most of them online, and my FBI connection said he'd keep me posted. But if one of the Websters goes off the grid, I need to know about it."

"Sounds like that Webster bunch is one messed-up family. Prob-ably raised on rattlesnake venom."

"Something like that."

"Not that many of 'em left from the sound of it, though," Garrett said. "Let's see, one son killed in a boat explosion, the father shot by his wife, who is now under arrest——"

"Louisa Webster is out on bail. Claims it was self-defense. Joe says she's still on the island."

"Does she worry you?"

"You bet. She's already proven that she's willing to pick up a gun and kill someone."

"Which brings us to the one remaining son and his wife," Garrett concluded.

"Joe texted me a couple of hours ago letting me know that Travis's wife, Patricia, gave a statement to the local cops saying she had no idea her mother-in-law planned to shoot her father-in-law. Then she packed up and left the island on the late-afternoon ferry."

"Given what's been going on, I'd think any smart woman in her position would want to get out of town."

"It does appear that Patricia Webster is not going to play the part of the loyal politician's wife standing by her man."

"So that leaves Travis Webster. He's the one who worries you?"

"Never quite got a handle on him," Jack said. "And, yeah, that worries me."

Garrett snorted. "You did say he had what it takes to be a successful politician."

"True. They were calling him the ideal candidate, but now his world has fallen apart around him. Hard to know how a person will react when that happens."

"But your FBI pal is keeping an eye on him, right?"

"Definitely. Joe is extremely interested in Travis because he and his team would really like to know what happened to the millions Egan Webster made by defrauding investors in recent years. The money is probably stashed offshore, but there's always a chance Travis can lead them to it. If the funds are recovered, it would be a major coup for Joe's team."

"You think Travis knew his old man's secrets?"

"What I think," Jack said, "is that Travis is a little tougher, a little smarter, and maybe even a little more ruthless than Egan Webster realized."

"Any evidence that he murdered a few people the way his old man did?"

"No hard evidence," Jack said. "But it was Travis's decision to run for office that seems to have triggered the entire chain of events. It started with the murder of Edith Chase."

"You're sure the hotel fire was murder?"

"Given all that's happened, her death is just too damn coincidental."

"They say coincidence happens."

"I've heard that."

"So you're thinking that Travis is a little more dangerous than some people think."

"Right."

Garrett exhaled deeply. "Egan Webster wouldn't be the first man to underestimate his own son."

Jack nodded, but he did not speak.

The night settled more heavily around them.

"Charlotte likes your Madeline," Garrett said after a while. "So do I."

Jack focused on the glowing jewels scattered across the valley. "I like her, too. A lot. But she's not my Madeline."

"You said Travis Webster's world is falling apart and that makes him hard to predict."

"So?"

"So your world fell apart two years ago. But you're not unpredictable like Webster. We all knew you'd get back on your feet. But in the process you made some tough rules for yourself, thinking they would keep you from screwing up again."

"I got blindsided two years ago."

"It happens to everyone sooner or later," Garrett said. "Okay, maybe not quite as spectacularly as it happened to you, but still, it happens. And you won't be able to protect yourself with a lot of hard rules."

"What are you trying to say?"

"Might be time to reconsider those rules of yours. Cut yourself some slack, son."

"You make it sound simple."

"It is simple. You made those rules two years ago. That means you're the only one who can break them."

Garrett turned and walked back through the garden and into the house.

Once again Jack was alone in the night.

CHAPTER FIFTY-EIGHT

She heard the muffled sound of a door opening and closing somewhere inside the big house. It was the second time she had caught the faint noise in the past few minutes. Two people had gone outside into the desert night. Both had returned. One had retreated to the far end of the house. The other one was coming down the hall toward her. She knew from his stride that it was Jack.

The wall of windows in the great room where she sat looked out over a portion of the cactus garden. She realized that he had probably noticed the glow of the computer screen when he had started back into the house.

Max stirred, stretched, and got to his feet.

She sensed Jack's presence even as Max trotted across the room to greet him. The little frisson of awareness that shivered through her was probably nothing more than her body's response to a subtle shift in the shadows or maybe a faint change in the currents of air that drifted through the room. But it would always be like this, she realized. She would always know when he was nearby. In the past several days she had somehow become tuned to him.

"Working late?" he asked.

She turned her head to look at him. He watched her from the entrance of the big room. He was dressed in what she had come to think of as his uniform: dark trousers, a black crew-neck T-shirt, and low boots.

Automatically she started to blank the screen of the computer. But her fingers paused over the keyboard.

"No," she said. "My curiosity got the better of me."

She set the computer on the end table and turned the device around so that he could see the screen. She knew his eyesight was excellent, but she was pretty sure that even he could not read the small print on the computer from where he stood.

The familiar, icy stillness came over him. Then, very deliberately, he walked closer. He stopped when he was a short distance away from the computer.

"Your grandmother knew the facts when she hired me," he said without inflection. "You knew them, too."

"Yes. But tonight I got curious."

"About what?"

"Why you didn't tell anyone the whole truth." She indicated the news account on the screen. "Something happened in that underwater cave, but I don't think it was an accident."

Jack looked at her for a long time. "How did you figure it out?"

"Because I know you, Jack."

"Think so?"

She felt herself turning red. This was his personal business. She had no right to push for answers. She took a deep breath and uncoiled from the sofa. When she was on her feet, she faced him.

"I'm sorry," she said. "I shouldn't have searched for the details."

He moved one hand slightly toward the glowing screen. "It's all public knowledge. The high-tech-industry media covered it for days."

"I know. But still, I shouldn't have allowed my curiosity to push me into prying into your personal history. I had no right."

"It doesn't matter. Like I said, it's all a matter of public record."

"Maybe it shouldn't matter, but it does."

"Why?"

"We both know why," she said. "You let what happened two years ago change your whole future. It doesn't have to be that way. Not your future with me, at any rate."

"Where are you going with this?"

Anger flashed through her, overriding her guilt.

"You're the one who says there's always a pattern. Well, I can't find the pattern in your story. Everything fell apart for no obvious reason. Your company financials were sound but you let everyone think your security firm was in deep trouble. You deliberately closed down the business rather than sell it or run it by yourself. I can think of only one reason why you would do that. You're trying to protect someone."

Jack made a harsh sound deep in his throat. "You think you've figured it out."

"It's not that hard to figure out." She spread her hands wide. "You screwed up. You made a mistake, didn't you?"

"I'm the ace profiler, remember?" Jack's voice was raw. "I'm the one who is supposed to be able to see the pattern. But I missed all the clues with Ingram . . . and with someone else. I was a fool."

"I understand all that. But you didn't shoulder the responsibility for a failing company that wasn't, in fact, failing, just because you made a mistake. Who were you trying to protect?"

There was a long silence. She began to despair. And then he shrugged.

"I told myself I wanted to protect Victor's wife and kids. They all loved him. He was their larger-than-life hero. In the end, I couldn't destroy that image. It was all they had left."

She caught her breath. "If it wasn't about money, what was it about?"

"Victor and I were both on the FBI consulting team. Victor was good with the computer stuff. Very good. He thought he was the smartest guy in the room, and most of the time he was. It was his idea to go out on our own and set up a corporate security company catering to the high-tech industry. I was ready to quit the profiling. I wanted to be in control of my own business."

"You'd had enough of profiling the monsters."

"I was so eager to get free that I jumped at the idea of partnering with Victor. He was the wizard with the online stuff. I was the one who could figure out motives and see the patterns. We should have made a great team. And we did, at first."

"What happened?"

"Everyone has a weak spot. Victor's turned out to be a woman. She was very beautiful and she was working for some very bad people. Somehow she got Victor to give her access to some of our clients' secrets."

"Industrial espionage?"

"Yes." Jack went to stand at the window. "And fool that I was, I never figured out what was going on until that spearfishing trip in Mexico."

"But in hindsight?"

Jack glanced back over his shoulder. His mouth twisted in a humorless smile. "In hindsight, I did see the pattern—small stuff. Anomalies that Victor easily explained away. Remember, he was the tech genius, not me. So yeah, I saw the pattern and I refused to accept what it was telling me. But I was starting to ask more questions and Victor was getting very nervous."

"So he suggested the spearfishing trip."

"He was the one who wanted to check out the underwater cave," Jack said. "It had already been explored. There was a guide line toward the bottom of the cave. As long as we kept a grip on the line we would be safe. He motioned for me to go first with the flashlight. And then he took a shot at me with the spear gun. I got lucky. The spear hit my tank. That's what saved my life."

Jack stopped talking.

Madeline moved to stand very close to him. She put one hand on his arm. His battle-ready tension told her that he was reliving the scene in his mind. She did not speak. She did not take her hand off his arm. It was the only comfort she could offer in that moment.

After a while Jack started talking again.

"I turned around in the water and finally accepted the reality of what was happening. Victor planned to kill me. But what he hadn't planned on doing was missing the shot. He had no backup plan. Victor never had a backup plan."

"Because he was the smartest guy in the room."

"He started to panic when he realized he had missed the shot. He dropped the spear gun and grabbed his knife. He swam toward me. I went low, trying to get beneath him. And then I switched off my flashlight, thinking it would make me less of a target. Everything went . . . very, very dark."

"Ingram didn't have a flashlight?"

"He had one on his belt, but he wasn't using it because he wanted to have both hands free to take the shot with the spear gun. When he realized he'd missed, all he could think about was coming at me with the knife. When the world went dark, his panic exploded. There is nothing that will kill you faster underwater. Victor did what most divers do when they lose it. He instinctively tried to go up."

"But you said the guide line was toward the bottom of the cave."

Jack looked at her. "It was. And that's what I used to get out of the cave. I wasn't exactly levelheaded myself at that moment, either. My heart was pounding and I was using up air at a dangerous rate. Once I was outside in open water I realized that Victor had not followed me."

"You went back in."

"I couldn't just . . . leave him there. I kept thinking of his wife and kids. I was still trying to convince myself that maybe it had all been an accident. But by the time I found him he was dead. There was some air left in his tanks, but in his panic he had spit out the regulator and drowned. It happens more often than people realize."

"You never told Victor's family the truth, did you?"

"There didn't seem to be any point. It was bad enough that he was dead. I didn't want to add to their pain and grief. And I had absolutely no proof of what had happened in that cave."

"What about the woman with whom he was having the affair?"

"My fiancée? That didn't go well, either."

"Your *what*?" Madeline stared at him. "Your fiancée was the industrial espionage agent?"

"I know. Doesn't make me look too bright, does it? When I returned to California I finally took a good, long look at the pattern and I put it all together. Jenny and I had a very short conversation. She took off. Didn't seem to be any point calling the police because industrial espionage is very hard to prove and companies rarely prosecute, anyway. They don't want their secrets exposed any more than they already have been."

"What happened to Jenny?"

"Last I heard she was on the East Coast. Married a guy with serious money."

Madeline took a deep breath. "So."

"So? I tell you my big secret and that's all you've got to say?"

She thought about it. "No. What I'm going to say is that I get why you're gun-shy when it comes to relationships."

"I am not gun-shy."

"Yes, you are. Just like me. We're both afraid of making mistakes.

But what I'm thinking is, now that we both know each other's secrets, there's no reason why we shouldn't get married."

She had just stepped off a very high cliff and she knew it.

Jack didn't say a word for a full sixty seconds. She was aware of the time because she was counting under her breath. *One thousand and one, one thousand and two, one thousand and three . . .*

He framed her face in his powerful hands and looked at her with his fierce eyes.

"Did you just ask me to marry you?" he said.

She allowed herself to breathe. "Yes. Do I get an answer?"

"Yes."

She blinked, bewildered. "What does that mean?"

"It means yes."

He groaned and wrapped his arms around her, holding her tightly, as though fearing she might fly away.

"I love you," he said into her hair. "I've loved you from that first day in your office when you tried to fire me."

"I wasn't trying to fire you," she said into his shirt. "I was simply suggesting that the hotel security business might not be a good fit for you and that you ought to pursue other professional opportunities."

"You tried to fire me. But under the circumstances I'm willing to let bygones be bygones."

"Good. That's good."

He kissed her with the soaring passion of a man who has just been set free from a cage. She understood his response because she had only recently escaped from an invisible prison herself.

CHAPTER FIFTY-NINE

Becky Alvarez rapped once on the partially open door of Jack's office.

"What?" Jack said. He did not look up from his computer.

"I've got an update on that hotel fire that killed Edith Chase."

Jack stopped reading the data on his screen in midsentence and swiveled his desk chair around to look at Becky.

"Talk to me."

Becky moved quickly into the office. She stopped in front of the desk and flipped open a notebook.

"I finally tracked down the housekeeper who took care of the penthouse that Edith Chase was in the night of the fire," she said. "The housekeeper remembered seeing an unknown person on that floor earlier in the day—a man who was wearing a hotel maintenance uniform. The housekeeper didn't recognize him, so she made a point of speaking to him, per routine hotel security protocol."

"Go on."

"The maintenance guy told her that he was new on the staff and that he had been sent to the penthouse to take care of a problem with the air-conditioning system. After speaking briefly with the housekeeper, he left. Used the stairs, not the service elevator, which the housekeeper thought was odd because it was a long way down to the first floor."

"Did the housekeeper report the unknown maintenance man to her manager?"

"Yes. But that's where things get murky. The head of housekeeping checked with the head of maintenance. No one could find a work order for that particular floor and there was no record of a new hire. The head of maintenance went to the head of security. As a precaution, security did a walk-through of the penthouse and found nothing out of the ordinary. They also checked the videos from the security cameras, but you can't see the guy's face because he was wearing a cap and glasses. The best description I could come up with is that the man was a notch or two over six feet. Athletic build."

"That fits all three males in the Webster family."

"The housekeeper said she's pretty sure the maintenance guy was in his thirties. If it was a Webster, it was either Xavier or Travis."

"He went to the penthouse earlier that day to rig the wiring. Later that evening he went back to trigger the explosion and fire. He had to be present at the scene that night in order to make sure that Edith Chase did not escape the blaze. He probably went into the room and killed her first, figuring that the fire would conceal the evidence of murder. When he was sure she was dead, he exited the hotel along with everyone else. He went down the emergency stairs and vanished into the crowd and confusion."

"That would explain a lot," Becky said.

"Send me a copy of the video."

"Knew you'd ask. It should be in your in-box by now." Becky went toward the door. "By the way, your mother called. She said to remind you that you're in charge of the chiles rellenos for dinner tonight."

Jack turned to face the computer screen. "Thanks."

"I'm leaving now." Becky glanced at her watch. "Unless you need me to stay?"

"No, go ahead."

"Don't forget to set the alarm on your way out."

"I run a security firm, Becky. I'm really good with locking up."

"Just thought I'd mention it. You've been somewhat distracted lately."

"Had a few things going on."

"Believe it or not, I had figured that out. See you tomorrow."

Jack looked up. "Good work finding the housekeeper."

"Remember that when it comes time for a raise."

She went out into the reception area. A moment later Jack heard the front door close.

The video was interesting, but Becky had been right. It wasn't clear if the man in the maintenance uniform was Xavier or Travis. Only one of them, however, had a motive.

Travis.

Jack got up, grabbed the rumpled sport jacket off the wall hook, and headed for the door, turning out lights as he went. When you ran a small business you had to watch every penny.

He paused at the front door to put on his jacket and arm the security system. Mentally, he made a list of the ingredients he would need for the chiles rellenos. *Poblano chiles, cheese, eggs.* And then there was the salsa to consider. *Tomatoes, onions, serrano chiles, limes . . .*

He liked cooking for Madeline, but it would be even better cooking for her tonight because he would be cooking for the woman who would soon be his wife. The future looked brighter than it had in a long time.

He walked toward the elevator lobby. The insurance broker and the marriage counselor who shared the same floor of the building had closed for the day. The remaining two offices were empty, victims of the last recession.

A janitorial cart stood in the hall. Mops, brooms, toilet brushes, and bottles of cleaning products poked up out of the cart like alien foliage. There was no sign of the janitor.

Jack was still some distance away from the elevators when he heard the door of the emergency stairwell open behind him.

"Don't move," Travis ordered quietly.

Jack stopped.

"Turn around," Travis said. "Slowly. Open your jacket. I want to see if you're armed."

Jack turned around. Travis was dressed in the green uniform of the building's janitorial service.

Jack peeled back one side of his sport coat.

Travis snorted. "No gun, huh? What's up with that? You sure as hell had one on Cooper Island. But you come home to Arizona, land of open carry, and you stop wearing a gun to work? So much for the big-time security expert."

"I'm more of a security analyst."

"What's that supposed to mean?"

"I analyze people like you. Try to figure out what they'll do next. Got to admit, you surprised me, Travis."

"No shit."

"If you were half as smart as everyone thinks you are, you would have been out of the country by now, headed for that island where you've been stashing the profits you skimmed off your father's hedge fund operation," Jack said.

"You know about the offshore bank? Well, it doesn't matter. The feds can't touch me there."

"Did your father ever realize that you were siphoning off the money?"

"Nope. Never. He just kept thinking that the old program wasn't working as well as it once had. But three years ago I tweaked the system just a little. I knew I would need a lot of cash to get into the political game."

"Why didn't you just ask Egan to bankroll a run for office?"

"What Egan Webster gave, Egan Webster took away. Dear old Dad used money to control people. I didn't want him to be able to control me." Travis gestured toward the door of Rayner Risk Management. "Let's go. Inside."

"Why?"

"Shut up and do as I tell you."

Jack keyed in the code and opened the door. Travis followed him into the small reception area and closed the door. He surveyed the office with a derisive expression.

"You're really a small-time operator, aren't you? How the hell did you land the Sanctuary Creek Inns account?"

"I must have been very persuasive. Out of curiosity, is this going to be one of your mysterious explosion-and-fire spectacles like the ones you used to cover up Edith Chase's murder and to try to get rid of Madeline and me at the Aurora Point Hotel?"

"You put it all together. I'm impressed. In answer to your question, I don't have time to set up another arson scenario. No point anyway, now that Xavier's gone."

"Because the idea on those other two occasions was to let Xavier take the fall if it turned out there was any serious investigation."

"That was the plan. Shit. How the hell did you and Madeline Chase survive the garage explosion? There was a rumor going around that you told the cops you took cover in the old lube pit."

Jack ignored the question. "What was it like sending Xavier out in that boat you'd rigged to explode? Must have been a little weird arranging the murder of your own brother."

"You want to know how it felt? It was a huge relief. The golden boy was a walking time bomb."

"A time bomb you set off the night you sent him out to torch the house where my clients and I were staying."

"Xavier was like one of those old-fashioned clocks—want to see him explode? Just wind him up and point him in the right direction. I pointed him straight at you that day. Figured that even if he failed, which he did, I would at least be rid of him."

"What did you do to set him off?"

"Earlier that evening I took him out for a few beers and explained that good old Mom and Dad were getting ready to send him back to the Institute. I told him it was your fault. Then I put the idea of torching the house in his head. I assured him that after he'd had his revenge on you and Madeline Chase, I'd have the boat ready for him to get away from the island before Egan and Louisa realized he was gone."

"You didn't send him after Edith Chase, though, did you? And you didn't use him to rig the explosion in the garage. You took care of those two projects."

"Sure. Couldn't trust Xavier to do anything right. He was too unstable. I needed to be sure of Chase's death, as well as yours and Madeline's. But now it's all fallen apart. Because of you." Travis raised the gun a little. "Sooner or later someone will find your body here in your office and conclude that you surprised an intruder."

"And you'll be on your way to that island and all that money."

"Not the outcome I had planned, but it will do for now. Money changes everything, you see. And there's plenty of it waiting for me on Luna Verde."

"Well, actually, that's not entirely true."

"What the fuck are you talking about?"

"We here at Rayner Risk Management take pride in our hacking skills. I can't claim to be a whiz but I've got this brother who's unbelievably sharp on a computer. Shortly after four this morning, he siphoned off all but ten dollars from that account you opened on Luna Verde. He left the ten bucks behind because we didn't want to close out the account altogether."

"You're lying, you son of a bitch."

"Check the account for yourself."

"I don't believe you," Travis said.

He reached into one of the pockets of the janitorial uniform and yanked out a tablet. He set the device on the receptionist's desk. The gun in his free hand shook a little as he entered a code and then a series of numbers.

"He's in," Jack said.

Travis looked up, startled. "What—?"

But the room was suddenly plunged into chaos as agents wearing dark jackets with the letters *FBI* emblazoned on the front and the back exploded through the front door.

In the next instant Travis was facedown on the floor. His tablet was in the hands of one of the agents. Someone else confiscated his gun.

Joe emerged from the scene of controlled chaos, grinning his skeletal grin.

"Get everything?" he asked.

"Every word." Jack peeled off his jacket, reached inside his shirt, and took out the digital voice recorder. He handed the device to Joe. "It's all yours."

Travis looked up. He stared at the recorder and then he looked at Jack.

"Everyone said you were just a small-time security company," he said.

"I *am* a small-time security company," Jack said. "But I've got aspirations."

CHAPTER SIXTY

Daphne stood at the window of Madeline's office and looked out at the view of Sanctuary Creek.

"So this is where you've been for the past eighteen years," she said.

Madeline moved to stand beside her. "Sanctuary Creek has been home ever since Grandma and I left Cooper Island."

There was an unfamiliar tension about her friend today, Daphne thought. It was as if Madeline was braced to take a big leap but she didn't know how the landing would turn out.

"I always knew you'd wind up running your own business," Daphne said.

"Is this going to be another observation about my tendency to go to the bottom line?"

"Nope. This is going to be an observation about how right you look here in the executive suite of Sanctuary Creek Inns. You were born for this, Maddie."

"Well, I was raised in the business." Madeline paused. "What about you? Is Denver home or do you think you might consider a career move that involves relocating?"

"What do you mean?"

"I guess I'm asking you if you're really attached to Denver."

"There's nothing for me back in Denver. But I do have some clients there. Why?"

Madeline walked back across the room to stand behind her desk. "Sanctuary Creek Inns is embarking on a long-range series of renovations. All of the hotels need updating and a fresh new look. But each one must have its own personality. It's a core tenet of the company that while we encourage customer loyalty to the chain, we really focus on building a unique customer base for each inn."

"I understand. What is this about?"

"There will be a separate design team for each of the inns, but I need someone here at headquarters to oversee all of the projects. The timeline is five years, and by the end of that period it will be time to start over. Hotel renovation is a never-ending process."

A rush of excitement hit Daphne like a powerful drug. She was suddenly exhilarated beyond measure.

"Are you inviting me to interview for the position of designer in chief?"

"Actually, I'm offering you the job. I would be thrilled if you take it, but I will understand if you don't want to do interior designs for a chain of hotels. I realize it's not the same as designing private living spaces or offices. At Sanctuary Creek Inns we're all about the fantasy—"

"I accept," Daphne said.

Madeline blinked. "Just like that?"

"There's nothing pulling me back to Denver."

"I may have to lie down and put a cool cloth on my brow. First Jack says he'll marry me and now you tell me you'll move to Sanctuary Creek and take a job renovating my hotels. Life is good."

"Yes, it is."

"Something tells me I'm not the only one who will be excited to know that you're moving to town. Abe Rayner will be a very happy man."

"Yes, I got that impression when he told me that he was considering a move to Denver."

"Why am I not surprised?"

"But it turns out that everything I want is right here in Sanctuary Creek," Daphne said. "Abe won't have to relocate."

"It's home," Madeline said.

"I've been wanting one of my own for a long time."

CHAPTER SIXTY-ONE

The ghostly ruins of the abandoned hotel loomed in the heavy fog.

"Looks like a scene out of a horror movie, doesn't it?" Daphne asked.

"*Nightmare at Aurora Point*," Madeline said. She studied the scene through the windshield of the rental car. "I can't wait to get rid of the place. I just hope I can find a buyer."

When she had announced that she was returning to Cooper Island to finish cleaning out Tom Lomax's cottage and put Aurora Point on the market, Daphne had insisted on accompanying her. So had Jack. *You're not going back there alone,* Jack had argued. He had left Abe behind in Sanctuary Creek to catch up on business at the office.

The three of them had arrived on the island a short time ago. Jack had decided to take the opportunity to have one last conversation with the chief of police. He planned to give Dunbar the details of how the case had concluded. *Cops like answers,* he'd explained. *Dunbar has a right to some. In my business you need to stay on good terms with law enforcement. You never know when you're going to need a favor.*

They had dropped him off at the island's small police station before heading for Aurora Point.

Daphne unbuckled her seat belt and opened the passenger-side door. "There will be a buyer. Objectively speaking, Aurora Point is actually quite attractive. It has good bones, as we in the design business like to say."

"You're right." Madeline got out from behind the wheel. "That's why my grandparents bought it in the first place. I might be able to interest a company that specializes in setting up corporate retreats and seminars. I'll make some calls when we get back to Sanctuary Creek."

Daphne smiled at her across the hood of the SUV. "Good to hear you thinking like a businesswoman again."

"Good to have my secret sister back again," Madeline said.

She opened the back of the SUV and removed the two empty suitcases. Daphne took one of them. They started toward the cottage that Tom had called home for so many decades. The fog was so heavy that it was impossible to see the little structure until they were only a few yards away.

Daphne followed Madeline into the cottage and stopped short at the sight of the overwhelming clutter. "Do we have a plan here?"

"Yes, we do. We're going to ignore ninety-nine-point-nine percent of this stuff. We'll leave it for the buyer to deal with, whoever that turns out to be. Same with the furniture in the hotel."

"Some of that furniture in the lobby qualifies as antique."

"I know, but I don't want any of it. Do you?"

Daphne shuddered. "No."

"Today I just want to take a second look around for anything that might tell us whether Tom had some distant family connections. He was clearly willing to believe that he had a long-lost granddaughter, so maybe there's still someone, somewhere who will care that he's gone."

Madeline paused. "I think I'd like to keep a couple of his pictures, too—one or two of the framed scenes that he signed."

Daphne hesitated. "Maybe I will, too—one of the pictures of the two of us, I think."

"Same here."

"Okay, I'll start in the bedroom. We didn't get far there the other day."

Madeline went into the kitchen and started opening drawers.

It was a dispiriting job. Everyone had a junk drawer in the kitchen, but Tom's were world-class archaeological sites containing relics from decades past. She rifled through yellowed newspaper clippings that seemed to be utterly random in terms of subject matter. Faded photographs filled other drawers, but most featured Tom's favorite subjects—landscapes, sunsets, and the ruins of the Aurora Point Hotel.

She started to go out into the living room but stopped short when she noticed the clipping tacked to the wall. It was the picture of Travis's wife, Patricia, displaying a picnic basket filled with corn bread.

PATRICIA WEBSTER SHARES FAMILY
CORN BREAD RECIPE AT COMMUNITY PICNIC

In response to requests, Mrs. Webster explained that it was an old family recipe with a secret ingredient . . . sour cream.

Sour cream was underlined in red pen.

Tom had always been a canned-beans-and-rice kind of cook. Why in the world had he bothered to cut out the newspaper story featuring Patricia Webster? And why underline the words *sour cream*?

She pulled the thumbtack out of the clipping, intending to show it to Daphne. A photo fell out from behind the newspaper article. It dropped to the floor.

For a moment she looked at it, uncomprehending. It was a picture of Ramona holding a plate of corn bread. She was smiling at the camera.

Madeline turned the photograph over, looking for a date. On the back, scrawled in Tom's handwriting, were the words *Family recipe—sour cream. Sunrise Sisters.*

Madeline went cold. With the newspaper clipping and the photograph in hand, she went back out into the living room.

"Daphne, I need you to look at something I just found," she called.

She stopped in the middle of the room and studied the framed pictures that covered the walls. *Sunrise Sisters* was displayed in the center. It was a photo of the hotel taken against the fiery light of a copper-and-gold sunrise. The lobby of the old hotel was silhouetted against the brilliant colors. She and Daphne were pictured standing at the cliff's edge, looking out over the water. Two young girls excited about the future.

Tom's dying words came back. *You always liked my sunrises.*

She crossed the room and took the picture off the wall. There was an envelope taped to the back of the frame. Anticipation and dread whispered through her.

"Daphne? I think I've found something important."

She tore open the envelope and dumped the contents onto the desk. Photographs tumbled out. The first photo showed a man climbing out from behind the wheel of an expensive SUV. The vehicle was parked in a stall in front of a suburban condo complex. The man wore sunglasses and a peaked cap that concealed most of his face. But the SUV looked exactly like the car that Travis drove. The photographer had been careful to catch the license plate in the scene. It would be easy enough to verify that it was Travis's car.

The second picture was taken from a different angle but it showed a woman emerging from one of the condos. She, too, was wearing dark glasses. The hood of her stylish parka was pulled up to partially conceal her profile, but her lean, long-legged build was easy to identify. Ramona.

Tom must have grown suspicious of her at some point, Madeline realized. It must have been heartbreaking for him to realize that there was no long-lost granddaughter, after all. He realized he had been played. That was when he had called and told her that he had to talk to her in person.

She picked up the third photo. Shock jolted through her. She stared at it for a few seconds, trying to make sense of the picture. Then she put it down and dove into her tote for her phone. She entered Jack's number, even as she shouted down the hall.

"Daphne, come here. You've got to see what I just found—"

Daphne appeared. She was not alone. Patricia Webster was with her. Patricia had a gun in her hand and it was pointed at Daphne's head.

"I'm sorry, Maddie," Daphne whispered.

Patricia motioned briefly with her free hand and mouthed the words *end it*. She reinforced the command by pressing the barrel of the gun more tightly against Daphne's head.

"What?" Jack asked in his inimitable style.

"Sorry," Madeline said quietly into the phone. "I hit your number by mistake, Jack."

"How's the photo sorting going?"

"Not bad. Oh, I got the recipe for you."

"What recipe?"

"The one pinned to the wall in the kitchen. You remember. You said you wanted to try it."

"As I recall, what I said was that I would never use sour cream in corn bread."

"I think I'll try whipping up a batch. Got to go now. Lot of work left to do here."

She ended the call.

"Good," Patricia said, her voice brittle with tension. "You handled that well. Now just keep doing as you're told and this will all be over soon."

"You know," Madeline said, "I'm a little surprised to see you here. If I were in your shoes I would have been as far away as I could get from Cooper Island."

"I've been waiting for you to return, Madeline. I knew you would, you see. Sooner or later you had to do something about getting rid of the hotel. I was sure you would come back here to take care of things. What I didn't know was that you would bring some of your friends with you."

"Got it," Madeline said. "You've decided that I'm the reason your big plan fell apart. You want revenge. Tell me, how long did you and Ramona Owens, or whatever her name was, work on the con?"

"Two years, damn you. And it wasn't a con. It was my dream—everything I ever wanted. It was supposed to be my *life*. Simply seducing Travis Webster would have been easy enough. He's just like his old man when it comes to women. He'll screw any pretty face that comes along."

"But you wanted to be more than just another lay. You wanted to marry him."

"He had everything he needed to go far—the looks, the charisma, the family money—everything. But he wasn't interested at first. When I met him his only goal was to rob his father's hedge fund blind before the Webster pyramid scheme fell apart. I'm the one who made Travis dream big."

"You dazzled him with visions of real power—the kind that comes with high office—and he fell for the promise."

"Convincing a man that he has what it takes to be rich or powerful isn't really all that difficult," Patricia said. "Men always want to believe what you're selling, you see. Ramona and I had considerable success running cons on the hedge fund boys. But Travis Webster was going to be our ticket to a new future. He was the one who had what it took to break into politics. That's where the real power is."

"You convinced him that he needed you to make it to the top," Madeline said. "You got him to marry you. When did you realize that there were a few bits and pieces of the Webster family history that had to be erased?"

Patricia's expression tightened with fury. "The bastard didn't even hint that there was something off about the founding of his father's hedge fund until after the wedding. Then he admitted that he was afraid Egan had a couple of real skeletons in the closet. He found them when he went digging into his own family history."

Daphne stirred. "You knew that as soon as Travis became a serious candidate, the media would start excavating his past."

"We didn't think the deaths of Carl Seavers and Sharon Richards would be a problem. There was no *there* there, as they say. Absolutely zero evidence that Webster had anything to do with the deaths. Travis was more concerned that his crazy brother and his father's financial manipulations might be the real problems for the campaign. It was Travis who first suggested that something permanent would have to be done about Xavier."

"What made you realize there might be a more serious problem with the murders of Seavers and Richards?" Madeline asked.

"Travis talked to his mother about his plans to run for office. Louisa was thrilled. But when he mentioned that he was concerned about the unsolved killings in the past because they coincided with the founding of Egan Webster's hedge fund, Louisa got very nervous. She finally broke down and told Travis that she had hired a private investigator to follow Egan to see who he was sleeping with. The PI disappeared. The next thing she knew, Egan told her he had received a blackmail threat, supposedly about some insider trading thing. Louisa was horrified. She suspected the extortionist might have been the PI she hired, but she could hardly admit that to Egan. So she kept quiet."

"And then the blackmailer just disappeared. The demands stopped."

"Louisa told Travis she hadn't known what to think so she just kept silent. But Travis was worried. So he and I set out to discover what had happened to the PI Louisa had hired. Ramona assisted us. I trusted her, you see."

"Because the two of you had worked together on other scams."

"Yes. Eventually Ramona found Purvis's sister. She was a junkie who'd been living from fix to fix for years. Ramona gave her a free fix and the woman told her that her brother had borrowed her car and taken off for some island in the Pacific Northwest. Purvis had told her that he was onto something really big, a business venture that was going to make him rich. He promised to share some of the cash with her."

"But she never heard from him again."

"And being a confirmed addict, she didn't waste any money looking for her missing brother," Patricia said. "But after Purvis disappeared, the landlord of his office building cleared out the office. He dumped everything into a cardboard box and gave it to Purvis's next of kin—his sister. She stuck the box in a closet and never thought about it again. Ramona bought the whole box of files for the promise of another fix."

"And then murdered Purvis's sister with the final fix," Daphne said.

Patricia shrugged. "She just gave her a very pure dose. Junkies OD all the time."

"What did you find in the files?" Madeline asked.

"An unopened credit card statement. There were gas charges at stations all the way up the coast. The last fill-up was not far from the ferry terminal that services Cooper Island."

"So you and Travis concluded that maybe Purvis had made it to Cooper Island, after all," Madeline said.

"By then Travis was convinced that the PI had evidence linking Egan to the deaths of Seavers and the woman. He knew that if Purvis had made it this far and if Egan hadn't killed him—which was evidently the case, according to Louisa—then there was only one place on the island Purvis could have spent the night."

"The Aurora Point Hotel," Madeline said. "Everything ended here."

"We still had no idea what had happened to Purvis, but the fact that your grandmother had closed the place down less than a week after Purvis checked in made us wonder if there was a connection. Travis was afraid that Edith Chase had somehow gotten her hands on the blackmail evidence. He figured if anyone knew the truth, it would be old Tom Lomax."

"Ramona posed as Tom's granddaughter," Daphne said.

"Yes."

"So if Ramona had been so helpful at every step of the way, why did Travis murder her?" Madeline asked.

"He didn't," Patricia said.

"Oh, crap," Madeline whispered. "It was you, wasn't it?"

Patricia's face turned a blotchy red. The gun in her hand trembled. "I was the one who went to meet her that night in the parking lot behind the diner. She was expecting Travis, who had promised to give her a few hundred thousand dollars as payment for the work she had done. She wanted out, you see; she wanted to leave the country. She was getting scared. She demanded her commission."

"Who was Ramona?" Madeline asked. "Why did you think you could trust her?"

"She was my sister," Patricia shouted.

Rage electrified the atmosphere around her.

"You murdered your own sister?" Daphne said.

"She was sleeping with him," Patricia said, her voice very tight. "I found out they were having an affair behind my back. She betrayed me. My own sister betrayed me with my husband."

"Why come back here?" Daphne said, stunningly calm, as though there weren't a gun at her head. "Maddie's right. You should be on your way out of the country."

"She can't go," Madeline said. "Not until she finds the pictures. Right, Patricia? I don't think you came here just to murder me. You're here because Ramona warned you that Tom Lomax had figured out that the three of you were all involved in the plot."

"She said he had photos." Patricia gave the crowded room a desperate survey. "I tried looking for them but it's hopeless. Lomax was a hoarder. So today there's going to be another fire. And when the ashes cool they'll find your body and the body of your friend. An electrical wiring problem. Very common in old houses. I learned that from Travis. He had a flair for the technical stuff."

"Are these the photos you're looking for?" Madeline asked.

She held out the first of the three incriminating photos. Patricia snatched it with her free hand and looked at it, distracted for a few seconds. But the barrel of the gun did not waver. She looked up quickly.

"That's Travis outside the condo that Ramona was renting in Seattle," she said. "The bastard met her there. That's where they fucked. Let me see the others."

"Sure. My favorite is the one of you and Ramona having coffee together in a small diner. It's clear you two knew each other. I imagine that will interest the police, since they're having a problem pinning Ramona's murder on Travis. This picture makes it clear that you knew the victim quite well. That will make you an instant suspect."

Panic flashed across Patricia's face. "Lomax saw us together? Let me have that picture."

Daphne watched Madeline very steadily. Madeline tightened her grip on *Sunrise Sisters* and tried to send a silent message.

"Help yourself, Patricia," she said.

She tossed the remaining photos toward Patricia. The pictures sailed across the room, fluttered wildly, and rained down on the floor.

"Bitch," Patricia yelped.

She started to swing the gun toward Madeline.

Daphne lurched to the side, crashing awkwardly into Patricia. The move didn't take Patricia off her feet, but she staggered.

The gun roared. Madeline felt an icy sensation on her left thigh but she was already in motion, the framed picture gripped in both hands.

The leading edge of the frame slammed into Patricia with Madeline's full weight behind it.

Patricia screamed, stumbled back, lost her balance altogether, and went down hard on her rear. The gun fell to the floor. Daphne went after it.

Madeline slammed the picture downward. Patricia threw up an arm to ward off the blow. Glass shattered.

"You murdered both of them," Madeline shouted. A volatile cocktail of pain and grief and rage splashed through her in hot waves. She slammed the steel frame down hard on Patricia's upper arm and shoulder again and again. Blood flowed. "It's because of you that Grandma and Tom are dead. It's your fault."

"No," Patricia got out. Shock and panic blazed in her eyes. "No, stop. Stop. You're crazy."

She tried to scramble out of the way, but she was trapped between the wall and the end of the ancient couch. Madeline moved in for another blow with her steel weapon.

"Maddie, stop," Daphne yelled. "That's your blood. *Stop.*"

The frame was snatched out of her hands before she could strike.

"That's enough," Jack said gently. "I've got this now."

She stared at him through a haze of fury and grief and pain.

"Jack," she whispered.

"I know you want to kill her, but trust me, it's better if you don't," he said.

She thought about that, trying to make sense of it. Jack eased her away from the sobbing Patricia.

"Okay," Madeline said finally. "Okay."

"Shit," Jack said. "Daphne is right. Most of the blood is yours."

She looked down and saw that the denim on her left leg was soaked with blood.

"Oh," she said.

The room started to spin around her.

Jack scooped her up and put her down on the sagging sofa. He clamped a hand over the bleeding wound and pressed down hard.

"Hurts," she said.

Jack ignored her complaint. He pressed harder.

One of the cops—it had to be the chief, Madeline decided—looked at an officer.

"Get the first-aid kit, Mike," he said. "Then get an aid car out here."

The officer slammed out of the cottage.

Daphne peeled off her jacket and crouched beside the sofa.

"I can handle this, Jack," she said.

Jack hesitated and then, seeing that she had created a makeshift pressure bandage with her jacket, he moved aside.

Madeline looked up at Jack. His eyes were very fierce.

"You got my message," she said.

"The idea of you making homemade corn bread with sour cream was enough to make me very nervous," he said.

She nodded, satisfied. "Love you."

"Love you."

Daphne kept up the pressure on the wound. "How are you doing, Maddie?"

"It hurts like frickin' hell," Madeline said. "Oh, God, Daph, I thought she was going to kill you."

"But she didn't. You saved my life, Maddie."

"I did?"

"Yes, you did. You saved both of us, in fact. I was terrified."

"Just like I was the night you saved me. We'll both be okay, though."

"Yes, we will be okay."

"Secret sisters forever and all that stuff, right?"

"Forever," Daphne said.

Madeline gave up trying to fight the spinning universe and the pain. She slid into the night.

CHAPTER SIXTY-TWO

"It's hard to believe that the corn bread recipe was what made Tom start to wonder if Ramona really was his granddaughter," Madeline said. "After all, he wasn't much of a cook. I'm surprised he even noticed the secret ingredient in both recipes."

"My guess is that he had probably picked up several small clues along the way but had tried to ignore them," Jack said. "Posing as a long-lost relative is a tricky con. Hard to stay in character over time."

They were gathered in Madeline's hospital room. The hospital was in Seattle. She had been airlifted off Cooper Island almost immediately after the shooting. Jack and Daphne had followed in the rental car. They had made it to the hospital just as Madeline was coming out of surgery. Neither had left her bedside during the night. Abe had flown in from Phoenix early that morning.

The surgeon had assured everyone that the wound would heal well and leave an interesting scar.

"I'll bet Ramona messed up several times," Abe said. "But that recipe might have been the final touch. What were the odds that the new Mrs. Travis Webster had exactly the same secret ingredient in her corn bread recipe?"

"It wasn't the recipe," Daphne said.

They all looked at her.

She reached into her purse and took out one of the photos of Ramona that Tom had taken. She set it on the bedside table. Reaching back into her purse, she removed a photocopy of the newspaper picture of Patricia displaying her corn bread.

"Tom was an artist with his camera," Daphne said. "He looked through the lens with an artist's eye. If you compare the picture of Patricia Webster with one of Ramona, you can see a certain family resemblance in the profile. I have a hunch that Tom noticed the similarities at some point and started to wonder."

"That's it." Abe snapped his fingers. "You're right and you're brilliant. And if Lomax had already started to doubt Ramona, the corn bread recipe might have been enough to make him really curious."

"So he started following her when she left the island," Jack said. "He located the condo she was renting and took those pictures of Ramona and Travis together as well as the shot of Ramona and Patricia having coffee. He knew then that he had been conned, but it was too late. He had already told her about the briefcase and what it contained. By the time he put it all together, Ramona and the briefcase were long gone."

"He wasn't planning to try to blackmail Webster?" Abe said.

"Maybe, but I don't think so," Jack said. "I think Tom Lomax made the mistake of confiding his secret to his so-called granddaughter. She took the briefcase out of the wall. Later, after he realized that he couldn't trust Ramona, Lomax went back to room two-oh-nine—probably intending to move the briefcase to a safer location. But by then it was gone."

"That's when Tom called me," Madeline said. She pushed herself higher on the pillow stack, sucking in a sharp little breath when fresh pain lanced her thigh. Jack frowned and started to lunge for the call button. She shook her head. "I'm okay."

Jack did not look convinced, but he subsided back into his chair.

"Tom told me that he had to talk to me in person," she continued. "I arrived just as Travis was staging Tom's death to look like an accident or an interrupted burglary."

"Travis heard your car in the driveway," Abe said. "He hid upstairs. And then he concluded that he might as well take the opportunity to get rid of you, too. He had already gotten rid of your grandmother. But he couldn't be sure how much you knew about what was in the briefcase, especially since it was obvious that Tom had contacted you. He tried to take you out at the same time."

"But he didn't get the opportunity because I had already called the cops," Madeline said. "And then I made the call to my new hotel security agency."

"After that, the bad guys never stood a chance," Daphne declared.

"We at Rayner Risk Management pride ourselves on providing first-class service," Abe assured her.

"We're sure it was Ramona who searched my condo in Denver?" Daphne asked.

Jack nodded. "Travis admitted that he sent Ramona there to try to get a handle on how much you knew about the events of eighteen years ago. Ramona didn't find anything in your condo, but she took your computer just to be on the safe side."

"So, what with one thing and another, I'm out a computer," Daphne said.

"You'll want to replace it," Abe said. "I could help you select a new one."

"Thank you," Daphne said.

Abe grinned. "Like I said, we're a full-service agency."

Daphne winked at Madeline and then turned a glowing smile on Abe. "What do you say you and I go get a latte? I hear they actually have a Starbucks in Seattle."

"No kidding?" Abe pushed himself up off the windowsill. "Very progressive town."

They went out into the hall, leaving Madeline alone with Jack. He got up and moved to stand beside the bed. He loomed over her and took one of her hands in his. The strength in his fingers felt good, she thought. It was the kind of strength you could rely on for a lifetime.

"You're sure you're okay?" he asked.

"I'm okay." She smiled. "I know things have been a little hectic lately, but you haven't changed your mind, have you? We're still getting married, right?"

"Hasn't anyone told you that once I make up my mind to do something, I'm like a freight train?"

"I believe that particular personality characteristic has been mentioned once or twice. As I understand it, anyone who happens to be standing in your path has two choices—get out of the way or get on board."

"You're on board?"

"For the whole trip."

He leaned over the railing and kissed her. When he raised his head, she saw the promise of a lifetime in his eyes.

"It's going to be good," he said.

"Yes. It's going to be very good."

She belonged to him.

He was locked inside a cage the size and shape of a coffin. A dark thrill heated his blood like a powerful, intoxicating drug.

When the time came he would purify the woman and cleanse himself with her blood. But tonight was not the time. The ritual had to be followed correctly. It was a crucial part of the sacrament. She must be made to comprehend and acknowledge the great wrong that she had done. There was no finer instructor than fear.

He huddled inside the concealed lift, listening to the sounds of someone moving about in the bedroom on the other side of the wooden wall panel.

He peered through the narrow crack in the paneling. Excitement sparked when he caught a glimpse of the woman. She was at her dressing table, adjusting the pins in her deep brown hair. It was as if she knew he was watching and was deliberately taunting him.

She was passable in appearance but he had seen her on the street and had not been particularly impressed with her looks. She was overly tall for a woman and her forceful character was etched onto her face. She was dangerous. It was all there in her unnerving eyes.

No wonder he had been sent to purify her. He would save her from herself.

She was not the first woman he had saved. Perhaps this time he would finally be cleansed.

The lift had been installed inside the thick walls of the old mansion for the purpose of conveying an elderly, infirm lady from one floor to another. But the woman had died a few years ago, leaving the big house to her granddaughter and grandson. He had been told that neither of them made use of the device. Having been locked inside the cage for what felt like an eternity, he understood why. The air was close and still and the darkness was almost as absolute as that of the grave.

The woman rose from the dressing table and moved out of sight.

He was free to descend in the lift at any time. It was operated by an arrangement of ropes and pulleys that could be controlled from either inside or outside the compartment.

He'd had a helpful chat with one of the many tradesmen who came and went from the mansion on the days when the woman held her salons. The man had informed him of the usefulness of the lift for conveying heavy items between floors. He had also mentioned that the woman and her brother never used the lift. Evidently the woman had a fear of being trapped inside the cage.

He heard the muffled sound of the bedroom door opening and closing. And then silence.

He slid the cage door aside and opened the wooden panel. The wall sconce had been turned down quite low, but he could make out the bed, the dressing table, and the wardrobe.

He moved out of the lift. The heady exhilaration he always experienced at such moments roared through him. With every step of the ritual he came closer to achieving his own purification.

For a precious few seconds he debated where to leave his gift. The bed or the dressing table?

The bed, he decided. So much more intimate.

He crossed the room, not concerned about the soft thud of his footsteps. The guests were gathering in the library on the ground floor. Voices were raised in conversation and someone was playing a piano to entertain the crowd. No one would hear him.

When he reached the bed he took the velvet pouch out of the pocket of his overcoat and removed the black jet ring. A fashionable item of memento mori jewelry, the stone was engraved with the image of a skull. The woman's initials were painted in gilt on the black enameled sides—C. L. When the time came, a small twist of her hair would be tucked into the locket concealed beneath the skull stone.

He slipped the ring back into the pouch and placed the gift on the pillow where she could not fail to notice it.

He stood still for a moment, savoring the intense intimacy of the experience. He was in her most personal space: the room where she slept; the room where she believed herself to be alone; the room where she felt safe.

That sense of safety would soon be destroyed. She belonged to him. She simply did not know it; not yet.

He started to go back to the concealed lift but paused when he saw the framed photograph on the wall. It showed the woman as she had been some ten years earlier, a girl of sixteen or seventeen. She stood on the brink of womanhood, still innocent and unknowing, but already there was something disturbing about her eyes.

Her brother was also in the picture. He appeared to be about nine or ten years of age. The two adults in the photograph were no doubt the children's parents. He could see something of the man in the boy.

He took the picture down from the hook and hurried to the lift. Stepping inside, he closed the panel and then the cage door. Darkness as deep as the black jet stone in the ring enveloped him. He dared not light a candle.

He groped for the cables and breathed a sigh of relief when they worked. He lowered the lift to the ground floor.

When he emerged he found himself back in the small antechamber behind the rear stairs. There was no one about. The elderly housekeeper and her equally aged husband, the butler, were busy with the social gathering in the library.

In the old days, when the mansion had housed a large family and a dozen or more servants, it would have been nearly impossible to slip in and out of the place unseen. But now there was only the woman, her brother, and the old housekeeper and butler in residence.

He made his way out through the tradesmen's entrance. A moment later he was lost in the fog. Once he was safely in a hansom he allowed himself to sit back and reflect on the satisfaction of his night's work.

The woman with the unnerving eyes would soon understand that she belonged to him. It was her destiny to be the one to cleanse him. The connection between them was a bond that could be shattered only by death.

RIVER ROAD

Jayne Ann Krentz

It's been thirteen years since Lucy Sheridan was in Summer River.
The last time she visited her aunt Sara there, as a teenager, she'd
been sent home suddenly after being dragged out of a wild party,
by the guy she had a crush on, just to make it more embarrassing.
Obviously Mason Fletcher – only a few years older but somehow a
lot more of a grown-up – was the overprotective type who thought
he had to come to her rescue.

Now, returning after her aunt's fatal car accident, Lucy is learning
there was more to the story than she realized at the time. Mason
had saved her from a very nasty crime that night – and soon
afterward, Tristan – the cold-blooded rich kid who'd targeted her –
disappeared mysteriously, his body never found.

A lot has changed in thirteen years. Lucy now works for a private
investigation firm as a forensic genealogist, while Mason has quit
the police force to run a successful security firm with his brother –
though he still knows his way around a wrench when he fills in at
his uncle's local hardware store. Even Summer River has changed,
from a sleepy farm town into a trendy upscale spot in California's
wine country. But Mason is still a protector at heart, a serious (and
seriously attractive) man. And when he and Lucy make a shocking
discovery inside Sara's house, and some of Tristan's old friends
start acting suspicious, Mason's quietly fierce instincts kick into
gear. He saved Lucy once, and he'll save her again. But this time,
she insists on playing a role in her own rescue . . .